"IS THIS YOUR ROOM OR MINE?"

He didn't answer. The door swung open and Ray was pleasantly surprised to see the room wasn't ritzy at all. In fact, it was almost utilitarian with one full bed, a nightstand, and a dresser with a small television sitting on it. It was clean and neat, but not what she had expected after the first-class airfare.

"Well, you've managed to surprise me, Eli. But I thank you. The room is perfect." She smiled.

He stepped inside with her and closed the door.

Ray's smile slipped. "Did I misunderstand?"

He shook his head, but leaned on the door as if he fully intended to stay.

"Is this your room and not mine?"

Eli crossed his arms over his chest. "It's your room."

"Good, that's what I thought." It wasn't necessary, but she added, "I couldn't imagine you willingly staying in a room this plain. I figured you'd get a suite or something."

As if she hadn't spoken, he said, "It's also my room."

More from Lori Foster

Anthologies

Published by Kensington Publishing Corp.

LORI FOSTER

UNEXPECTED

ZEBRA BOOKS
KENSINGTON PUBLISHING CORP.
www.kensingtonbooks.com

ZEBRA BOOKS are published by

Kensington Publishing Corp.
119 West 40th Street
New York, NY 10018

All Kensington titles, imprints, and distributed lines are available at special quantity discounts for bulk purchases for sales promotion, premiums, fundraising, educational, or institutional use.

Special book excerpts or customized printings can also be created to fit specific needs. For details, write or phone the office of the Kensington Sales Manager: Attn.: Sales Department. Kensington Publishing Corp., 119 West 40th Street, New York, NY 10018. Phone: 1-800-221-2647.

Zebra and the Z logo Reg. U.S. Pat. & TM Off.

First Brava Books Trade Paperback Printing: September 2003
First Kensington Books Mass-Market Paperback Printing: November 2004
First Zebra Books Mass-Market Paperback Printing: May 2014
ISBN-13: 978-1-4201-4947-0
ISBN-10: 1-4201-4947-4

ISBN-13: 978-1-4201-4948-7 (eBook)
ISBN-10: 1-4201-4948-2 (eBook)

20 19 18 17 16 15 14 13 12 11 10 9

Printed in the United States of America

Chapter One

_____

She'd already signed the contract.

Backing out now would blow her reputation with the agency, and besides, this mission would be a piece of cake. There was no reason to drag her feet. She needed the money, she was free at the moment, and it'd be a routine run, nothing more, nothing less. It'd be easier now than in the past. Everything had changed.

Herself included.

She shook her head at that errant thought. True, she was older now, wiser, more settled. But at the core, she was the same—unacceptable to most, invaluable to others. Her skills, an innate part of her, were still finely honed. She knew what she could do, and damn it, she'd do it. Hell, she'd _missed_ doing it.

So why, when she pushed the door open and stared into the dim, smoky room of the bar, was her heart so heavy in her chest? It wasn't the depressing gray cloud that hung thick in the air, not only from cigarettes, but from disgust and ambivalence and antagonism. This was far from a happy place, but then, she'd known it wouldn't be. By necessity, it was an obscure hole in the Chicago slums where meetings like this one, with people like her, could be handled with discretion.

It was stupid to borrow trouble or dwell in indecision. Doing so undermined her credibility, so instead, she'd concentrate on getting this over with fast and easy, with no complications.

She had everything planned out.

Flipping her bangs off her forehead, she strode into the room, ready to get things started.

Several heads turned her way, scrutinizing her, making note of her appearance. Calculating. For much of her life, she'd gotten undue attention for one reason or another, most of the reasons uncomplimentary. She'd long since gotten used to the stares and the whispers. She ignored them all, and with luck, they'd show her the same courtesy.

Peering through the obscuring smoke, she scanned the tables and booths, searching out each darkened corner. Country music blasted through tinny speakers, vying with the boasting and bragging of drunken men. It was the typical atmosphere of a seedy bar. Without thinking, she rubbed her stomach, sick with a rush of vivid memories that never failed to surface.

Then her gaze locked onto his. Wow. The past faded away under the impact of the present—*his* impact. She felt . . . invaded.

Bright hazel eyes, radiant in the otherwise dismal interior, held her captive. She stared at him; he stared back.

Never before had she seen such intense emotion in a man's expression. For a moment, it knocked her off guard. Without moving, he appeared turbulent, frustrated, filled with determination and impatience.

Because of his situation, or because she'd arrived late?

She watched him a moment more, taking his measure. He was bigger than most of the men she knew or had worked with. And he had a more self-assured air. That he'd be trouble she didn't doubt—he pretty much screamed it with a capital T. But how much trouble, that's what she needed to know.

Lounging back in his chair, he allowed her perusal, and even took the time to look her over, too. But then, amazingly enough, he dismissed her by giving his attention back to the entrance of the bar.

Cynical amusement nudged away the lingering nervousness. He hadn't realized her identity? She wasn't what he'd been expecting? Typical. And for a second there, she'd thought he might be more astute than the others.

Anticipating his reaction when she introduced herself, she started toward him. He sat at a solitary table at the far end of the room, his back to the wall so he could face the bar, a rear exit to his right. It was a guarded position she would have chosen, but probably just a coincidence for him.

She wove her way around tables, drunks, and proffered drinks without once taking her eyes off him.

As was her usual habit at such meetings, she'd dressed in plain black clothes. It made it easier to disappear if necessary, and didn't draw added attention that more complimentary clothes might have.

Her long-sleeved tunic hung to midthigh, loosely fitted so it wouldn't impede her movements should she need to take physical control of the surroundings. Her jeans were slim, her low-heeled boots only ankle high. She never wore jewelry—in fact, she didn't own any—but she did carry a black briefcase. The case was an annoyance, but it usually proved necessary to have it handy.

When she stopped in front of him, his gaze came to her face, arrested for only a moment. Then slowly, very slowly, he looked her over again, his attention lingering in certain places like her chest, below her waist, her thighs. His look was so intimate, so personal that it brought on a mélange of sensations—outrage, disgust, and strangely enough, heat. Surely not embarrassment, she told herself. She was too old and far too jaded to be disconcerted by the likes of him.

His visual inspection was appreciative and felt like a tactile touch. Damn it, she didn't like being touched, not without permission.

Her eyes narrowed, prompting him to a softly uttered, reluctant rejection. "Sorry, honey. It's unfortunate, but I'm already busy tonight."

The nerve. Despite her exceptional control, antagonism bristled to the surface. Her every movement rigid, Ray hooked a chair and drew it out. She seated herself, placing the briefcase at her feet for safekeeping.

He cocked one dark brow upward and braced his forearms on the rough, scarred table. The new position emphasized the width of his shoulders, the brawn of his arms. She'd expected another wimpy, slim *GQ* look-alike, but this man could be a barroom bouncer. He wasn't bulky, just big and hard and solid.

Added to the fine physique were the eyes of a predator, now filled with annoyance. He leaned toward her with a scowl.

"I'm Ray Vereker," she drawled, stopping him in his tracks. She didn't say anything more, didn't offer her hand in polite greeting. She just waited for the usual signs of disbelief and disparagement.

They were slow in coming.

Rather than gape, he leaned back and studied her anew. If she'd thought his earlier perusal was intimate, it was nothing compared to how he looked at her now. For a lesser person, for someone without her skills and background, it might have been an unnerving process. His eyes were such an unusual shade of hazel, cat eyes, bright with intelligence, almost menacing. They went from heated notice to cool regard.

Deciding to mock his up-close and personal inspection with one of her own, Ray draped one elbow over the back of the chair and slouched down in the seat to get comfortable. Wearing an air of unconcern, she took in his appearance, from his dark brown hair cut in precise lines to his straight, masculine nose and high cheekbones to his mouth, now flattened with irritation at her boldness. He had a stubborn jaw, she noted, proving he'd be plenty of trouble, indeed.

The black tee he wore looked softer than heaven, fitted over that broad chest. Even his open jacket screamed wealth, made of fine leather and deliberately scuffed to appear fashionably worn. The watch on his thick wrist probably cost as much as her truck. Maybe more. And his nails were impeccably clean.

Thanks to the table, she couldn't see below his waist, but she'd be willing to bet the rest of him was as sturdy and strong as what she could see. Maybe it was a good thing half of him was hidden. Half was about all she could take at one time. The man made her heart race.

Though she doubted he'd ever been in such a ramshackle bar in his life, *he* didn't look the least bit ill at ease. Even her presence, which had to be a shocker, hadn't really rattled him.

To be honest with herself, she admitted he was very fine to look at. She appreciated strength and self-control. From what she could tell, he had both in spades.

Not that it mattered. He was still rich, and given what she'd seen so far, too arrogant for his own good. What fool came into such a place and advertised himself as an easy mark? By wearing the watch and the jacket, he'd done exactly that.

He was a fool, all right. And for the next few days, she owed him her service.

As the silence stretched on, Ray sighed and crossed her legs. She knew his tactic. He hoped to remain silent so long that she'd begin to babble nervously. He underestimated her. He could sit in strained silence as long as he wanted. Time was money, *his* money, and she didn't mind wasting it if he didn't.

He looked at her mouth, rubbed his own, then pinned her in place with a laser-sharp gaze. In a flat tone devoid of any telltale emotion, he said, "I requested the meanest son of a bitch they had."

She gave a slow smile. "I know what you requested. I have your papers with me."

"And?"

She lifted one shoulder, held up her hands to indicate her presence. "They complied."

Eyes closed, he pinched the bridge of his nose, muttering under his breath. Ray noticed that his hands were large, sprinkled with brown hair. They looked like capable hands, not the pampered, smooth hands of a rich boy.

Catching herself, she jerked her attention back to his face. He scrutinized her, then asked with some disbelief, "Do you have any idea what it is I want from you?"

"Sure."

With a touch of disbelief, his gaze slid all over her again, appraising, before both brows lifted. Ray never moved a muscle. He could look a dozen times if it made him feel better. She wouldn't be changing.

"I assumed 'Ray' would be a man."

"Assumptions are nasty things. They can get you into trouble."

He waved that away. "What's your real name?"

"Ray is my real name."

"Your whole name then."

"Why does it matter?"

Ray could feel his growing tension deep inside herself. It was an odd sensation, one she'd never experienced before. She half expected an explosion at any minute and braced for it, making herself tense, too.

"I'm wondering," he said slowly, his unnerving attention on her mouth again, "if there's some feminine nuance I'm missing."

She smirked. "In me, or my name?"

His gaze snapped back to hers and he barked a laugh. "Honey, despite the hard attitude, your appearance is most definitely *un*manly."

He said that with . . . interest? No, no way. She was lousy at judging men and their various moods in regard to the whole man/woman thing, but she understood reality very well, thank you. No man in his right mind would be thinking of anything but the mission. Not with her. Not now.

And most definitely not after the mission ended, when her special skills had been revealed.

During her ruminations, the silence grew, and finally, because she had no reason not to, she said, "Ray Jean Vereker. But I go by Ray and only Ray. You're given fair warning right now not to use my middle name, ever."

Oddly enough, her warning evoked amusement. Oh, he didn't laugh, didn't even smile. But she saw the mischievous twinkle that entered those mysterious eyes. "Yeah? Or what?"

Done with the small talk, with the nonsense, Ray said, "Or I'll walk out and you'll be left to settle for the second meanest son of a bitch there is."

A reluctant, slightly crooked grin tugged at his mouth, adding to his appeal. "You're really that good?"

Ray didn't hesitate. "I'm really that good." She waited for his sarcasm, perhaps some outright derision.

Instead, he said, "Will you be offended if I ask for credentials?"

He wasn't dismissing her out of hand? Well . . . that surprised her. Bemused, Ray straightened in her seat. "'Course not." She pulled the briefcase up to the tabletop and with quick, deft movements opened the lock. She extracted the topmost papers and slid them across the table. "I'd think you were an idiot as well as a fool if you didn't."

He'd been reaching for the papers, but paused with her words. "You want to explain that?"

What the hell? He didn't sound particularly insulted, more like intrigued. They needed to start out on the right foot, and that meant making him understand that if he accepted her, she was the boss and her rules were to be followed.

Her first rule would be to get him out of his

fancy clothes and into gear much more suited to their purpose. That thought roused an image of the process, and unfortunately, it stalled at the part where he was out of his clothes, rather than in them. She'd be willing to bet he looked real good naked.

And if she didn't stop thinking that way, things were going to get *way* too complicated.

Clearing her throat, Ray leaned on the table, making certain she had his undivided attention. "We'll be lucky if we get out of here without someone trying to take your wallet or watch or both. And the men in here wouldn't care if you got hurt in the bargain. Not that I'd let it happen," she assured him. "When you're with me, you'll be safe. Part of my job is to protect you, and as I already said, I'm good at my job."

"Like my own personal bodyguard, huh?"

His amusement stung. "An astute man adapts to his surroundings. An astute man knows it isn't always necessary to flaunt his position in life. We'll have our hands full without borrowing trouble for reasons of vanity."

His expression sharpened as the amusement faded away. She'd made him mad. Very mad. It shone in every line of his taut face, the fire in his gaze.

Ray rolled her eyes. He wasted his time trying to intimidate her. Regardless of his good looks, she knew he'd be no different from any other wealthy man. Easy to take, and easier to leave. "Look, Mr. Connors . . ."

He snorted rudely. "You feel comfortable enough with me to throw out insults, so you may as well call me Eli."

He'd surprised her again. She'd expected a blast of his anger, reciprocal insults, anything other than that calm, dry wit.

Ray didn't like surprises. They were dangerous and could easily lead to trouble. She had to stop thinking she had him figured out. Maybe, just maybe, he *was* unique from the rest.

"It wasn't an insult I gave you—"

"Fool? Idiot?" He snorted again, forcing her to fight off a smile.

"All right, it was, but I didn't really mean it that way. Think of it more as an instruction."

"An instruction on survival?"

"Why not? I was told you wanted to stick close, that you insisted on accompanying me when I go in." And that's what really nettled her. She worked alone. Always. Not since that awful time long ago had she allowed a partner. But damn it, she needed the pay a job like his would bring.

She drew a deep breath and continued. "Since it appears I have no say in that half-witted decision—"

"You don't. It's my brother over there, so I'm going along."

"—and since I have no intention of causing myself extra worry just so you can dress in your finest, you're going to have to follow my lead. In everything. Do I make myself clear?"

There was another long hesitation while Eli searched her face. She felt . . . *touched* again, as if he somehow saw below the surface. Impossible. She excelled at hiding all thought, all expression, and no one, certainly not a fancy-pants rich boy, would discern anything about her that she wanted kept private.

Finally, coming to some silent conclusion that

he didn't share, Eli said, "The watch is from my grandfather and it never comes off."

Never wasn't acceptable, but for now, Ray let it go. "And the jacket?"

His crooked grin reappeared. "The oldest one I own."

She would not be charmed by that boyish smile. Straightening the papers on the table between them gave her something to look at other than those devastating eyes. "Gotcha. Well then, we'll just need to shop before we leave." Ray glanced up and away. "That is, if you still want me."

Uncertainty hit her the second she said it, and she shoved the papers toward him. Affidavits, referrals, and recommendations made up her resume. There were no specific details on any missions because every case was covert, guaranteed high-priority privacy protection.

The papers would detail her abilities, her experience, and her success. But they wouldn't give names or dates. Eli would never know that her missions had grown farther and farther apart—or why.

He accepted the documents, giving all his attention to her credentials. He took his time, carefully reading everything.

Without looking up, he said, "You've been to Central America before."

The words wanted to stick in her throat, but she forced them out. "I've been there."

"More than once?"

"More than once." She wouldn't give him specifics about those other times. The papers told him she'd succeeded in her missions, and anything more was none of his damn business.

But she could tell him what she'd already found

out about *this* mission. "Your brother's in Mataya." That snared his attention. Hungry for info, he put the papers aside to listen. "It's a small village that's usually pretty peaceful. Now that they've got your brother, though, they see him as the pot of gold. You don't have to worry. They're treating him like a prince."

"How can you know that?"

"I've had dealings with that village before. In the past, they've helped me with other rescues. In fact, that's probably where they got the idea to try snatching your brother."

"From helping you rescue other men?"

"Maybe. I have it on good authority that they won't hurt him, but I doubt he'll be comfortable with their standard of living. He won't be dining on prime rib or soaking in the sauna, that's for sure."

Eli leaned toward her. "I was told by some of his friends who'd been with him that he wasn't hurt, but no one knew how to get him back. There's been no ransom demand, no official notice."

She shrugged. "They probably don't know what he's worth." She could just picture the bunch of them, pseudo guerillas, hashing over the dollar amount with hopeful greed. "The guys who took him are new at this."

"How do you know for sure who has him?"

"I checked before agreeing to the job."

"Your connections in Central America are that good?"

"Of course." She didn't tell him that she had befriended some of the people in years past. Locating a fair-skinned rich boy wasn't all that hard. He stuck out like a broken thumb. "I know where he is, I know that he's fine, and I know how to get him out with the least amount of hassle."

"We don't yet know what they want for him."

She rolled her eyes again. "They want money— the only issue is how much you'll have to actually pay, and that'll be negotiable. It won't be exorbitant. They're so poor, ten thousand would seem like ten million to them."

He seemed relieved by her confidence. She could actually see some of his pent-up anger easing. "I was told you were good."

She accepted that tribute without modesty. "Yeah, I've been told that, too."

He made a face of hesitant acceptance. "Your grasp of the situation verifies it, and certainly everything in your papers looks credible."

She heard that "but" loud and clear. "So?"

"It's still a little hard to believe."

Here we go. "Because I'm female."

"Because you don't look cutthroat enough, powerful enough, or hardened in any way." His drew a slow breath, his gaze locked on hers. "Hell, if anything, you look soft. Very soft."

The way he said it kept her from actually hearing the words for a moment. When they did register, indignation exploded, causing her to slowly straighten. She felt her muscles—sleek, not obvious, but there all the same—quiver at the insult. Her body automatically went on alert, her senses rising to an acute level of awareness, ready to move with fluid speed.

Ready to kick his ass.

No man had ever dared to tell her she was *soft*. Most never gave it a thought one way or the other unless her talents were needed, and when she proved how hard she could be, they no longer cared. Her voice was silky and filled with menace when she purred, "You require a demonstration?"

He didn't grin, but he definitely looked amused again. "Offering to beat me up?"

His humor rubbed her on the raw. "Don't think I can't."

This time he actually laughed, but with incredulity and astonishment. "I probably outweigh you by ninety pounds, none of it fat. You really think you're that good?"

Before the mission was finished, Ray vowed to show him just how good she could be. It'd be a well-deserved lesson, and one he wouldn't forget. "I'm alive. That's good enough for me."

"Alive, but still a woman." He tilted his head, laughing quietly. "It's tough to swallow."

Much more of his provocation and the lesson would come sooner rather than later. She wasn't usually so prickly, but the majority of her jobs weren't with a man like him. Most who hired her were obnoxious, arrogant, belligerent men who she could easily dismiss as unimportant and unworthy of her temper. They treated her as a lesser person. They did *not* dare to tease her, or smile at her with masculine pleasure.

They did not size her up as a woman.

Before she ruined everything by dislocating his shoulder, she got her temper under control. "Are we staying here? I want a drink if we are, and if not, well then, I suggest we get going. We're drawing a lot of attention."

Instantly alert, Eli's piercing gaze swept around the room with hasty caution. "Where?"

Motioning with a tilt of her head, Ray said, "At the bar."

He looked, and scowled at whatever he saw. "The bar is behind you. How do you know anyone's paying attention to us?"

"Feminine intuition?"

His mouth flattened. "It was a legitimate question, Ray."

With his mood soured, hers improved. "Yeah, all right. Don't get your briefs in a bunch." She watched with satisfaction as his expression tightened even more, then admitted, "I can feel it."

"It?"

"Yeah. The growing tension, the static charge. Someone is plotting." She gathered her papers and put them away, locking the briefcase and keeping it on the table in front of her. "I can feel the eyes, feel the hush in the air. The anticipation."

When he only stared at her, she sighed. "It's what I do, Eli, what I'm good at. Without gut instinct, I wouldn't be here now."

Eli considered that. She waited for his mockery, but after a thoughtful moment he nodded. "All right then. Let's get out of here." He pushed his chair back.

Triumph surged, but Ray didn't give in to it yet. She wanted a commitment. She needed this job, much as it galled her to admit. There'd be hell to pay when Matt found out, but she'd handle him. "Then you do want me?"

Before Eli could answer, another voice, slurred with drink, sounded close behind her. "I want ya, honey." A damp, meaty hand closed around her upper arm. Ray didn't so much as flinch. She'd expected at least one battle before the night ended, and she wasn't disappointed that she'd get it. Just the opposite.

Eli scowled, but Ray said only, "Looks like you'll get your demonstration after all."

He gave her an incredulous glance before surging forward. *To her rescue?* Ray grinned. What a joke.

She stood and shoved her briefcase against his abdomen, halting him in his heroic attempt. "You wanna help? Watch my case for me." The man still held on to her arm. "And you might want to get out of the way."

"Like hell." Eli dropped the case on the table, took one step forward—and was forced to duck as Ray went into action.

Smiling, she grasped the man's arm just above his elbow, turned and bent to put her shoulder into his soft gut, and sent him flipping onto his back by the simple means of straightening. It had all happened in less than three seconds.

The big man sprawled out at Eli's feet. For one moment his eyes were open in glazed shock, then they crossed and his head lolled to the side.

The comical expression on Eli's face delighted her. With one novice move, she'd surprised him good, but there wasn't time to relish her small victory.

A roar sounded behind her and a man lunged forward. Ray spun around, leg extended, and sank the heel of her boot into his groin. He screamed like a girl as he crumpled on the spot.

"Man, that must've hurt," she said to Eli, who blinked at her in astonishment.

In typical barlike fashion, chaos exploded around them. For the first time that night, Ray felt good. She was in her element. Meeting Eli had filled her with some strange roiling emotion, and this was just what she needed to rid herself of it. It had been too damn long since she'd had a good workout. Bouncing on the balls of her feet, she shook her hands to get them limber and looked around for fresh meat, waiting for the next attack, grinning all the while.

"Jesus."

She turned to see Eli staring at her with appalled incomprehension. Big as he was, strong as he appeared to be, he still looked aghast at the various scuffles quickly escalating to brawl proportions. Damn. No time for fun now. Her first priority was keeping Mr. Moneybags safe.

"Come on." Ray grabbed his hand and her case and started for the back door. He allowed himself to be towed along.

Another man reached out, snatching at the back of Eli's jacket. Ray moved to defend him, anxious to get in one more lick, but Eli didn't give her the chance. More aggravated than alarmed, and with no hesitation whatsoever, he punched the man in the side of the throat. The poor fellow gagged and staggered back into a table, knocking over drinks and starting another quarrel.

Impressed, Ray looked at Eli with new eyes. Surprise of surprises, he could defend himself. What about that?

As if he'd read her thoughts, he shook his head, flexed his knuckles, and somehow took the lead, yanking her out the door and into the chill night air.

Now that he was relatively safe, Ray tried to release his hand, but Eli held on, his grip unbreakable unless she wanted to stop and prove a point. Which she didn't, not yet anyway. They were still in a darkened alley in a disreputable part of town, and anything could happen. Men were known to leave bar disputes with a knife in hand, or worse, a gun. It wouldn't do her reputation a damn bit of good if someone shot at him or managed to prick him with the tip of a switchblade. Rich people bled a lot.

That didn't mean, however, that she'd let him be in charge. Ray pulled him to a stop. His hand was large and lean, swallowing hers, making her feel almost . . . dainty. How absurd. She could kill a man with one blow. Nothing dainty about that.

But he kept her hand cradled in his like a little bird in a nest. His palm was incredibly warm, his fingers long and strong and rough with calluses.

She was trained to notice every small detail. The calluses on a wealthy man didn't make any sense, but now wasn't the time to ask personal questions. "Where's your car?"

Eli gave a mock bow. "I hate to disappoint you, but I'm not as stupid as you want to think. I took a cab."

"Perfect." She nodded her approval. "Then we can both take my truck."

Several more men spilled out of the bar, fists and rank curses flying.

Ray got Eli moving again with a jerk. "Come on."

They jogged out of the wet, smelly alley into the incredible star-filled night. Ray breathed deeply of the cool moist air. She felt strangely stirred by the sequence of events that had just taken place. Sort of antsy and restless and way too warm. She wanted to run, to throw a few more hits. She wanted to sit down and just smile.

Shaking her head at her own odd mood, she continued at a fast clip down the road to the first side street. The moon was fat, providing plenty of light to guide them.

Eli easily kept up with her pace, but then, given his height, his legs were a whole lot longer than hers.

There, parked against the curb under the dubious protection of a bright street lamp, was her truck. She owned the most disreputable-looking piece of transportation on the road, and the most reliable. Ray again tried to pull away from Eli's hold, and he again resisted her efforts.

She looked at him over her shoulder. "It's going to be damn tough for me to drive a stick one-handed."

He surveyed her truck with curiosity but no condemnation. Looking down at her, he asked, "It runs?"

Ray didn't take offense. "Turn me loose and I'll show you."

He did.

Keys in hand, she unlocked her door, slid behind the wheel, and reached across the seat to unlock the passenger door for Eli. He had a little trouble getting it unjammed. It was a deliberate alteration to the door, making it tough for anyone to jump into her truck without her invitation.

She turned the engine over, proud of the throaty, rumbling purr of power, and was already coasting when Eli finally threw his shoulder into the door, jarring it loose so he could pull it open and jump in.

She flipped on her headlights, put the truck in gear, and rolled onto the main drag, quickly gaining speed. Eli snapped on his seat belt, drawing her notice.

Expecting his complaints to start at any second, she was surprised that he had his head back on the seat, eyes closed, looking very at ease. He didn't seem the least put out by what had transpired thus far. Amazing, she thought, even as she admired the angles and planes of his face that, together, made a very striking appearance. What really got her, though, wasn't his looks, but rather that small, secret smile he wore.

He'd had fun, maybe as much fun as she'd had. To be sure, Ray asked, "Enjoying yourself?"

"Just reminiscing."

She didn't understand him at all.

Because wealthy men were the only ones who could afford her, she'd become well acquainted with their idiosyncrasies. They sometimes considered her work sport and were titillated by the threat of danger—which they thought less than real. They didn't want to be inconvenienced, dirty, or at risk. And they most definitely didn't want to put out much physical effort.

Yet Eli had held his own in the bar, ruthlessly defended himself, and now smiled about it.

He was one mystery on top of another. She wouldn't question him about it because getting to know him personally wasn't part of her job. She didn't want to know him, to maybe start to care. Caring was a liability, a weakness she couldn't afford. "We'll shop in the morning and pack in the afternoon, then leave the next day."

His eyes opened. Without raising his head, he turned his face toward her. Moonlight played over his features and illuminated his hazel eyes. "You can be ready that soon?"

"You can't?"

His smile had been replaced with a kind of pensive reflection. "I'll be ready. I just assumed these things required more planning."

Ray shrugged with feigned indifference. "What's to plan? I already know where he is and I know how to get in. Over the years, things have gotten easier, not harder in Central American. All we really need is a few supplies and some luck."

He shifted closer. "If all they want is a little money, why don't I just pay them?"

"Because they might wait another week or more before even asking. And in the meantime, your brother is in Central America. The guys who have him aren't much to worry about, but what if someone else finds out about him and decides they'd rather ransom him? A rich American is tough to resist. It could get ugly. With me in the picture, we get him out pronto, they get some cash to keep them happy, and all's well that ends well."

Even to herself, she sounded convincing, and still her stomach twisted with dread. Memories were a bitch, and illogical to boot. What she'd said was true. This would be a joyride.

But it was the first time she'd returned with a partner.

She squeezed the steering wheel. "I took care of everything before meeting with you."

Eli nodded, but asked, "Everything, meaning . . . ?"

"Travel arrangements, weapons, cover once we're there. It's all set."

He shook his head in awe. "You're not lacking in confidence, are you?"

"Modesty isn't one of my virtues." Considering that topic dead, Ray went onto the next item of business. "Where do you live? Or do you expect me to guess?"

She found he wasn't easy to rile when, after a look of censure, he gave her simple directions. "Do you want me to pick you up in the morning?"

Ray stopped at a red light. So late at night, the roads were deserted. Other than the mellow purr of the truck's engine, silence filled the cab to the point she thought she could hear her own heartbeat. Or maybe it was his.

She twisted toward him, caught him watching her, and her stomach got jumpier than ever.

She thought about altering the plans, thought about insisting on a necessary distance between them. But at this stage, it wouldn't make sense. Not now, and not because of some vague awareness she'd never sensed in herself before. So, Eli was an appealing man? He wasn't the pansy-ass she'd expected him to be, and he wasn't rude or condescending. Big deal. He'd still bought and paid for her service. She'd have to keep that in mind.

"Pick me up? No way. I'm sleeping at your place." Her words were casual but commanding. Now that she'd made up her mind, she wasn't about to let him change it.

Eli looked blank. "My place?"

The light turned green and Ray eased forward. "No reason for me to spend the night in a motel when you have plenty of room. Right?"

After a hesitation, he said, "Right," but he didn't sound convinced.

"We're going to be getting real familiar soon, anyway." She spared him a glance and saw his intent frown of consideration. "Get used to it."

Since Ray had needed very specific directions, Eli asked, "You're not from around here?"

"Illinois, yeah. Chicago, no."

"Where are you from?"

Just as she didn't want his personal details, she wouldn't give her own. "Did you notice that wasn't in the papers you looked at?"

He shrugged. "So?"

"My private business is just that, private. In return, I don't want to know any more about you than what you need from me, the facts, and any pertinent information. That's it."

"I see."

"I hope so." She meant to let it go at that, she really did, but before she knew it, more words tumbled out, making her sound defensive. "I can't stomach biased assumptions." The truck jerked as Ray shifted, giving away her unease. Damn it, she didn't need this. Why the hell was she babbling?

Eli sighed. "Once again, I'm afraid I miss your meaning. Do you care to explain, or is that forbidden also?"

Ray wanted to bite her tongue, but she was the one who'd started this. "My life and how I live it is nobody's business but my own."

"I agree." He tilted his head and, very softly, asked, "So what was that about biased assumptions?"

Damn her loose lips for getting her into this. She drew a breath and tried to think of the simplest, least emotional way to explain. "Based on the job you've hired me to do, you probably already have preconceived notions of the type of person I am." He neither confirmed nor denied that, so she demanded, "Don't you?"

"I don't know. I'm still trying to figure you out."

"Well, don't." Her voice had been an octave too high, and with ruthless determination, she sought the unfeeling façade of a hired mercenary. It took her five endless seconds before she said, with more control, "Who I am and what motivates me can't be shown on a paper. Just trust that I can do the job and keep any other thoughts to yourself."

"Right. Got it. No speculating." Then he ruined that reassurance by saying, "So you're actually two different women. That's what you're getting at?

And I'll only have the privilege of meeting the mercenary. The other woman, the one I can't discuss, is off-limits."

Oh God, she should throw him out of the truck and head home right now. Her teeth locked together. "You can put it that way if you like."

"This is interesting."

"No. It. Is. Not." She glared at him. "As long as you stay away from personal questions, we'll handle this business just fine. *Like a business*. But get nosy and you won't like the consequences."

"Meaning you'll beat me up?"

She barely swallowed down the feral sound of frustration, then muttered, "Don't think I won't."

Eli made an annoying tsking sound. "I had no idea mercenaries were so touchy."

That did it. Her spine snapped straight and her temper peaked. Through her teeth, she said, "I am *not* touchy."

"Well, you're sure as hell overreacting." His voice rose in volume, too. "I didn't ask for a listing of your most recent lovers or what religious organization you belong to. I don't give a damn if you dance naked on a stage or spend your free time as a brain surgeon. In the civilized world, people make small talk. That's all I was doing."

And there was the crux of the problem. Ray had never fully fit into the civilized world. Oh, for the most part she'd left the mercenary life behind. If it weren't for Matt's college fund, she wouldn't have taken this mission. But her job as a carpenter only took them so far and she wanted her brother to have every advantage. She wanted his life to be different.

Outwardly, Ray did her best not to react to Eli's barbs. But inside, she felt every single one. She had been touchy, damn it. Pass her the Midol, because she'd acted just like a woman with PMS.

She thought to apologize, she really did. But it had been years since she'd bothered to excuse herself to anyone, for any reason, and she wasn't certain she still knew how. The silence had gone on too long, anyway.

She'd just have to concentrate on ignoring him—as if anyone could. God, she could *feel* him next to her. She knew right where his muscled thighs rested on the seat, where his long fingers tapped restlessly on the door. She knew how his coat had opened over his abdomen, how the wind had ruffled his dark hair.

If only he'd been the same as the other arrogant jerks who'd hired her. Or if he weren't so damn handsome, and so accepting of her instructions.

She drew a deep breath—and smelled his rich scent.

How did he manage to smell so good? Moments ago her stomach had been jumpy over the thought of returning to a place that held only painful memories for her.

Now her stomach jumped because sitting beside her was a man who didn't fit any of the previous molds she understood. He was different, but in all the right ways.

She'd done a lot of preparation for this mission. She had it planned down to the minute. In and out fast. No time for complications.

But she hadn't planned for Eli Connors. What a sexy complication.

She had a feeling this was going to be the hardest mission of her life.

Chapter Two

Eli told her to turn at the next street, then leaned back in his seat to watch her. From the moment she'd stepped into the bar, *not* watching her had been impossible.

Truth was, she fascinated him. And it wasn't just her delicate looks, which were beyond deceiving, given the way she'd handled herself at the bar. She'd thrown a man, and flushed with the sheer pleasure of it. She'd made another into a choirboy, and grinned with delight.

What a woman.

But her staunch attitudes and constant blustering had revealed, at least to him, a lot of vulnerability, too.

What type of female became a mercenary? What type of woman lived a life that made her feel so defensive? Despite her warnings, maybe because of them, he wanted to get to know her better. She was a link to his brother, reassurance at a time of uncertainty, and something about her appealed to him on the most basic level. Even though she kept telling him not to pry, she was more up front and open than anyone he'd ever met. She didn't have an ounce of guile. No, Ms. Ray Jean Vereker called 'em as she saw 'em. And she'd insulted him several times.

Not many women, from the slums of his past or the present boardroom, had ever done that.

Trying for subtlety, hoping to provoke her into giving more away, Eli smiled toward her. "You think you're pretty tough, don't you?"

Keeping her gaze on the road, she lifted one narrow, straight shoulder. "I'm tough enough when I need to be. That's all you have to worry about."

He'd always been attracted to assertive women. Okay, so a mercenary was a bit over the top, but as he'd told her, she didn't look hardened enough for the job. If she'd had a string of rattlesnake tattoos and a mustache and a figure like a tank, maybe, just maybe the persona would be more creditable.

"You're a very attractive woman, Ray." Her back stiffened in what he already thought of as her battle mode, and he had to bite back a laugh. "I'm not getting personal," he assured her with grave sincerity, "just making an observation."

He watched her gather herself, saw her tucking away her real reactions to deliver what she considered a suitable response. Her laugh sounded rusty, as if it'd been a long time since she'd felt any real humor.

What kind of life did a female mercenary lead when she wasn't on the job? Did she live as a hermit, was she a bully, or did she somehow manage to fade into regular society? Was she engaged, even married?

Without meaning to, Eli pictured all kind of awful scenarios until he shifted in his seat, disgusted with himself and his possessive thoughts.

"If someone had taken the time to tell me it was

a woman they'd send me, I still wouldn't have envisioned a woman like you."

With silky menace, she repeated, "Like me?"

"It's not an insult, Ray." He shook his head. "In fact, it was a compliment."

"There's more to capability than brute strength, and looks can be deceiving. But as far as trying to compliment me, don't. We'll be spending at least one night in Central America, maybe two. Trust me, I look pretty bad after a couple of days roughing it. More importantly, I don't care. I don't waste time caring." Her dark gaze swept over him before she turned down the road that led to his building. "Remember that."

He didn't believe her. She wanted to be cold and indifferent, but she bloomed with warmth. For whatever reasons, she just didn't want to admit it.

Minutes later, she parked the hideous, rust-covered truck in the parking garage amid the array of expensive, richly colored cars. Ray didn't seem the least bit impressed with the difference. In fact, she almost seemed contemptuous of his money.

He liked that about her.

Part of her present nasty attitude was due to surprise, he thought. She'd apparently expected some resistance on his part when she'd first shown up. What she didn't know was that he'd called her agency primarily for a guide and only secondarily for backup in case of any physical confrontations.

He could hold his own, so he didn't expect her to have to engage in any physical battles, despite her more than capable display at the bar. She knew her way in and around Central America, and that was her value. The necessity for stealth made bringing along more than one person risky, and she had the credentials to prove she was the best, so she'd have to do.

Ray walked to the front of the truck and waited for him. Long-legged, slim but with subtle curves, she had the appeal of natural, healthy good looks. She wasn't classically pretty, not with that strong jawline. But her full lips and wide, very dark eyes were quick to catch and hold attention. And that attitude . . . He smiled. Ray wielded her attitude like a sledgehammer, using it to clear the way of any resistance.

She riffled her fingers through her long, midnight black bangs, watching as he left the truck. Eli raised an inquiring brow. "Do you have a bag or anything you need for the night?"

"It's under the seat." She cocked out a hip in an impatient pose. "I was waiting for you to get out of the way."

Except for the few times he'd managed to take her off guard, her voice was soft and husky, seldom raised above a moderate tone. To maintain that air of control, she also kept her stance deceptively casual.

Even when she'd thrown the man at the bar, she hadn't tensed. She'd just sort of . . . maneuvered, bent the right way, and the big man had gone flying. Eli figured it was a necessary pretense on her part because she couldn't really be that calm and indifferent to the circumstances of her ability. Much of what she presented to the world was a ruse.

He intended to sift fact from fiction.

Pulling the bag out for her, he started forward, but when he reached for her arm, she casually sidestepped, evading his grasp.

To cover the nervous gesture, she said, "You're taller than I first thought."

Eli stared down at the top of her short, glossy black hair. Usually towering over most women and a fair amount of men, he was pleased, though he didn't know why, that Ray was only about five inches shorter than him.

"I'm six-four. But you're pretty tall, too." And then, just to tease her, he added, "For a woman."

Somehow, when she glared at him, she managed to look him dead in the eye without seeming to tilt her head at all. He liked it. "Is this your only bag?"

"There're two changes of clothes." Ray turned away to contemplate the building. "That's all I need."

The bag was very light, making Eli curious. "What about shampoo and soap and . . ."

"You don't have those things?"

"Of course I do. But don't most women have their own brands? Mine might smell a bit masculine."

She made a show of mild disgust. "We're going to a tiny, nothing village in Central America, not a formal ball. Does it matter what I smell like?"

In his defense, he'd never before met a woman who wouldn't care. At the moment, she smelled like . . . warm, soft woman, and that was about as good as it got.

To lighten her mood, he said, "You do have your own toothbrush, don't you?"

"I have my own toothbrush," she agreed. Then she turned toward him. "You don't live here."

Eli stared into her eyes, so opaque they seemed fathomless. Her lashes weren't real long, but they were inky dark and thick. He saw a tiny scar near the corner of her right eye and another near her temple. How had she gotten them? Did he even want to know?

She stared at him, unblinking and defiant. Eli shook off his preoccupation with her appearance. "I have an apartment upstairs."

"Maybe, but it isn't your home."

Playing along, he asked, "Why not?"

"Because no one who could afford me would live in a complex this simple."

"It's a nice place," Eli defended.

"Nice. But not nice enough. Where are you taking me?"

Eli gave up. "I have several offices, and I keep an apartment close to the locations I visit most often. My home—that is, where I prefer to be—is in Kentucky. I have a ranch there."

That appeased her. "It would have been too much of a coincidence for us to both live in Illinois."

"True. I'm staying here now because you're here."

He waited for some sort of reaction to that, but Ray only nodded and started into the building. "You own a chain of department stores?"

Technically, they were his grandfather's, but that was probably more information than she wanted. "That's right."

A gentleman by nature, it was difficult for Eli not to take her arm as they walked. But she'd been quietly obvious in her wishes not to be touched. It was one more thing to add to her mystery. "We can do the shopping you think is necessary in my Chicago store tomorrow."

"No. We'll do the shopping at the local thrift shop. I don't want you standing out or I'll be rescuing you and your brother both."

Behind her, where she couldn't possibly see him and take offense, Eli grinned. She was a bossy little thing, giving orders without thought and fully expecting them to be obeyed. It was a novel sensation for him, since he was usually the boss, commanding hundreds of people.

She had a slow sassy walk, too. She may have thought wearing the dark clothing would make her less noticeable, but Eli doubted anything could make her fade into the woodwork. Her confident, take-charge aura was too out there and in-your-face.

Even the shortness of her shiny, coal black hair appealed to him. It had a slight natural wave and curled over her ears and nape. Her wispy bangs were longer and she fiddled with them a lot. Eli wondered if that's why she'd left them long—to give her fingers something to do.

Despite the mannish swagger, her hips swayed gently as she made her way up the hallway to his door. Eli pulled his gaze away from her derriere and fished in his pocket for his door key.

He wasn't disappointed that the moment he had his keys in hand, she reached for them.

He lifted them over her head. "I think I can manage." His words were gently teasing.

She actually flushed, then forced a nonchalant shrug. "Habit."

The blush nearly did him in, so sweet and so telling about the real woman. If he weren't careful, he'd spend more time contemplating her than rescuing his irresponsible brother.

Eli unlocked the door and pushed it open. They

stepped inside, and for the briefest moment, they stood in the dark. Ray was so vital, bursting full of energy and life. He could smell the light, feminine fragrance of her skin and hair, see the glimmer of her witchy eyes as she watched him. Then he flipped the wall switch and the room became flooded with light.

Ray looked around, but showed no reaction to the lush furnishings. "We need to talk, but first, you want to show me where you want me to sleep?"

The lady was full of loaded questions. First, she'd asked if he "wanted her," and now she left the sleeping arrangements up to him. If he hadn't already seen her emasculate one guy with a kick in the jewels, he might have offered a suggestion or two. But judging by the flat look in her beautiful eyes, she expected some snide sexual comment on his part. He wasn't about to oblige her.

Regardless of her biased views, he was not an idiot.

He'd needed a distraction from his worries, and Ray Jean Vereker, lady mercenary, was certainly that.

"I'll fix us something to drink while you put your things in the first room on the right down the hall. It's a guest bedroom with a private bath."

"Fix something to eat, too. It was a long drive for me and I'm so hungry my ribs are clanking together."

Eli shook his head, bemused. She certainly didn't pull any punches. "What would you like?" he asked politely.

"What do you have?"

That threw him. "You know, I don't have the faintest idea. I told the cleaning lady to stock a few things since I knew I'd be staying here. Do you want to take a look yourself?"

"No. Just surprise me. I'm hungry enough to eat anything."

Five minutes later when Ray came in, Eli had a can of soup simmering on the stove and had just finished making sandwiches. "Baloney and cheese. That okay?"

For an answer, Ray took the sandwich from his hand and sank her teeth into it. As she chewed, she pulled out a chair and lounged back in it, reaching for her case at the same time. "What exactly did your brother do to get himself in this fix?"

"You don't know yet?" That surprised him. She seemed to know everything else.

She swallowed before answering. "It wasn't pertinent. Mercenaries don't have a conscience. We don't decide who is right or wrong in a situation. We just work for the highest offer." She saluted him with her last bite of sandwich. "Your offer was right."

He knew, damn it, *he knew* it was all an act—and still he stiffened. "Then I suppose I'm lucky the guerillas didn't want you to kill him."

"I told you that particular village isn't violent, and they're far too poor to afford me."

She didn't deny that she might kill for money and it pissed him off. He knew her rules, but still he said, "And if the circumstances were different?"

"If they were violent and rich?"

"Yeah."

"Your brother would already be dead—but not by my hand."

Eli chose to take that as reassurance on her morals, whether she meant it that way or not. "My brother Jeremy foolishly went to the wrong place at the wrong time."

"Why?"

He slashed a hand through the air. If Jeremy were here now, he'd get an ass-kicking that'd last him a lifetime. "He wants to be a photojournalist. He's a good student, but he hates to study. I suppose he had this half-baked idea about firsthand experience. Since parts of Central America are still accounted to be underdeveloped, he hoped to get some prime photos and ace his finals report."

"You allowed him to go?"

"He's nineteen, too old for me to forbid him anything. But no, I didn't know he was going. He asked for the money to fund the trip, but he told me he was going to Europe with some friends over semester break." Eli glanced away, silently cursing his own gullibility. Time and again, he tried to make up for the fact that Jeremy had lost his parents, and with Eli's entrance into the family, his position as heir apparent. In the process, he'd spoiled him. "If I hadn't been so preoccupied with business, I might have known what he was planning."

"Blaming yourself won't help him, and you didn't answer my question. What happened to get him in trouble?"

Rubbing his face, Eli stood and walked to the stove. He was amazed by how quickly Ray put her food away. She didn't seem indelicate, but the food rapidly disappeared. He ladled a bowl of the soup and placed it on the table. Not bothering to sit, he said quietly, "Jeremy isn't really a bad kid, but he has this stupid chip on his shoulder. He was in a bar with the friends he'd taken along. They were drinking, showing off, trying to pick up some local women, and they managed to offend a few of the men."

Ray laughed, a genuine laugh this time. "I hadn't heard that part of the story. Your brother has to have a screw loose to go provoking a guerilla."

Eli couldn't argue with that assessment. "A disagreement erupted, things got heated, and they took him."

"How long ago was this exactly?"

"Less than a week. It took a few days for his friends to return home and contact me. They first tried getting him out on their own, but they're young and . . ."

"And if they'd pushed it, they might've ended up hostages, too."

"That's how I figured it." His hands curled into fists as he paced the confines of the kitchen, reliving that moment of helplessness. "Rather than wait for a ransom demand, I tried contacting the local officials. They gave me a huge runaround. Either they truly knew nothing about it, or they didn't give a damn."

"You have to know who to ask."

"And obviously I didn't." Eli hadn't told his grandparents the truth about Jeremy. It would have worried them sick. Instead . . . He turned to Ray. "So I called that damned agency."

"And got me." She winked. "Lucky you."

He *did* feel better, knowing she was familiar with the area and the people. Instinctively, he knew she wouldn't lie to him. If Jeremy were in serious danger, she'd say so. Quietly, he agreed, "Lucky me."

She gave him a sharp glance. Eli didn't look away. He felt a connection with her that went beyond her reasons for being with him tonight.

The seconds ticked by while she appeared to be thinking things over. Finally she straightened in her seat and nodded. "First off, stop worrying, okay? Your brother really is fine. I got a firsthand account. A trusted source told me he's full of complaints, driving everyone crazy, but unharmed."

Eli rubbed his hands together. "So how soon can we get him, do you think? I don't want to wait around until he does get hurt."

Ray looked him over with a critical eye. "Is your brother like you?"

"Like me?"

"Semitough," she clarified. "Or is he a typical pampered rich kid?"

Eli didn't know if he liked being labeled "semitough" but at least he understood her meaning. "Jeremy's worked on the ranch most his life. He's strong. He's a man."

"A nineteen-year-old man. God knows, those are the worst kind." Her expression softened with some hidden, inner thought that curled the corners of her mouth. "At that age guys are full of testosterone and vinegar, without much room for common sense."

"True," he agreed in the same soft tone, beguiled by that smile. "That's Jeremy."

Ray finished off her soup, then pushed out of her seat. "They'll have him sleep in a casita with the insects for company. His selection of food will likely be rice and beans or beans and rice, and they can offer only the crudest means of bathing."

"Shit."

"It's not a Boy Scout campout, but if he can handle roughing it, it won't be so bad." She squeezed his shoulder, surprising him with the gesture of comfort and the strength of her grip. He looked at her hand, slender and pale, and had to fight the urge to lift it to his mouth and kiss her palm. "We'll have a long day tomorrow. You'd better get some sleep."

Since he'd gotten word of his brother's predicament, he'd barely slept at all. Not only was he worried about Jeremy, but his grandfather and grandmother were too old to suffer through such concerns. "In a bit."

She treated him to another show of her bossiness. "Now. Sitting out here stewing isn't going to help your brother. You'll need to be in fit shape for a rescue. *We* have the hard part. All he has to do is wait for us."

Eli rubbed the back of his neck. "I can't seem to get it off my mind enough to sleep."

Moving behind him, she pushed his hand aside and took over the task of massaging tight muscles. Her fingers were cool against his heated skin, strong but gentle, kneading with a practiced ease. "Concentrate on how you're going to box his ears for doing this to you when you get him home."

The massage wasn't working.

With Ray so close behind him, her hands touching him, his muscles were in danger of going into a cramp. "I've already done that a thousand times. And I've envisioned the rescue at least double that." Over his shoulder, he gave her a piercing look. "You, however, I couldn't have imagined in my wildest dreams."

Her hands remained in place, but were no longer moving. A hushed quality had invaded the air between them. "I won't disappoint you."

He felt the heat of her on his back. As they

stared at each other, her breathing deepened and her fingers contracted.

"What makes you the best, Ray?" He wanted to better understand her, all of her. "Men are stronger, with more endurance. They can be taught anything you've been taught, right? So why you?"

She answered without hesitation. "Just as you can't believe it, no one else can either. That's an advantage that I use. No one sees me as a threat until it's too late." She squeezed his shoulders, breaking the moment of intimacy with camaraderie, and turned to leave the room. "I know when to brazen it out, when to make my move. Because I'm smaller and lighter, I can slip in and out of camps without making a sound. I don't play macho games, and most importantly, I never lose my focus."

"Never?"

She looked back at him and slowly shook her head. "Doesn't matter how tempting the distraction might be."

Was she saying he tempted her? He couldn't have been more stunned if she'd plopped into his lap and kissed him. "Ray . . ."

"No. Don't say it. Whatever it is, just let it go." Her eyes, deep and mysterious, held his for a long moment. Then she whispered, "Good night, Eli." And she was gone.

The whispering woke her.

Feminine whispering.

Ray jerked up in her bed, alert to danger but disoriented by the strange room, the soft bed, and the expensive sheets. In less than a second, everything fell into place. Eli. She'd left him sitting at the kitchen table on the assumption he'd soon retire. Instead, he'd invited over company? That didn't make any sense.

Straining her ears to hear, Ray could just make out Eli's voice, quiet but firm and determined. There was silence, then more whispering—and the unmistakable sound of a soft female moan.

That bastard.

Ray didn't hesitate. She slipped out of bed and, not bothering to dress properly, cracked her door open to eavesdrop. She couldn't see down the hall but she no longer needed to. Eli had a female guest, and he was obviously being romantic.

Indignation hit her like a slap in the face.

Hadn't he been overwhelmed with concern for his baby brother only hours before? Hadn't she forced herself to offer comfort when she was so lousy at doing so?

She should have known the truth. Despite seeming different, Eli was wealthy and the rich never concerned themselves long with anything other than their own pleasure.

She knew she wasn't being fair, but damn it, she'd lain awake for over an hour trying to get him out of her mind, trying to reconcile just how different he really was from the other men who'd hired her.

Trying to dredge up that damned focus she'd bragged about.

Ray was tired and suddenly quite irritable. They had a job to do in the morning and they both needed their rest. If he'd wanted a last-minute romp, he could have at least been quiet so she could sleep through it.

Having made up her mind, Ray flipped her disheveled bangs off her forehead, pulled her thin olive green men's undershirt down so it covered her panties, and strolled nonchalantly down the hall. Stealth was her middle name; her bare feet made no sound on the plush carpeting and her compressed lips ensured that even her breath was silent.

She slipped into the room without either of them noticing, giving her a chance to observe. Immediately, she realized that Eli wasn't quite the participant she'd imagined. He tried valiantly to disengage himself from the clinging woman. His success was nominal.

Though the female looked small and delicate— a deliberate affectation, no doubt—she had the tenacity of a cat determined to get attention. She rubbed herself against Eli the same way a cat curled around your legs.

Ray observed her with objective criticism and had to admit she looked classy. And definitely moneyed. Her pale blond hair, styled to skim her shoulders with each move of her head, had professional streaks. Her simple tan dress was tailored but still managed to emphasize her boobs and backside to draw masculine attention.

Narrowing her eyes in disgust, Ray leaned one shoulder against the wall, crossed her ankles, and folded her arms over her breasts. With a discreet "Ahem" she finally and quite suddenly drew their attention.

Eli pulled free of the woman's hold and his gaze zeroed in on Ray like a beacon.

The woman was speechless for several seconds before she gasped. "Eli, who *is* this person?"

Eli's attention never moved from Ray. But it did

move all over her, slowly, thoroughly, from the top of her rumpled head to the tips of her bare toes. Ray could feel that look scorching her, touching on her like a heated breath. Strangely, though she wasn't cold, goose bumps rose on her exposed skin and she became suddenly, severely aware of just how little she wore.

The undershirt concealed every part of her body that proclaimed her a woman, but still, it clung to her, the neck scooped low, the armholes wide so that the tops and sides of her breasts were visible. It molded over her upper thighs, stopping just short of revealing her panties. Used to being in predicaments where modesty had no place, Ray was surprised to feel her cheeks heating in concordance with Eli's rapt observation.

Of course, he noticed. The flare of heat in his eyes told her so. His slight, nearly imperceptible smile told her so. His carefully drawn in breath told her so.

To regain her equilibrium, Ray said to him, "Who am I, Eli? It's up to you." Without knowing who the other woman was or what she knew of Eli's intentions, it seemed safest to leave the story up to him.

As if he'd only just then remembered the other woman, Eli turned his attention back to her with a frown. "I told you I'd be busy for a while, Jane. You shouldn't be here."

Jane's gaze skipped between the two of them and it didn't take a mind reader to know she'd drawn some hasty and incorrect conclusions. But to Ray's surprise, she didn't get angry at the suspicious presence of another woman.

She pouted.

Her bottom lip stuck out and she stroked Eli's arm while pressing her breasts against him. "I missed you, Eli. You wouldn't tell me where you were going or why, or how long you'd be away. Of course, now I understand." She emphasized that with a pointed glance at Ray.

Ray wanted to puke over the nauseating display. "Here we go with the assumptions again."

Eli gave Ray a quelling frown before peeling the woman off his arm. "I didn't tell you, Jane, because it doesn't concern you."

"Of course it does." Her voice dropped to a whisper, but Ray could still hear her—just as Jane intended. "You were forced to resort to . . . *her* type, because I've denied you."

Ray scoffed. *"My* type?" How ridiculous. She wasn't a woman a man would go to for that sort of thing. The very idea of it made her laugh.

Judging by his glare, Eli didn't share her humor.

"But Eli, you can send her away now." Jane's smile trembled, shy and so sickeningly sweet, Ray's teeth started to ache. "I came to tell you I'm ready. I simply hadn't realized how . . . desperate you had gotten."

Jane was a small woman, and it seemed to Ray that Eli had to look down a great distance just to frown at her. Not that it had any visible effect on good old Jane. She clung like a limpet, cooing and puckering and turning Ray's stomach with the overblown display of affection.

If I ever coo at a man, Ray thought privately, *I hope someone shoots me.*

She should probably leave and give them their privacy, but she wouldn't. She was responsible for Eli until the mission ended successfully, and he did need his sleep. Both those reasons were plausible enough to suit Ray, so she didn't budge from her position on the wall.

And then Jane slipped her little hand into Eli's open shirt, stroking him, toying with him, and Ray got a brief glimpse of his chest. It looked warm and hard, sprinkled with curling dark hair.

Fascinated, Ray took in the play with the same attention she'd give a peep show, but the show only lasted a moment before Eli forcibly set Jane a respectable distance from the undeniable lure of his body.

His shirt, however, remained open, and Ray continued to admire his obvious strength and fitness. She hadn't expected that from a man of wealth and leisure. She'd expected him to be soft. She'd expected him to be unappealing.

Assumptions. She shook her head, knowing herself to be as guilty as most.

"Jane," Eli warned as she tried to snuggle closer again. "Ray isn't here for that and you owe her an apology for suggesting such a thing."

"Really?"

Jane seemed pleased that Ray wouldn't be occupying Eli's bed after all. How she'd come to such an asinine conclusion in the first place left Ray boggled. If the woman had clear vision, she had to have noticed Ray wasn't exactly a femme fatale. She could kick Eli's ass, but no way could she seduce him.

"Then why is she here, Eli, in your home, dressed—or rather, *undressed*—like that?"

Ray saw the muscles in his jaw flex. "She's here because I hired her to do a job. And she's dressed like that because she was in bed, as I should be, and we woke her."

Jane wouldn't be that easily appeased. Her eyes slanted toward Ray with raw suspicion. "What job?"

Growling in frustration, Eli briefly closed his eyes. When he opened them again, he looked toward Ray. She grinned, enjoying his predicament.

Giving up, he explained, "Ray is a guide to help me get my brother back."

Ray took offense at being termed a mere guide, but held her tongue. Jane obviously wasn't about to believe such a thing anyway.

"What kind of guide runs around half naked? And why is she spending the night here?"

Eli lost his patience. "That's enough, Jane. It's time for you to leave."

Throwing herself against him, Jane gave Eli no option but to catch her. Over the top of her head, he glowered at Ray.

Now how was this supposed to be her fault?

Surely he didn't expect her to offer some magical solution. The workings of the average female mind had always been a mystery to her. Eli likely understood women better than she ever would.

Jane started crying, which didn't surprise Ray in the least. The woman had the appearance of a professional watering pot—her hair was pale, her complexion was pale, and she cried without smudging her makeup even a little. Very professional.

Eli struggled to free himself without actually hurting the woman. Jane's narrow shoulders squared and her tears miraculously disappeared. "I'm going with you."

Eli groaned, stuck one hand in his hair, and knotted his fingers. He looked ready to detonate.

Ray decided to take pity on him. "No, you're not. Eli will just have to make do without your company for a few days, because there's no way I'm going to be responsible for the both of you."

Jane stood frozen in appalled disbelief. "Eli would be responsible for me, not you!"

"If you want Eli home in one piece, he'll have to be responsible for himself and no one else." Ray pushed away from the wall and strode forward until she towered over Jane. With a wide-eyed look of worry, Jane scuttled closer to Eli's side as if for protection. It was hard not to laugh, but Ray had excellent control. She summoned her meanest expression. "You'd only distract him."

Jane sputtered. "I'm his fiancée. I should be with him."

Fiancée? Ray allowed the single moment of crushing disappointment, then shook it off. Eli's life, outside of the mission, was no concern of hers. "You'd only be a hindrance."

Ready to crawl back to bed, Ray turned to Eli and, seeing his relief, added, "I'm putting my foot down on this, Eli. If you want me, you'll have to send her home."

She gave him the easy out, taking the blame fully on herself, but Eli didn't look grateful. No, instead, he looked . . . *hot.*

His hazel eyes seemed to smolder in the evening light until Ray felt unsettled and uncertain and ready to bolt.

She never ran, damn him, and definitely not from a man. She thrust her chin up. "Make up your mind, Eli."

His gaze dipped to her mouth, lingered, before he turned to face Jane. "I'm sorry, Jane. But I need her help."

Jane gave one more pitiful sob, flinging herself into Eli's arms and nearly smothering him with a long, drawn-out kiss. Ray couldn't be sure, but she thought tongues might have been involved. Standing there watching that kiss, she felt like a voyeur, and worse, she felt pathetic. She wanted to walk away, yet her feet remained glued to the floor.

Eli didn't fight Jane. He merely waited her out. When Jane finally pulled away, he flattened a large hand on her back and started her toward the door.

"Go back to your hotel, Jane. I'll call you when I get home."

"Please be careful, Eli."

Prodded by some evil imp, Ray called out, "I'll take real good care of him, Jane, don't you worry none."

Jane started sobbing again.

Ray could hear Eli's strained reassurances. Deciding that she'd gotten into enough mischief for the night, she started down the hall. Just as she reached her room, she heard the front door close. She stepped inside and quietly closed her door, leaning back against it. Eli's footsteps sounded softly on the carpeting, then stopped outside her door. Ray held her breath.

"Good night, Ray," she heard him whisper, his tone laced with amusement. Then he went on to his room.

Ray turned out the light and crawled into her bed. She curled into a ball on her side and tucked her hands beneath her cheek. Her thoughts were jumbled and confused. She wasn't certain what to make of her feelings because it had been so long since she'd felt anything like them. She was appalled that this could happen, that she would let it happen, but she had.

For the first time in a very long time, she was interested in a man. She actually felt desire.

What rotten timing.

Chapter Three

Eli was already up and dressed when Ray came into the kitchen the next morning. It was early, only six o'clock, and the sun had just begun to rise. Ray yawned as she sauntered in and casually seated herself at the table.

She still wore that damned provocative shirt, but now she had on loose matching shorts, too.

It didn't help.

The army green, mannish getup should have looked ridiculous. It didn't. With her trim healthy body, a burlap sack would be sexy.

"Coffee?" His voice emerged as a low rumble. He'd awakened with thoughts of Ray on his mind, which had caused his morning erection to linger. Now, with her here in the flesh looking sleepy and tender, his dominant male instincts surged.

"Yeah, that'd be terrific." She yawned again. Assuming he'd serve her, assuming he could ignore the provocative way she dressed, she lounged back in her chair.

Her legs were sleek with muscles, smooth and straight. Her shoulders were toned, proud. She showed a lot of skin and all of it looked creamy enough to kiss. When she'd first appeared last night, he'd been hit with such a wave of lust it had almost staggered him.

Throughout the long night, his thoughts had centered on her, and when he had managed to sleep, he'd dreamed of her. Restlessness had driven him from his bed nearly an hour ago.

He handed Ray the coffee, then settled himself across from her. Unwilling to alarm her or put her on guard, he tried to be casual, too, but damn, he'd never known a woman so completely comfortable in her own skin.

Her short, midnight hair stuck out at very odd angles, and her eyes were alert but puffy from sleep, the lids heavy. Her cheeks were flushed, one of them bearing a small crease from her pillow. She obviously hadn't suffered the same distractions he had.

He propped his head up on an elbow and smiled at her. "You don't look like you could take on a rescue right now."

Sipping the hot coffee, she peeked at him over the rim of the cup and shrugged. "It isn't necessary that I do any rescuing right now, is it?"

"And when it is necessary?" he asked, doing his best to keep his gaze on her face rather than the sleep-warmed skin of her upper breasts, revealed by the low neck of the undershirt.

She paused in the middle of a drink, then gulped down a good portion before plunking the mug onto the tabletop. "What's the matter, Eli, getting cold feet? Your fiancée convince you I wasn't right for the job?"

Her comment gave him the perfect opportunity to clear up at least one misunderstanding. She'd run off to bed last night, taking away his chance then. Which was maybe a good thing, because the way he'd felt last night, he'd have ended up kissing her before she reached her room, and Ray being Ray, she might have crippled him for it.

"Contrary to what Jane might say, she's not my fiancée. She was just being possessive." He grinned, remembering Jane's expression. "You made quite a grand entrance last night. Really took her by surprise."

Ray snorted in doubt. "Not a fiancée, yet she came all the way from Kentucky to declare herself, to offer up her body and her undying love?"

Beneath the sarcasm, Eli could hear Ray's genuine curiosity. And the way she didn't quite meet his eyes was telling. He knew her question wasn't just to pass the time and that pleased him, especially since she had been so careful to remain impersonal. "Jane has a business office here, also. She probably had a meeting to attend and decided to kill two birds with one stone. Actually, she travels a lot more than I do. We generally don't see each other all that often."

"Then how did the two of you ever get together?"

Briefly, Eli considered teasing her about the forbidden nature of her personal question, but he didn't want to discourage her. It'd give him leverage when he got around to asking his own questions.

But he also wasn't willing to go into detail, sensing that Ray would find too many differences in their backgrounds. "With each of us in the department store industry, we have similar interests."

Ray's dark eyes were enigmatic and unconvinced. But as if she'd belatedly recalled her rules, she said "Whatever." She had one arm crossed over her stomach, the other holding her cup. "You have anything for breakfast? I'm starved."

Her outspoken manner and brazen attitude delighted him. She was so different from other women he'd known. Hell, she was different from the men he'd known, too. "Tell you what. Why don't you get dressed and we can go out for breakfast?"

She shook her head. "No, I'd rather eat here. We still need to get you some clothes, and you need to gather up some cash and book our flights into southern Texas this afternoon."

"Cash?"

"To pay off the informants. It'll be cheaper than the ransom would have been, but it's going to cost you." She gave him a suggested amount to have on hand, her sharp gaze waiting for any resistance. It was less than he'd anticipated paying, so he didn't argue.

"After we land in Texas, we'll meet up with a friend of mine who'll fly us into Mataya in the morning. We may have to spend one night there depending on how things roll out with my contacts. Then we get your brother and come home."

"Just like that?" He was amazed by how simple she made it sound, how nonchalantly she discussed invading a foreign country and enacting a clandestine rescue.

"I hope. Things can always go wrong, but there's usually a way to correct problems before anything disastrous happens."

She stood and walked to his cabinets to scrounge for food. Eli leaned back and enjoyed the sight. She had a terrific body, honed and sleek like a female jungle cat, sexy in a way only a female body could be.

She was on the slim side, her hips flaring gently from a narrow waist. Her breasts weren't large, but they were high and firm, displayed beneath the cotton shirt when she stretched up her arm to reach for a bowl.

Her nipples pressed against the soft cotton and he felt his muscles twitch. Damn.

After locating a loaf of bread, some eggs, and the bologna and cheese, she searched for a pan. "I'm going to cook. You want some?"

"Uh, what are you making?" Eli was pleased that she'd offered to fix him breakfast, but he wasn't sure he wanted to eat whatever she intended to concoct with her ingredients. Bologna for breakfast didn't seem particularly appetizing.

"I'll just scramble the eggs and the bologna and cheese together. Sort of a lazy man's omelet. Trust me, it's good."

Actually, he would have said "yes" just so he could stay and watch her cook. Every movement was agile and flowing without deliberate effort and she seemed to get a great deal done without rushing.

That was something he'd noticed about her. She seldom hurried, but she was always productive. At one point, she stopped stirring the eggs to give an elaborate stretch. Eli nearly strangled on his coffee.

Though she'd assured him Jeremy would be fine, and he trusted her experience in the matter, he wouldn't relax completely until he had his brother home safe and sound. He should have been concentrating solely on that, not on Ray, not on the firmness of her ass or how sweet her belly looked and how he'd like to kiss her there . . .

She glanced up, saw where he was looking, and rearranged her undershirt so it again covered her stomach.

Her expression was devoid of emotion.

Because he normally went after what he wanted, and he definitely wanted Ray, he had a hard time restraining himself. "Sorry."

She turned away, an odd introspective mood clouding her previous lack of inhibition. The kitchen remained silent while she finished cooking. But when she returned to the table to dish up the eggs, she made a wry face at Eli.

"I guess I don't have any modesty left. Being in this line of work has a way of forcing you to get to the core of survival. After being around men so often, I've begun to feel like one of the guys, and men have always treated me just that way."

Eli had a really hard time believing any man, young, old, single, or attached could be around Ray without complete and total acknowledgement of her as a woman. It didn't matter what she wore or how she acted with the men. Unless they were blind, they'd be noticing her.

She gave a self-conscious shrug. "I'm only in this mode when I'm on an assignment. There're just too many other things to concentrate on to worry about my appearance. I hope you don't mind too much." She pushed her bangs away. "I'll try to remember a little more modesty."

He didn't want her to do that. But after that speech, where she took everything so seriously, concentrating solely on the job of saving his brother, mentioning that he had enjoyed the show might seem insensitive.

He'd just have to try harder to hide his reaction to her.

But then she took her seat, reached for her toast, and the strap of the undershirt slid down her arm. For one breathless, heart-stopping, anticipatory moment, Eli thought the shirt would give way to gravity and reveal the fullness of her breast. Neither heaven nor hell could have pulled his gaze away from her.

But she caught the strap and tugged it back up, oblivious to his turmoil.

Eli rubbed his face. Much more of that and he'd be making a fool of himself at the kitchen table. He concentrated on the food, on his brother, on anything and everything other than Ray.

Eating eggs and fried bologna while feeling like an anxious adolescent preparing for his first intimacy wasn't easy to pull off. His lack of control annoyed the hell out of him.

As she wolfed down her portion of breakfast, Ray pulled out a map and laid it on the table between them. Using her fork, she pointed to a spot in Central America. "This is where they have your brother, just a couple of miles from the Macal River."

He glanced at the map. "A plateau?"

"Yeah. Real pretty land, but riddled with caves, some pretty treacherous. There's a clearing here," she said, pointing to the map, "that used to be an old logging camp. It's being reclaimed by the forest, though, and isn't really passable except on foot. Deadfalls are everywhere. The wood makes good campfires, but it also houses some deadly insects and snakes."

Eli wasn't worried about a few bugs. "Is the pilot you mentioned reliable?"

Her eyes came up to his with a suddenness that was both startling and provoking. "Would I suggest him if he wasn't?"

With the morning sunlight flooding through the window, her eyes appeared a shade of brown, rather than black. But there were flecks of gold and ebony in them. They were beautiful eyes, eyes that could eat a man alive. Without thought, Eli reached out and took her hand where it rested on the table. "I didn't mean to insult you, Ray. The truth is, despite everything, I'm still anxious."

A strange expression came over her face, and she nodded. "I understand. All I can tell you is that worrying won't help. In fact, it's the worst thing you can do because it weakens you, both physically and emotionally."

"So you never show fear and you never worry?" He said it teasingly, while wondering what kind of restrictive life she'd led when she didn't want to laugh, didn't want to connect with people, didn't want to care enough to feel concern.

"I try not to. Sometimes . . ." She shook her head and sighed. "I have my weaknesses like everyone else, Eli. But if I hear you repeat that, ever, I'll make you sorry."

Her threat lightened his mood and gave him a smile.

As if that had been her intent, she smiled, too, then curled her fingers into his and gave his hand a hardy squeeze. "Distract yourself. Think of pleasant things, fond memories, whatever. But don't dwell on it."

He already knew what those pleasant thoughts would be, and they all centered around her. Still holding her hand, glad that she hadn't pulled away yet, Eli asked, "What do you do to distract yourself?"

"Exercise to the point of exhaustion, which I'll probably do tonight. Sometimes I read a book. If I'm home, I play with my dog."

Doing a double take, he said, "You have a dog?"

She smiled, a full, genuine smile for once, and

Eli felt his stomach muscles contract in reaction. The smile transformed her face, taking her from cool and aloof to warm and open.

"Yeah," she whispered, "I have a dog. He's about the meanest mutt you'd ever want to meet. Growls at everyone, and wow, he *hates* men." Then, very softly she added, "But he loves me."

Eli was entranced, there was no other word for it. He sat there staring at her, knowing he'd just been sunk, that he was in over his head and didn't even care.

Ray was so tough one minute, so oblivious to her femininity, then within a blink of the eye, she turned gentle and sweet. His gaze drifted over her face, taking in every nuance, every small detail. There were tiny lines at the corners of her eyes, testimony to the seriousness of her missions. And those small scars . . .

She looked fragile, if such a thing were possible for a person of her capabilities. But with her shoulders bare, no makeup on her face, and her features relaxed, she looked utterly female and frail. He wanted to protect her, from the world and her own sense of herself. Even more than that, he wanted to mark her as his own.

And if Ray had any idea of his thoughts, he'd be in trouble for sure.

She broke his pensive mood by saying, "If you're not going to eat your eggs, can I have them?"

The hilarity of the situation hit him. Here he was mired in profound ruminations of the heart— and she'd only been coveting his eggs.

Laughing, he pushed his plate toward her. "Go ahead. I wouldn't want you to deplete your resources."

She gave him a very prim "Thanks," then dug into his food.

Eli knew it wouldn't be wise to push her, not yet, maybe not ever. He couldn't tell her the carnal course his thoughts had taken, but he could tease her, perhaps get another smile from her. "You know, your naturalness is refreshing—I think."

Ray glanced up from her contemplation of the map. "My what?"

"The way you say and do just as you please. It's nice not to have to wonder what's in your head."

She blinked at him lazily while storm clouds gathered in her eyes. "You think I have it so easy? You actually think you know my thoughts?"

Uh-oh. Apparently, he'd stepped in it again. "Ray, you haven't exactly been circumspect in your speech or"—he glanced at her body, teasingly displayed—"in your attire."

Her eyelids narrowed just the tiniest bit. She propped her chin on a fist. "You didn't by any chance think to get to know me better, did you?"

Eli wasn't quite certain what was going on now. Seconds ago she'd been open and friendly. She'd told him about her dog, damn it. Of her own accord, she had opened up. "I'd like to get to know you better."

"Why?"

He couldn't tell her that he wanted her, that despite the situation with his brother, he couldn't get her off his mind. He shrugged and settled on saying, "You fascinate me."

Her smile was mean. "Kind of like the strange animals at the zoo, huh?"

"No." He resented the gibe, especially since it had come on so suddenly. "I think you're very independent and honest and up-front. I like and admire that about you. You don't meet too many people with those traits."

She continued to scrutinize him. "You don't know me, Eli. If you did, you wouldn't say such a stupid thing."

From bad to worse. She was so damn defensive, so hurt. "I want to know you."

She laughed without humor.

"When this is over, we could see how things go."

Before he'd finished that statement, she was already shaking her head. "Not possible."

"Why?"

Ray stood and paced to the sink, put her empty dish inside and ran water over it. She was gathering her thoughts, her arguments, but Eli didn't know how to reassure her.

He knew for certain she didn't realize the picture she made, leaning against the sink with the undershirt hugging the soft lines of her hips. She turned, putting her hands behind her on the counter, which only served to push her breasts forward. Again, she seemed oblivious to the sensuousness of her stance.

"I never see the people I work for after the job is done."

"Why, Ray?" His gaze held hers, taking in her carefully wrought expression of indifference. "Explain it to me."

"What's to explain? I just don't."

"You must have a reason." He pressed her when he knew that could be dangerous. But he sensed an emotional opening and he fully intended to take advantage of it. "I would think you'd get pretty close to a person if you rescue him."

She shook her head. "No, that would be stupid."

"Why?"

Exasperated, she said, "You wouldn't understand."

"You sound so sure of that." Despite his efforts to remain calm and in control, his brows pulled down. "You know, it's just possible I'm not really as shallow as you think."

Her arms came around to cross over her chest. It was a protective gesture, and Eli wondered at it. Why did she feel threatened? How could she feel threatened by a man when she was comfortable traipsing about in her underclothes in front of him? That alone denoted a certain amount of self-confidence and trust.

He stood, crowding in close to her. Her face turned up to his and he stared into her eyes. He wanted to touch her, to make the physical connection between a man and a woman. The compulsion was almost too great to resist. "Explain it to me, Ray," he insisted quietly.

Her chin tilted stubbornly in a sign of defiance. She was always so contained, so laid back, she wouldn't have cared enough to be defiant. But this topic got to her, threatened her in some way, and damn it, he wanted to know why.

"It would be like mixing two entirely different worlds. And I know from experience it doesn't work. People like you—"

"What the hell does that mean, 'people like me'?"

"People with *money*," she clarified, drawing the word out like a curse. "You hired me, Eli, you did not make a social call. This is a business arrangement, that's all. Quit trying to make it something more."

Her insistence only made him more determined. "Maybe it could be something more if you'd let it."

"For what purpose?" she almost yelled.

"Because I want you."

Her eyes flared, color rushed into her cheeks— anger or embarrassment, he had no idea which. Her chest rose and fell, then her expression settled into lines of rage. As she turned to stalk away, he grabbed her shoulder.

Big mistake.

Within a heartbeat, his thumb was twisted backward at an awkward angle. Eli locked his jaw in serious discomfort. Feeling his own anger erupt, he growled, "Let go, Ray."

She did, backing up a step and looking very sheepish. "I'm sorry. It was pure instinct." Then she caught herself and her brows snapped down. "You shouldn't touch me. Especially not after spewing garbage like that."

"Garbage?" He rubbed his thumb but it continued to throb.

Going on tiptoe, she stuck her face in his and snarled, "I'm not out for a quick toss in the hay, Eli. Save that for Jane." Her sneering tone irked him all the more. "Just because I have some unusual habits doesn't mean I'm easy."

He wanted to turn her over his knee. His anger had risen until he had to speak through his teeth. "If you had let me finish instead of being so damned prickly—*just like a damn woman*—you'd know that wasn't what I meant at all." He tried shaking his hand, but the pain continued to pulse through his thumb. He glowered at her. "I only meant that I like you and I'm attracted to you."

"Why?"

"What do you mean, why? You don't think you're likable? Hell, Ray, you're giving me your expertise and assistance, and if that's not enough—"

She curled her hands into fists. Not a good sign.

"I'm not *giving* you anything. You're paying good money for it."

Eli didn't appreciate that little reminder. His expression became stony. "You didn't have to agree to help. Money or not, you could have said no."

He tried bending his thumb, and grimaced instead.

Just that easily, Ray relented. Dropping her weight onto one leg, thrusting out the other hip in an arrogant slouch, she said, "Here." She grabbed his hand, turned his thumb sharply, making him grunt, then asked, "Is that better?"

Strangely enough, it was. Feeling less than pleasant, Eli said, "I'll live, thank you very much."

She looked at him, shook her head with a short laugh, then attempted to wipe away her grin. "You're funny, Eli, you know that?"

"Putting a torque on my thumb amuses you, does it?"

She shrugged, which wasn't much of an encouraging answer. "Look, let's forget all this nonsense about getting to know each other, okay? We need to concentrate on getting through this job." Her natural confidence restored, she sauntered lazily toward the door. "I'll shower first, then we can get things going."

Eli watched her go, but just before she disappeared from sight, she turned to him again. "Eli?"

"Yeah?"

"Thanks."

In a tone as reverent as her own had been, he asked, "For what?"

"For wanting to get to know me. Even though it's impossible, it was a nice thought."

She turned again, but Eli's implacable words stopped her. "Like hell, Ray. It isn't impossible,

and I will know you. You might as well get used to
the idea now."

That particular challenge had her shoulders
stiffening, but as she walked away, Eli was almost
positive he'd seen a small smile on her mouth.

Deep down, she was exactly like other women—
confusing as hell.

They were almost ready to leave for the airport,
and Ray looked Eli over approvingly. He'd flat out
refused to shop anywhere except at his own store,
but she had to admit, he'd done well. Now wearing
faded black jeans and a fashionably worn black
T-shirt with low boots, he appeared much more casual. Of course, the watch would have to go, but Ray
put off telling him so since he'd been so adamant
about wearing it.

That morning he'd started to shave, but Ray
had caught him in time, insisting he leave the
whiskers alone. His beard shadow wasn't heavy yet,
but by tomorrow it would be. He looked downright rugged and disreputable and all too appealing for her peace of mind.

Eli nodded at the bag she'd carried from the
mall. "So what'd you get?"

It had been a frivolity on her part to purchase
anything, but she'd felt compelled to obtain one
particular item. Pulling a sour face, she opened
her bag to show Eli her new pajamas.

He laughed, shaking his head, and then in a
husky, intimate whisper, said, "Personally, I preferred what you wore this morning."

Didn't she know it. He'd been plain about it to
the point he had *her* thinking of it, even though
she knew better. "And that's why I thought it might

be a good idea to get something a little less revealing. It'd be stupid to let old-fashioned lust be a bother on this mission."

Ray almost flinched when his palm cupped her chin, turning her face up to his. His hand was big and hot and rough, and everything in her curled in response.

The pajamas were coming a bit too late, in her opinion. She was already way too bothered.

"I love the way you state your case, Ray. Old-fashioned lust? Are you feeling it, too?"

She cleared her throat—and lied. "Oh, I think I can control myself." Her statement was meant to be sarcastic, but the words emerged as a breathy whisper, losing some of their impact. Eli smiled knowingly.

"For now." His thumb brushed her bottom lip, prompting her to pull away. "For now, we'll control ourselves."

He took liberties she'd never allowed before. "You're taking a lot for granted."

That had his left eyebrow raising a good inch. "Am I? And I thought I showed incredible restraint." He chuckled at her disgruntled frown. "Now don't get riled. We still have to finish packing our stuff and that'd be tough for me to do with a mangled thumb."

He kept teasing her instead of getting mad. She didn't understand him at all. Ray shook her head and went off to her room to add the absurd pajamas to her duffel bag. She was most comfortable sleeping nude and had worn the undershirt out of modesty. She could just imagine how uncomfortable sleeping in the stupid cotton pajamas would be. They were lightweight, made like a T-shirt and short pants, and would cover her from the scooped neck to just below her knees. Much as she hated to admit it, she knew the purchase had been necessary.

For her as well as for him.

No way could she give in to her attraction to Eli, remarkable though it seemed. He was of the elite, richer class. He was involved with Jane. And damn it, employers didn't get seriously involved with their employees, especially not when the employee was in effect a hired thug. She liked to think her talents were more refined than that, but he wouldn't think so. How could he? She'd attacked him in the kitchen, for crying out loud. When she thought of what she'd done to his thumb, she wanted to groan. It had been her equivalent of a slap—and that was too emotional to suit her.

Yet around him, her control was obliterated. Her reactions were involuntary, out there for him to see before she even realized what she might do. It made her feel raw, exposed.

As she packed and prepared, Ray tried to remember how long it had been since she'd been so attracted to a man. She'd given up on finding a "happily ever after" about five years ago, when she was only twenty-six. Since that time, she'd met a few men who had momentarily piqued her interest. None of them had known she could muscle her way out of a mob or load an AK-47 with lightning-fast reflexes. She'd kept the most basic part of herself hidden, and still it hadn't lasted.

Not that she'd mourned the ending of any relationships. Men had a way of opening their mouths and destroying whatever illusions of suitability she tried to give them. True, she was more independent than most and likely that was a problem, because she just couldn't take the natural arrogance that seemed to accompany most men. They saw women in one-dimensional ways, small, weak—all the things she most detested.

Funny, but Eli's arrogance had only sharpened her interest. Maybe because she felt his was more deserved. He was self-confident, strong, and hard. And big.

He stood a head taller and his shoulders were twice as wide. In comparison, he made her feel small, a circumstance she hadn't encountered too many times since she'd matured.

Of course, they hadn't gotten to the thick of it yet, where she'd really test Eli's mettle. Once they were in Mataya and he had to follow her lead, he wouldn't find her quite so amusing. He'd back off on his own, so she really had nothing to worry about.

He was in a chipper mood when they left the apartment, which only served to annoy Ray further. She was disgruntled, but with herself, not Eli. It seemed that despite everything she'd just told herself, she already felt a sense of loss. Eli wasn't hers, would never be hers.

But damn it, she wanted him to be—at least for a little while.

Chapter Four

After they stuffed their baggage behind the seat, Ray tossed Eli the keys and told him to drive.

"Really?"

Well, what about that? She'd expected an argument, not a look of anticipation, as if getting behind the wheel of her battered truck appealed to him. "Yeah, really. You do know how to drive a stick, don't you?"

"Learned when I was ten, as a matter of fact."

"Ten?"

"Yeah. I was a . . . rambunctious kid." He adjusted the seat to fit his longer legs, turned the key, and smiled at the low rumble of the engine. "Know what I think, Ray?"

She wasn't sure she wanted to. But he didn't wait for her to ask anyway.

"I think most of the wear and tear on your truck is camouflage, kind of like your blustering and bravado."

That tore it. "Blustering and bravado?"

He put the truck in gear and drove out of the lot, shifting with practiced ease. "The truck looks bad, but it's a real gem." He flicked a look her way.

"You can pretend to be cold and heartless, but you're a sensitive woman."

Being compared to her truck wasn't the best compliment. In a flat voice, she said, "The windows are bulletproof and the frame is reinforced with body armor. It doesn't matter how the truck looks, Eli. It's a kick-ass machine, meant to get me safely where I'm going, not for joyriding."

His big hands opened and closed on the steering wheel in a near caress. Mesmerized by that, Ray almost missed it when he murmured, "A fast, fun joyride wouldn't hurt anything now, would it?"

Her eyes narrowed in suspicion. Was he talking about the damn truck, or her? It didn't matter, not when her mind took the comment in the most explicit, sexual way possible. Damn it, how did he keep doing this to her? She wanted to put him in his place, she really did.

Only at the moment, she wasn't sure where that might be.

She slouched in her seat, propped her feet on the dash and turned her face to stare out her window. She'd ignore him and his innuendoes.

The problem was, she knew he was looking at her. She could feel his gaze, moving over her, filling her with throbbing turbulence. Eli was not a man to be ignored, in any way, shape, or form.

"You're awfully quiet, Ray. What's the problem now?"

"I'm thinking." She slanted him a look, her sense of injustice rising. "Maybe you should try it rather than indulging all this idle chitchat."

"Getting on your nerves, am I?"

He didn't sound the least contrite. "Yes, actually you are." His hands were still now, and that allowed her gaze to zero in on something she could tackle without unsettling emotion. "I see you didn't take the watch off like I told you to."

"My watch stays."

She was ready for a confrontation. "No, it doesn't. If it's noticed in Mataya, we'll have our hands full getting out with your arm intact."

Eli merely grinned at her. "I trust you to take care of me, Ray. That is what you promised Jane, remember?"

She resented having her own words thrown back at her. She resented more the fact that she'd had to promise Jane anything. "It looked to me like you needed some help getting rid of the lady." And with a sneer: "Is she always that clingy?"

"Not usually, no."

That wasn't enough of an answer to suit her. "She hinted you two haven't exactly been . . . *close.*"

Eli chuckled. "You mean sexually?"

The turbulence expanded, feeling almost like pain. "Yeah. So why her sudden change of heart?"

"Her heart wasn't involved, Ray. Just her tactical mind."

"What do you mean?"

Eli grimaced as if pained. "My grandfather is playing Cupid. He wants our two families to join, and evidently, given her recent performance, Jane is all for it."

He couldn't possibly mean . . . Skeptically, Ray asked, "A business alliance?"

Eli shook his head. "My grandfather is old-fashioned. He likes to keep it in the family."

Her heart skipped two beats. "Meaning?"

"Marriage."

She didn't care, she didn't care, she did not care. "Why the hell would she marry you if she didn't love you?"

That had him laughing, but not for the reasons

Ray thought. "You make marriage to me sound like a heinous fate worse than death." His laugh was nice and deep. Real. "Our marriage would unite major competitors in the same industry. It'd be a match made in boardroom heaven."

Because her privacy was so important to her, it amazed Ray that Eli didn't seem to have an aversion to discussing his private affairs. "So you're supposed to marry a woman for the sake of money?"

He frowned at her curt generalization. "That was the plan, I suppose, though I never agreed to it."

Ray didn't bother trying to hide her shock. "That's disgusting. How much money do you people need, anyway?"

"I never said—"

Anger brought her feet off the dash to land on the floor with a thud. "Marriages of convenience went out a long time ago." She crossed her arms over her chest. "The whole idea is pathetic."

Eli absorbed her annoyance with a slow smile. "Are you willing to make me a better offer?"

Her arms fell to her sides. "Now what are you babbling about?"

"I haven't fallen in love with anyone yet, including Jane, but I'm thirty-three. It's time for me to settle down and start a family of my own."

"Do wealthy people have a schedule for that sort of thing?"

"Not a schedule, no, but I do have a responsibility, especially to my grandfather to carry on the tradition of a family-run business. I can't very well do that without more family." He reached over and patted her knee. "Just think of the strong, independent kids we'd have."

She shoved his hand away. "You aren't the least bit funny, Eli."

He laughed again and Ray thought about socking him. In the end, she decided that would only inconvenience her, since she'd be the one to have to take care of him afterward.

"What's the matter, Ray? Don't you want to supply me with a couple of small Connors to carry on the family name? I promise I'd be a good dad."

Oh, she believed that. He'd probably be a wonderful dad. But the idea of her as a mother was utterly ludicrous. She didn't think she'd ever held a baby, much less cared for one.

A little melancholy, Ray leaned her head back on the seat and closed her eyes, all but dismissing Eli. But she couldn't refrain from one last parting shot. "It appears to me Jane is now more than anxious to give you as many heirs as you want."

"Ray," he chided in a more mellow tone, "you don't need to concern yourself about Jane."

She kept her eyes closed, refusing to look at him. "Which is your way of telling me to mind my own business? Hey, I can handle that. If you feel compelled to sell yourself for money, who am I to complain? It makes no difference to me."

Eli sighed. "This is ridiculous. I never said I was going to marry her. I only said that my grandfather wanted me to."

"And evidently so does Jane."

"Maybe, not that it matters what she wants since I'm not going to marry her and that's the end of it. So drop it."

"Fine."

"Great."

She didn't want to talk about marriage anyway.

"*But,*" Eli added, making her groan, "I am serious about wanting a family." He waited a moment in silence, then asked, "Don't you?"

Ray swiveled her head toward him, pretending boredom. "Do I what?"

"Want a family." And then with a start, he said, "Or do you already have one? Damn, Ray, I don't know anything about you. You're not married, are you?"

Slouching farther into her seat, Ray grumbled, "I think this falls under the heading of personal information."

Those expressive eyes of his lit up with exasperation. "Don't give me that, not after the way you've been grilling me." When she only shrugged, he appealed to her sense of fair play. "Come on, Ray. I answered your questions."

"I didn't twist your arm."

"You twisted my thumb earlier. Almost the same thing."

She shot him a baleful frown. But really, telling him wouldn't make any difference, and maybe it'd get him off this subject and onto one that didn't rattle her. "No, I'm not married, never have been. I'm thirty-one years old. I have an eighteen-year-old brother and two highly annoying, prissy female cousins who, thank God, live a fair distance away."

Typically, he took what information she gave and picked for more. "What about your parents?"

She stared out the windshield. "They died when I was eighteen."

"Both of them?"

With a nod, she said, "A stormy night, slick roads . . ." She flapped a hand, unable to say more. "My aunt took us in. I joined the service shortly after that."

"That's awfully young to be a soldier."

Young, but also angry and eager to find her place in the world. It had been a life-altering decision, one she'd never allowed herself to regret. "A little over five years ago, my aunt got cancer and she died, too."

Eli glanced at her briefly. "You recite that like a grocery list when I know it had to hurt like hell."

Ray stared out the window at the passing scenery. Hurt? The death of her parents had damn near killed her, too. She'd felt broken and lost, but so much had changed since then, it now seemed as though it had been someone else who'd suffered that loss, who had tried to find a place for herself when there was no place available. She'd been a different woman then, a girl really, young and naïve. It sometimes galled her to remember how small and afraid and weak she'd been.

She wouldn't allow anyone or anything to ever make her feel like that again.

"What good would it do for me to mourn the past? I'm a realist. I deal with life, good or bad. Besides, if you learned from the hard times, if they made you a little wiser, more self-sufficient, well then, they weren't all bad, were they?"

The gentleness of his tone nearly undid her when he whispered, "What could you have possibly learned from your parents' deaths?"

More than she had ever wanted to know. "I learned that you shouldn't depend on other people for the things you need."

"Like love?"

She snorted. "Like food or shelter or protection. Even good people can suffer circumstances beyond their control so it's best to be independent, to take care of yourself, and to need only what you can supply. My life wasn't a tragedy, Eli, so don't make it out as one."

After that heartfelt outburst, Eli finished the

drive to the airport in silence. But his brooding wore on her. She knew he was chewing over the conversation, applying maudlin sentiments even though she'd told him not to. Every so often, he looked at her, and like the first time she'd seen him, his eyes mirrored so much sentiment, it unnerved her. She chose not to look at him again, to ignore him. It was the only way she could concentrate on the job she had to do. She needed a mindset, a detachment from other things to perform the job well.

Usually she could compartmentalize her thoughts, storing away those that might distract her, honing in on the pertinent considerations.

Her reaction to Eli was unexpected. She couldn't detach herself from him no matter how she tried. He seemed to like that.

Ray did not.

Eli parked her truck in the long-term lot. Their timing was perfect, because there was only a fifteen-minute wait before the plane was ready to be boarded. Ray wasn't surprised that Eli had booked them first-class but that didn't mean she had to like it. Though it wasn't her money, she still considered it a waste, especially when she realized how out of place they looked with their ordinary, worn street clothes and Eli sporting a day's growth of beard. She was used to people staring at her, but now it disconcerted her. And with the take-off imminent, she didn't need any more tension.

Leaning close to her ear, Eli suggested, "Ignore everyone, relax and enjoy the ride. Trust me, it won't kill you."

Ray drew a slow breath, prepared herself to look

bored, and then peered up at him. "Actually, I was thinking of taking a nap. You'll let me know when we land, won't you?"

But instead of answering that question, Eli studied her. As usual, he saw too much. "Getting nervous?"

She knew he referred to their jaunt into Mataya, which she wasn't the least bit nervous about. The flight, however, was another matter. And the way he attended her every move with so much concern only added to her jitters.

"Of course not. I told you everything will be fine."

"You seem tense," he insisted.

The big airplane began taxiing down the runway, going faster and faster while her stomach clenched and her nerves unraveled. God, she hated flying. "I'm mentally preparing for what we'll do and when we'll do it." Keeping her voice calm and even wasn't easy. There was no spit in her mouth, no air in her lungs. "That way," she gasped, tightening her hold on the chair arms, "everything will go like clockwork."

Eli drew back, his gaze moving over her face, then her posture. Damn him, why didn't he look out the window or read a magazine or something?

The plane lifted—and so did her stomach.

Without a word, Eli pried her right hand free from the armrest. His long, warm fingers curled around hers and his thumb began stroking her knuckles, gentle, easy. He drew her hand onto his hard thigh, faced forward, shifted his shoulders to get comfortable and sighed as if utterly relaxed.

Now that he wasn't watching her, Ray squeezed her eyes shut, praying Eli wouldn't notice. She couldn't bear the thought of him seeing her like this.

Normally when on a flight, she could concentrate hard on other things: her brother, her dog, or the impossibility of a normal life. It helped her to overcome her unreasonable fear of flying. But this time, because Eli was with her, she couldn't let down her guard. If she allowed herself to become melancholy, he'd notice. The man was far too astute for his own good.

Though sleep would surely elude her, she decided to pretend to doze off. It'd keep her fear masked and keep Eli from making small talk that she'd only be able to babble through. Even better, she wouldn't have to see the fat, fluffy clouds now drifting past the small window, reminding her that they were well above the ground.

She concentrated on Eli's breathing, deep and even and calm. She felt the warmth of his strong hand holding hers, his powerful thigh beneath her wrist.

She didn't wake up until they landed.

The jarring motion of the wheels on the runway nearly sent her into a panic. Her heart shot into her throat, but her survival instincts were honed razor sharp, so she didn't scream, didn't even move. She shifted her eyes around to take in the seat in front of her, the aisle to her left. Still on the plane, she realized with little comfort, but she was now warm and cozy. Safe.

Beneath her cheek, she felt firm muscle along with the slow thud of a steady heartbeat. Eli no longer held her hand. Experimentally, she moved her fingers and found another firm muscle—that twitched and throbbed.

Good God.

It didn't take a rocket scientist to recognize *that.*

Everything came together. She was cuddled against Eli, her head on his shoulder, his arm around her back, supporting her neck and keeping her close. And her hand was in his lap, right over the zipper to his jeans.

The plane completed its landing without her notice. She was too busy praying that Eli had fallen asleep, too, despite the evidence of his arousal. But when she dared a peek up, she found him watching her, his eyes heated and tender at once. She went breathless, warm and trembling.

His hand came to her cheek, his thumb brushing her temple gently. "You must have been exhausted. Didn't you sleep well last night?"

His words were whisper soft, his head bent toward her so their noses almost touched. Feeling his breath on her lips, Ray swallowed a groan from the unexpected need that suddenly crashed through her. She wanted to put her head back on his shoulder. She wanted to breathe in his scent, taste his warm throat, curl her fingers around the lengthening erection that grew beneath her palm.

Instead she tightened her jaw and straightened, then carefully shrugged away his arm. "No, I didn't sleep well at all." She rounded on him. "You and your girlfriend woke me up, remember? And I'd had a long drive the night before."

The heat left his gaze, but the tenderness remained, tinged with amusement. "We'll be off the plane in just a minute."

It wouldn't be soon enough to suit her, but she couldn't let him know that. "So?"

"So it's been a busy day with the shopping and packing. Breakfast was a long time ago and we've already missed lunch. You want to stop at a restaurant or go straight to the hotel?"

"We'll eat."

Eli smiled. "Now, how did I know you were going to say that?"

Few men ever dared to tease her—usually only Matt or her best friend, Buddy. Few men left her feeling awkward. She'd been on many jobs where she was the only female around, and it had never before mattered. The men were just people, not people of the opposite sex. With Eli, she saw him strictly as a man with a capital, throbbing *M*.

Maybe it was her age. Maybe her hormones were different now. If so, she'd ruthlessly beat them into submission because she wasn't about to start acting like a silly female.

Yet, as they left the plane and traveled through the airport, she was keenly aware of Eli beside her—and not because she felt responsible for him. Damn it, she knew his scent, the heat of his body. When he took her arm, it no longer offended her. Instead, a small thrill jolted her senses. And when he smiled at her, she suffered the queerest melting sensation in her belly.

She hated it.

Never in her life had she suffered so much frustration. The loss of control was unacceptable.

They ate at a crowded fast food place in the airport. All through their meal, Ray pondered the situation. But for now, there was no way out. She'd just have to get her act together.

The ride to the hotel was accomplished in silence. Ray stared out her window at the hot sun. The sky was white, without a single cloud in sight to soften the glare. Mataya would be even hotter, steamy, too, and she wondered at Eli's endurance. Would the change in weather drain him? Plenty of people had trouble bearing up under the sweltering temperatures. Some even became ill . . .

She realized she was fretting and stabbed Eli with a glare of fury. She *never* fretted, damn it, definitely not over an employer. But her indignation was wasted. Either Eli didn't notice her volatile mood, or he ignored it.

The cab stopped in front of the hotel and Ray climbed out, struggling to moderate her thoughts. Heat rose from the pavement in waves, instantly turning her skin damp.

Seconds later, Eli stepped up beside her. He carried both their bags. When she reached for hers, he held it away.

"Eli . . ." she said through her teeth, ready, even anxious for a fight.

He disarmed her by smiling. "What's the matter, Ray? You look like a thundercloud."

She went mute. Damn but that smile felt like a lick in all the right places.

"Ray?"

Trying to think of a plausible reply other than being in estrus, Ray swung around and stormed to the hotel doors, holding them open for him since he wouldn't relinquish her bag. Once inside the lobby, she didn't have to worry about answering him. The small hotel was filled to overflowing with milling guests, making casual talk impossible.

"What the hell?" Eli asked no one in particular. He tried to catch a bustling bellhop but had no success. Finally, he led Ray to a sofa and dropped the luggage at her feet. "Watch the bags and I'll check us in."

Ray snagged the back of his shirt, regaining his attention. He raised a brow in query.

"You're forgetting who's the boss on this trip, Eli."

"Oh? Did you want me to watch the bags so you can check us in? I don't know if they'll allow you to use my credit card, *boss,* but if you insist, then . . ."

She felt like a fool. "Check us in. I'll wait here."

"Now why didn't I think of that?"

She considered dropping him to the floor, but he was already gone, trying to obtain the key cards to their rooms.

It was a good ten minutes before Eli returned and he looked entirely too disgruntled.

"Tell me there's not a problem with our reservations." She wanted a long hot shower and some quiet time alone.

"No problem. They're just crowded from a convention." Eli didn't look at her, and in fact, he seemed so distracted she didn't voice a single complaint when he hoisted both bags and herded Ray toward the elevator. When he saw the mob there, he changed his mind and turned to the stairs instead.

"Okay, I give," she said to his back. "Why are you looking ready to do bodily harm?"

"This from the woman with an expression so dark she could scare grown men."

"Are you afraid, Eli?" she taunted.

"No, but then I know you intend to protect me, not murder me in my sleep." He stared down at her. "Isn't that right?"

Undaunted, she said, "You admit you need my protection?"

"Of course." Then he mused, "Funny that you're the only one threatening me, huh?"

Oh, it'd be *so* easy to throw him right now, to land one well-placed hit to a tender muscle. He wouldn't laugh at her then.

Her eyes narrowed in contemplation, and Eli leaned down close to her ear with a husky whisper. "Ray, I swear you look sexy as hell when you go into combat mode."

Like a sail caught in the wind, she snapped straight. Sexy? She opened her mouth to blast him, but nothing came out.

Appalled at herself, Ray stormed ahead of him, taking the lead up the stairs. Eli gave her a room number for the seventh floor. Ray was in excellent shape, but still she was huffing by the time Eli finally stopped in front of a door.

He wasn't even breathing hard.

She eyed him with distaste, shoved her bangs from her forehead, and propped her hands on her hips. After balancing both bags in one arm, Eli slid the door card into the slot.

Ray thought to ask, "Is this your room or mine?"

He didn't answer. The door swung open and Ray was pleasantly surprised to see the room wasn't ritzy at all. In fact, it was almost utilitarian with one full bed, a nightstand, and a dresser with a small television sitting on it. It was clean and neat, but not what she had expected after the first-class airfare.

"Well, you've managed to surprise me, Eli. But I thank you. The room is perfect." She smiled.

He stepped inside with her and closed the door.

Ray's smile slipped. "Did I misunderstand?"

He shook his head, but leaned on the door as if he fully intended to stay.

"Is this your room and not mine?"

Eli crossed his arms over his chest. "It's your room."

"Good, that's what I thought." It wasn't necessary, but she added, "I couldn't imagine you willingly staying in a room this plain. I figured you'd get a suite or something."

As if she hadn't spoken, he said, "It's also my room."

Her eyes widened and she examined the room again. The single bed and his earlier, outrageous compliment took on new meaning. Very slowly, she brought her accusatory gaze around to his. "Oh, I get it now," she growled. He stared back without a single flinch. "One thing you ought to know, Eli."

"What's that, honey?"

"My protection only goes so far—and you're really pushing it."

Eli peeled himself away from the door, starting toward her with a measured stride. His eyes never left her face.

Rather than backing up with his advance, Ray widened her stance and faced him defiantly. Her preparation for battle only got her a look of appreciation, reminding her of what he'd said: he found her battle mode sexy.

And if she believed that, he could sell her a bridge.

He stopped right in front of her, forcing Ray to look up at him. Once again, she noted the differences in their sizes. She knew what she was capable of, and still he made her feel small and helpless.

"The hotel made a mistake, Ray. They gave away our rooms."

Ray said nothing.

"They're having a convention and someone fouled up the reservations. This was the only room available. I couldn't imagine trying to find another hotel tonight, so I accepted. Under the circumstances, and considering you slept at my place last night, I didn't think you'd mind."

Of course he didn't think she'd mind. Eli had no way of knowing her frustration. She'd never felt this level of sexual attraction before, so she didn't know how to deal with it. And that scared her.

But short of explaining to him that he made her so hot she couldn't stop thinking about jumping his bones, there was no way to refuse. Locking her jaw, she said, "You're right. The room is fine."

"You don't look like it's fine." Eli scrutinized her. "You look ready to flay me alive. I think that's exceptionally strange given how you strutted around in your underclothes just this morning."

Much more of this and her teeth would be reduced to powder. "I do *not* strut."

With a small smile, he said, "Yeah, you do." His voice and his expression gentled. "What's changed, Ray? You don't trust me?"

Trust him? Ha. It was herself she couldn't trust anymore.

Needing some physical distance, Ray walked around the bed, pretending to look things over. "I'll admit it." She summoned a credible laugh. "For a second there I thought you were getting ideas."

Eli didn't share her humor. "And if I was?"

She jerked around to face him from the other side of the bed. "Don't."

Briefly, he closed his eyes. "I would never force you, Ray."

Of all the . . . "I wouldn't let you!"

He smiled. "It's just . . ." His gaze wandered from her face to her body and back again.

Against her better judgement, Ray whispered, "What?"

It seemed Eli wanted to say more, but then he

shook his head. "Nothing." After shoving his hands through his hair, he picked up their bags and set them on the bed. "It's getting late. Why don't you get ready for bed and I'll ring the desk to make certain we get a wake-up call."

So many strange emotions churned inside her. Disappointment, anticipation, and wariness. She didn't know herself anymore and that was dangerous. Digging through her things, she located the hideous pajamas and did her best *not* to strut as she headed to the bathroom.

Her shower, consisting mostly of cold water for obvious reasons, only lasted a mere three minutes. It wasn't long enough. God, she hadn't been this jumpy on her first mission, back when she'd been a green kid.

It was stupid to hide in the bathroom, so she threw the door open and strode out.

He was already propped up in bed.

As if someone had suddenly stapled her feet to the floor, Ray stopped dead in her tracks.

He'd removed his shirt.

The sheet only came to his hips and the sight of his bare chest, muscled and enhanced with dark hair, was enough to unravel her. It just wasn't fair.

On top of being funny and strong and accepting, why the hell did he have to look so good?

Chapter Five

Ray consoled herself with the fact that she could see the waistband of Eli's boxers. She didn't think she could have gotten into the bed if he'd been bare-ass naked.

Eli looked up at where she stood in the bathroom doorway. He took note of the new pajamas but kept whatever opinion he had to himself.

Still she stood there, and he sighed. "Would you feel better if I slept on the floor?"

That brought her out of her stupor. "Don't be stupid. We both need a good night's sleep." After all, she told herself, she'd slept in the open with men, side by side, and she'd shared tents when they were available. This would be no different. She tried to convince herself, but the effort was wasted because her voice trembled when she said, "I don't have a problem with it if you don't."

Watching her, alert to her every move, Eli lifted the covers and waited.

It was a good thing she was a sturdy woman in good health, with the way her heart punched inside her chest. Utilizing every ounce of control she possessed, Ray walked to the bed and slipped in beside him.

Eli waited only until she lay back, her arms propped behind her head, before he dropped the covers over her and turned off the light.

The darkness brought out her other senses with the acuity of a predator.

She could smell him, feel the heat of his body seeping over to her, weakening her muscles, penetrating deep inside her.

And she could hear him breathing, light, even breaths.

She knew without being able to see that he was propped on one elbow, staring toward her. An invisible fist tightened on her lungs, then in a husky whisper, his voice a caress, he said, "Good night, Ray Jean. Sleep well."

Eli wasn't prepared for the impact of her body landing full against his, or her thumb pressing into his vocals.

"I told you *never* to call me that."

If he wasn't strangling, it would have been funny. Lying still with the shock of her breasts squashed to his bare chest, the warm, smooth weight of her inner thigh against his hip, Eli barely noticed the menace in her tone. "Ray?" he rasped, faking confusion to keep her exactly where she was a bit longer.

"You called me Ray Jean," she snarled in a low, mean voice. "I warned you not to." Her breath fanned his mouth and her eyes were a bright glimmer in the dark room, only inches from his. She was in full mercenary mode—and damn, he had a boner.

Very slowly, Eli brought his hands up to frame her waist. She was narrow, firm; his thumbs nearly touched over her midriff, his fingers meeting over her spine.

As hot as he suddenly felt, he still had to struggle to keep from laughing. He found her defense of her name ludicrous—and endearing. Why? What significance did the name hold for her? He wanted to ask, but that'd fall into the category of personal stuff and he didn't want to scare her off. Other than not being able to breathe, he loved feeling her so close. Given a choice, he'd have kept her right there all night.

"You're choking me, Ray." His voice was rough with the pressure she exerted on his throat.

Ray jerked, inadvertently tightening her hold. As if she'd only then realized what she was doing, her eyes widened, apparent even in the darkness of the unlit room. By small degrees, her fingers loosened and she started to pull away. Eli's grip on her waist stopped her.

"Eli?"

"Hmmm?" It would be so easy to slip his fingers beneath the pajama top and encounter warm skin.

"What do you think you're doing?"

Though she spoke in a mere whisper, he heard the fury, and the confusion. She'd been comfortable enough challenging him physically, but sexually she was at a loss.

"Me?" He tried to sound innocent. "All I did was say good night and you attacked me."

She remained stonily silent, awaiting her release. Eli moved his fingers in a subtle caress, allowing his thumbs to move tantalizingly close to the soft fullness of her breasts.

It was very tempting . . . No, better not, he decided. She was rigid enough to break already. "Why, Ray? Why are you so touchy about your name?"

"Let. Go."

He didn't want to. He wanted to pull her down flush against him, to feel all that vital energy directed at him. He wanted to take her mouth and . . .

"Don't make me hurt you, Eli."

He couldn't help himself. The situation was so novel, and she was so deadly serious in her determination that he chuckled.

Bad idea.

Her hand moved so fast, he barely caught it in time. But he *did* catch it. The other moved, too, and he grabbed it as well, keeping both her wrists securely held. Ha. Now what would she do?

In the next instant, her forehead smacked against his. The blow was hard enough to ring curses from him and instantly gave her the release she'd requested.

She started to scramble to the side, saying, "You deserved that, Eli. I told you not to—"

Her words were cut short as Eli reacted, turning fast and hard, flipping her onto her stomach beneath him. Before she could counter the move, he had her pinned down. His ears were still ringing and colorful stars danced before his eyes. Had she meant to knock him out?

It seemed probable—and hilarious. He was in bed with a woman he wanted more than any other he'd known, and she had tried to scramble his brains.

He covered her completely, the weight of his big body crushing her smaller frame into the mattress. His fingers wrapped firmly but gently around her wrists, not giving her a chance to get hold of his digits, trapping her arms above her head. His legs were between hers—a nice position, that—totally immobilizing her. He pressed his face into her shoulder, which also held her face down so she couldn't bite him.

They were both breathing hard.

Without even meaning to, Eli pressed his hips inward, nudging his swollen cock against her firm buttocks, groaning at the feel of her, her softness, the carnality of their positions.

If they were naked, he'd be inside her right now.

Damn. He didn't want to frighten or hurt her, but he needed a moment to rid himself of the pounding in his head, as well as the insistent throb in his groin, before he let her loose. She didn't move, didn't make a sound, and he started to worry. "Are you always so physical, Ray?"

When she didn't answer, he wrongly assumed her silence was shock.

"Ray? Honey, you okay?"

Her voice was cold, remote, and beyond furious when she growled, "I'm not your honey."

Relief brought back his amusement. "Such a nasty temper," he chided. That had her struggling anew, which only caused her rounded behind to push into him again. Eli was caught between the pain in his head and the pleasure her movements brought him.

But given her current mood, pleasure wasn't too wise. "Settle down, Ray."

"Get off of me."

A note of hysteria tinged her command. She wasn't used to anyone else having the upper hand.

He wondered how many times a man had done this to her?

The thought of someone else making love to her, taking her from behind, made his possessive urges riot. But the thought of a man holding her down as a true captive, intent on hurting her, made him want to kill the faceless bastard.

He closed his eyes, and though he knew she hated it, he hugged himself closer to her. "Not yet, honey. You'd only lay me low again, and my brains can't take much more. I think I'll wait until you forgive me for calling you Ray Jean. And until you explain why you're so touchy about your name."

Her silence sounded with the same effect as a scream. Hurting for her, though he wasn't certain why, Eli lowered his head until his breath fanned her nape. It was a risk, getting that close to her. His little soldier knew how to defend herself, and at the moment, she might not mind causing him real pain. On the other hand, he'd rather be shot than hurt her. So if she wanted to, she could probably get loose.

Did that mean she didn't want to?

"What's the matter, Ray? Talk to me, please."

He felt her shuddering breath. Not tears, because she would never let herself cry. He kissed her temple.

"Why do you care?"

He countered that with: "Why would you think I shouldn't care?"

Her forehead dropped to the mattress; her muscles, tensed and coiled only moments before, went lax. Several seconds passed before she spoke. Her defeated voice was muffled by the covers. "My aunt . . . used to call me Ray Jean, just to remind me that I was female."

Unable to resist, Eli rubbed his nose against her neck. "She was actually in doubt?"

Her shrug jarred the bed. "She just didn't think I was very ladylike, and she hated that—she hated *me*. She tried to insist I curl my hair, that I wear dresses and makeup. Whenever I did, she made fun of me for doing it wrong."

Eli pressed his face into her neck and just held her.

"She ridiculed the way I walked, the way I talked. Everything. Her prissy daughters were held up as a constant example of what I wasn't."

Understanding came, and with it, an ache in his heart that nearly did him in. "So you became just the opposite?"

She made a sound of disgust. "Don't be an imbecile, Eli."

He smiled at the insult. No woman had ever called him names before. "Sorry."

"I was already the opposite. No matter how my aunt pushed, I couldn't be like them. It's just not me."

Eli breathed in the light, natural fragrance of her. Her wrists where he held her were small, the skin silky smooth. He could feel the contours of her body, the dip of her waist, the rise of her rump. God, he wanted her in so many ways. He wanted to hold her, to fuck her and make love to her and talk to her all night.

He also wanted her to trust him. "I think," he whispered, forcing the words out despite his raging lust, "that you're about as much as any woman can be."

Ray didn't say anything. She held completely still beneath him and that bothered him more than her curses or insults ever could.

When the silence stretched out uncomfortably, Eli said, "I'm sorry for upsetting you."

She still didn't answer.

"Ray?"

In a small voice very unlike her usual commanding tone, Ray admitted, "I'm not used to someone getting the best of me. It's . . . disconcerting."

Eli wasn't certain, but he thought he detected a touch of admiration in her tone. It pleased him. "I am a lot bigger, Ray. And stronger."

She shook her head, and her hair brushed against his jaw and chin. "It's not that. I could still take you."

Eli laughed outright. "You think so, do you?"

"I know so."

"Then what happened?" He settled himself more firmly against her, spreading his legs a little, which forced hers wider, too. "Why are you beneath me instead of the other way around?"

She stiffened. "If you're going to be a jerk about it, I'll admit that I didn't want to hurt you."

"Really?" She was so full of surprises. "What do you call choking me?"

She huffed. "It didn't shut you up, did it? I could have put you out then, but I didn't."

The idea that she might have held back intrigued him. "Why not, Ray?" Did her restraint mean she cared?

"The agency would frown on it."

He hadn't laughed so much in a long time. "That's your only reason, huh? Well, not to brag, you understand, but I held back, too." Her head came up in surprise, affording him the chance to kiss her cheek. With his mouth still touching her, he said, "You may as well know there's no way you could ever best me. No holds barred, I'd come out on top." And he was just horny enough to press into her and whisper, *"Again."*

"That cocky attitude is going to get you into

trouble." She looked over her shoulder to add, "Next time I won't concern myself with returning you whole hide."

"So we're to battle it out, huh? I'll look forward to your efforts, Ray. Not that it'll change the outcome."

Ray snorted in derision. "You want me to believe you'd actually fight me?"

He nibbled on her ear. She had very small, delicate ears, and his control weakened by the moment. "No. But I think I could appreciate holding you beneath me for a nice long time. What do you think, Ray? Is that threat incentive enough for you to think twice before attacking me again?"

Fury, or maybe interest, deepened her breathing. Eli couldn't tell which. "No."

She had guts and gumption, and he admired both. "Good. I'm glad."

"You're nuts is what you are," she grumbled. "Now will you get off? We need to get some sleep."

"If you promise to let bygones be bygones."

"All right." A heartbeat passed and she added, "For now."

Very slowly, Eli removed his weight and rolled to the side. He waited until Ray had resettled herself, her body stiff beside his. He wanted to hug her, but knew better than to even try. "Good night. Ray."

He was pleased when she returned grudgingly, her words barely audible, "Good night, Eli."

Despite the heat in his body and the turmoil of his mind, he relaxed with a smile. Ray was unbelievably, delightfully unique from any person he'd ever known, especially the women. With all her outspokenness and arrogance, she was somehow more real. And he already looked forward to spending time with her, without the restrictions of familial duty and worry occupying his thoughts.

When his brother was back home where he belonged, he'd give Ray all his attention.

He was determined to have her, one way or another.

Bored but too restless to sleep, Jeremy stirred in the small confines of his hut. His own body odor, ripe as month-old fruit, rose to assault his nose. Good God, he needed a bath. The one time he'd mentioned it, though, the guerillas had offered to let him use the stream to wash. Of course, he'd refused. Hell, there were *leeches* in there. He'd seen some of the men—fastidious bastards who bathed every day—peeling the slimy, blood-bloated things off their legs, arms, even their groins.

Jeremy's stomach jolted with the horrible memory. No thank you. They were all barbarians, forcing him through inhuman conditions. They'd taken him, so they should provide proper means of bathing.

His once comfortable, custom-tailored shirt had gotten dirty during their trip to the make-do prison, thanks to miles of foot travel. The men had tried to "exchange" it for a roughly woven tunic. Right. Like they thought he'd take a nickle's worth of coarse cloth to replace a shirt that cost more than their damn village.

He'd accused them of only wanting to steal it. That hadn't gotten him a better shirt. Just the opposite. His soiled shirt had been tossed back at him and not once since had they offered him another.

Unreasonable bastards.

Now everything he wore was grimy with filth
and sticky with his own sweat. He'd tried demanding that someone wash his clothes, but most of the
guards didn't understand his English and he didn't
understand their Spanish.

He shook his head in disgust, but no one noticed. He was all alone. For the most part, they left
him that way. Given how he smelled, he hardly
blamed them for that.

If only he hadn't lost his camera back at that damn
dive where he'd stupidly gotten drunk. Without the
photos he'd already taken, the trip was an entire
waste. Since he knew Eli was going to be majorly
pissed once he got him out of there, he'd hoped
to at least salvage the awesome shots he'd taken.
They'd go a long way toward justifying the sneaky
lies he'd told and maybe, just maybe, save his ass.

His self-pitying thoughts got distracted when
something rustled in the dry brush. Jeremy went
stock still, not even daring to breathe. Moving only
his eyes, he peered off the side of his narrow cot.

Oh shit. Through the rickety floor slats, he could
easily see the ground below. All the casitas were on
platforms, he suspected to keep them dry from
sudden downpours. Though the rainwater quickly
flowed into the underground caves, it also brought
out the insects. And here in Mataya, they had some
really nasty bugs.

Like the gargantuan tarantula creeping across
the dirt below him.

Jeremy's eyes widened like saucers to see better
in the shadowy light of dusk. Oh God, he hated
creepy bugs, most especially big hairy ones the size
of his damn fist. The last time Ferdinand, as he'd
named the hideous thing, had crawled from his
hole, Jeremy had jumped up screaming, practi-

cally climbing the walls. The ragtag soldiers had all come rushing, determined to protect their prisoner.

When they saw he was freaked out over the spider—who in their right mind called *that* a mere spider?—they'd roared with hilarity, falling down, pointing, wiping tears of mirth from their dark faces.

Still clinging to the casita walls, Jeremy had been left feeling like an idiot.

Even without a grasp of Spanish, Jeremy understood when one of the guards claimed he squealed like a little girl. Another mocked him by dancing around the yard, carrying on in a falsetto screech on his tiptoes.

Stung with humiliation, Jeremy had picked up rocks and flung them. How dare they treat him like that? Back home, as heir to the Connorses' estates, he got respect and admiration from everyone.

The guerillas had walked away grinning, treating him like a petulant little boy.

When the next man brought him his lunch of beans, he'd explained in broken English that only when tarantulas were scared or put on the defensive did they attack with their poisonous bite or project their spiny hairs.

God forbid the damn thing should feel defensive, so Jeremy didn't move. Luckily, after a while, it went away. He breathed a sigh of relief and relaxed back against the wall. When he got out of here, he was going to make them all pay for their crude treatment. He wasn't used to being dirty, to eating fried beans, or being taunted with insects.

With nothing else to do, he moved to look out the narrow window slit, taking in the view of the surrounding jungle. If he had his camera, he'd be snapping one roll of film after another.

The small hidden camp was a few miles from the outskirts of the village. Sitting atop a hill, they overlooked the Vaca Plateau. Mountains could be seen on the horizon, with tall trees spreading their bare branches like veins across the gray sky. At the base of the mountains, the jungle expanded, looking lush and filled with animal sounds. The howler monkeys were particularly obnoxious and often kept him awake. He remembered a time when he'd seen them at the zoo and thought they were cute.

The little bastards drove him crazy now with their deep-throated roars at dawn.

Tiny frogs, more poisonous than the tarantula, and night-hunting cats made the jungle a horrific place. So many times he could have escaped, because he wasn't watched *that* closely. But where would he go, other than into that dense jungle where he'd no doubt fall to the bottom of the damn food chain?

No, he'd wait. Eli would come, Jeremy knew that.

What Eli would do after the rescue was what kept Jeremy awake at nights. His brother wasn't going to be happy, and Eli in a rage was ten times more intimidating than any band of guerillas could be.

Ray awakened slowly—then went still.

She'd done it again! She'd gone sound asleep when she absolutely shouldn't have. She almost never slept that hard, definitely not when on an assignment. Yet she'd passed out for the duration and couldn't remember moving all night.

But she had moved.

If her body wasn't lying to her, and she was pretty sure it wasn't, she was now sprawled over Eli, her face cushioned against his hairy chest, her thigh resting over his lap. He had morning wood. After camping out with guys plenty of times, she understood that predicament—but she'd never been personally involved with it.

"Hey."

His soft greeting nearly stopped her heart. Now what?

"I know you're awake, Ray." His fingers threaded through her hair and rubbed her scalp.

How did this keep happening to her? It was as if her body just sought his out, drawn to him like a lodestone. Had *he* awakened when she crawled on top?

Did he help get her there?

She didn't move. She *couldn't* move. In so many places, she touched him. Skin on skin. Heartbeat to heartbeat. He was hot, his flesh taut. Her breathing hitched in primal awareness. When he raised his other hand to tip up her chin, she felt the muscles in his chest and abdomen flex, and even that sent a thrill coursing through her.

She had no choice but to look at him.

Big mistake. Eli's eyes plainly showed his thoughts, and once she knew what he was thinking, she thought it, too.

His beard shadow was more noticeable this morning, giving him a piratical appearance that seemed darkly appealing and far too suitable to the type of man she now knew him to be. Ray watched his gaze drop to her mouth and she unconsciously licked her lips while struggling for a clear thought.

Eli's fingers gripped her skull, holding her head still as he slowly leaned forward. His intent was obvious.

He was going to kiss her.

It was all the inducement Ray needed. She practically sprang from the bed, ruffled, confused, far too warm. Her normally agile limbs refused to work correctly. She got one foot caught in the sheet, staggered, righted herself. Once out of the bed, she tried to look blasé, but hiding her turbulent emotions and racing heartbeat wasn't easy.

Eli watched her like a hawk preparing to scoop up a mouse.

That image didn't sit well with her, so she forced a chuckle. "Sorry about that. I didn't mean to hog the bed." She ran her fingers through her tangled bangs, inadvertently making them more tangled. "I, uh, don't usually sleep like the dead."

"I didn't mind."

Ray had to turn her back to his deep, softly spoken words. God, she felt his husky voice reverberate through her entire body, settling like a weight in her lower belly. She resisted the urge to fan herself, unwilling to let Eli know how much she'd been affected by his touch.

The telephone rang, jarring her. Before common sense could sink in, she pivoted on the balls of her feet in a fighter's stance, ready to face the threat.

Eli gave her a long look, sat up on the side of the bed, and answered their wake-up call. Hot color stole up her neck, over her face, right up to her eyebrows.

After he'd hung up, Eli scrutinized her. "Are you okay?"

"Fine." Her voice was clipped, but hell, she'd almost kicked the phone.

He looked unconvinced, concerned, and protective. "You know, Ray, all I really need are directions. You can tell me what to do. There's no reason for you to go along—"

"No." He wrongly assumed her stupid jitters were in fear of the mission. Her throat squeezed tight, making it hard to breathe. If he thought she couldn't do her job, then she had no value to him, not now, not here. But she couldn't correct him either. An admission like that would probably have her right back in the bed. "I run the show, Eli, not you, and no way in hell are you going anywhere without me."

His eyes narrowed. She recognized the stubbornness in the set of his shoulders, the signs of impending arguments.

"Give it up, Eli." She crossed her arms over her chest. "We don't have time for macho nonsense. If we're going to meet my friend on time, we have to get rolling. From here on out, things will move quickly. We need to stay on schedule, so get your butt out of the bed."

The seconds ticked by while Eli ruminated in indecision, his eyes locked on hers. She didn't dare waver, didn't look away, and in the end, he nodded, filling Ray with relief.

"Whatever you say, Ray." Looking more manly than any man had a right to, he rose from the bed, grabbed up his overnight bag, and disappeared into the bathroom.

He was gone fifteen minutes, which gave Ray

time to collect herself. Not that it helped much when, the second she saw him, she wanted to melt all over again.

His hair was wet from his shower but he'd remembered not to shave. He wore only dark beard shadow, small droplets of water that still clung to his chest hair, and fresh boxers.

She wasn't a schoolgirl or an inexperienced virgin. She'd never led a sheltered life. More times than she could count, she'd seen men in similar states of undress.

This wasn't the same. This was Eli.

She silently cursed herself, especially when Eli looked up and caught her ogling him.

He held her gaze while stepping into his jeans. "I'm done in the bathroom if you want to dress. I'll be ready in five minutes."

Ray picked up her bag and hurried into the bathroom, then closed and locked the door. She was still washing up when she heard Eli open the hotel door and speak quietly to someone. Her curiosity pricked, she dressed quickly to investigate. No sooner had she stepped out of the bathroom than the aroma of fresh coffee and croissants had her stomach growling in appreciation.

Eli looked up as she walked in. He'd placed the tray at the end of the bed and was already filling two cups. Beside the plate of fat, flaky croissants were pats of butter, jams, and jellies. A small urn of creamer and several sugar packets rounded out the feast.

"I thought you might want a bite to eat before we take off. It's not much, but I didn't think we'd have time for a big breakfast."

The man was diabolical in his tactics. He'd probably make a good mercenary—if all his missions were to seduce women. He was certainly on the road to success with her.

He hadn't bothered with a shirt yet. His chest was the stuff of dreams, with just the right amount of dark hair and prominent muscles. He looked strong, without the bulk of an overblown body-builder.

Beneath his navel on his hard abdomen, Ray saw the start of a silkier line of hair. She knew where that happy trail led and almost wished he hadn't put on the jeans.

She busied herself with spreading two packets of strawberry jam onto half a croissant. She took a healthy bite and groaned in bliss. "Good stuff. Thanks."

When he didn't reply, she glanced up. He wore such a tender expression, she blinked. "What?"

Shrugging, Eli told her, "It amuses me that you enjoy eating so much, and you're so damn slender."

"Fast metabolism," she explained. "And you'd better eat something, too. It might be a while before we get the chance again. And when we do, it sure as hell won't be fresh pastry."

Eli dutifully walked to the tray to choose his own croissant. "You know, I've been wondering about a few things."

Ray paused in the act of chewing. "Yeah?"

"You keep saying you have everything planned, but that doesn't tell me anything."

"You know what you need to know."

"I hired you, remember?"

Like she could ever forget? "So?"

"Doesn't that give me a few rights?"

"No."

He pressed her. "If there's more to this than

you're telling me, if my brother is in serious danger . . ."

Huffing, Ray reached for his arm, then turned his wrist so she could read the face of his watch. "All right. You have about two minutes to get specific answers. Then we have to go."

He nodded in satisfaction. "How are we going to get past the border patrols?"

Arching a brow, Ray said, "That's pretty specific. Okay, first off, Mataya is coastal on two sides. We won't file a flight plan, so no one will be watching for us. The area isn't that hostile anymore, and they're so poor that they can't afford regular patrols. It won't be a problem. Going through legal channels not only costs a fortune in bribes, it takes forever. The rule is to never confront an official if you don't have to. They have a way of talking circles around you until you've emptied your pockets."

"And once we land?"

"We'll travel overland by foot for about fifteen miles to what the locals refer to as the town square, though that's misleading. It's a packed dirt courtyard surrounded by a few thatch-roofed *palapas*. It opens up to the main dock." She glanced up and away. "You'll see mostly fishermen, some outdoor cooking fires, and a brothel."

Other than a raised brow, he didn't react to that.

"I have a few contacts there who'll bring me up to date on things." And when Eli met her contacts, he'd likely swallow his tongue.

"What *things?*"

She shrugged. "When the plan is going down, how many men will be at the site with your brother, stuff like that."

"And the plan is?"

Ray hesitated to tell him. The locals weren't familiar with him, and while everyone in Mataya wore a smile and gave a hearty greeting, true trust for an outsider was a fragile thing. Eli, being a man, could easily blow it. Especially if he showed them any disrespect . . .

She shook her head. No, Eli wasn't like that. He was always polite to her, so she had no reason to think he'd treat others any differently.

She sat on the side of the bed. "Sarita Contreras owns the brothel. Her clientele is mostly guerillas. You see, her brother, Ignacio, and Miguel Bodden are the leaders of their small group."

"A brothel, huh?" Eli sounded more curious than condemning. "So Miguel is one of her customers?"

"No, Miguel is her man." Ray made a face. "He comes across as a very scary character, but not that long ago he was still farming sugarcane. You'll know him when you see him. He's really hairy."

Eli ran a hand over his bare chest. "I'm hairy."

The croissant stuck in her throat, forcing her to swallow twice. Eli was hairy, but nicely so, unlike Miguel, who looked like a shaggy rug. "On your chest, yeah."

"And my legs and my—"

Ray rushed to interrupt him. "Miguel has hair everywhere, even behind his knees. When he's naked, it looks like he's wearing a wool suit. He could pass for the missing link."

"You've seen him naked?"

That deadly calm voice caught her attention. "He hangs out a brothel, Eli, so what do you think?"

A dark scowl told her what Eli thought of that. He crossed his arms over his naked chest. "How do you know Sarita?"

She couldn't help but grin. "I didn't work for her, if that's what you're wondering."

He just continued to watch her, so Ray shrugged. In her mind, she censored the details, rearranging them in a way that she didn't mind sharing. "She's helped me on other missions, which is also how I know Miguel. He and I have tangled once before. Sarita gives me information, supplies when she has them."

"Because you pay her?"

"Sure. But also because if the men are hanging out at the camp, they aren't visiting the brothel. She'd rather have Miguel with her than risking his neck trying to survive. Most of them started out as farmers or fishermen, and only became guerillas because they had to in order to survive."

"That's the same reason the women work in a brothel?"

"They don't have easy lives. Miguel is a possessive ape, but Sarita knows they need money to survive, and other than the drug trade, that's the only way she can get it."

"You said you've met up with Miguel before?"

"Yeah. He tried getting in my way when I went there to retrieve a tourist. Miguel wasn't the one who had him, but he thought he could shake me down, maybe steal the ransom money from me."

"What happened?"

Eli had a knack for making a simple question sound like a growled demand. "Because I knew how Sarita would feel about it, I tried not to hurt him. But the big dope wouldn't let up, even after I'd broken his nose, two fingers, and bruised a few ribs. I ended up giving him a little tap between the legs, not enough to do serious damage, but enough to slow him down." Ray finished off her coffee and stood. "The women who help us will be paid. How much, I don't know yet."

"Depends on what you do to their men?"

Astute as well as handsome. Ray hid her grin. "That's right. Miguel was no use to Sarita for some weeks. She deserved extra compensation. Hopefully he's learned his lesson by now. But you can't expect the women to betray their men for nothing."

"Will the men be angry at them?"

"Of course. But Sarita does it anyway."

"Just for money?"

He sounded offended on the other man's behalf. Ray pursed her mouth. "That—and to protect Miguel."

"Protect him from what?"

Ray brought her gaze up to his. "Me." She turned away to repack her belongings. "When I make a deal with her, I keep it."

"And part of the deal is to spare Miguel?"

"Something like that. Now get ready. Buddy hates to be left waiting."

Eli reached for his shirt and pulled it on. "Buddy is the one we're meeting today?"

"That's right. He's an ace pilot and one of my best friends."

"And where do you know him from?"

Exasperated, Ray threw up her arms. "What is this, the Inquisition?"

"No, just simple questions."

True, and if she kept flying off the handle, he'd begin wondering what secrets she kept from him. "Buddy and I were in the service together."

Eli gave her a perplexed look. "Am I wrong in assuming you were a soldier?"

"No."

He frowned, then sat on the side of the bed to

pull on his boots. "I thought the military kept the sexes separate. How did you get to be such good friends with him?"

Memories bombarded Ray, some pleasant, most not. She resented Eli for dredging them up, forcing her to face them before she had to. "Wise up, Eli. The military can do whatever the hell it wants. Let's just say Buddy and I spent a lot of time relying on each other, and leave it at that."

Eli stared at her for a long moment, then asked with resignation, "You're not going to elaborate on that, are you?"

"Nope. Any other questions?"

"Yeah. Are we taking weapons with us?"

"Buddy'll have what we need on the plane. He puts together all my supplies—makes it easier than taking them through airport security."

Her dry tone left Eli with no doubt that she thought his question to be asinine. Still, he said, "One more thing."

Ray gave a sigh of annoyance. "What's that?"

"If we're walking fifteen miles to get Jeremy, how the hell are we going to make it out of there without being caught? Seems to me going in will be a lot easier than getting out."

"Checking in with Sarita first, then going through the mountain passes will be what takes so long. We'll take a more direct route back by road, so that's only about five miles. I thought I'd steal a jeep or something once we're ready to go."

Eli's expression never changed. "Steal a jeep?"

"Yeah." She almost laughed. "I don't suppose you know how to hot-wire a car do you?"

Eli stood, his eyes glinting with smug satisfaction. "As a matter of fact . . . I do."

Ray quickly covered her reaction. She shouldn't

have been so surprised. Eli had already proven himself to be a capable, resourceful man. "Well then, maybe you can take care of acquiring our transportation."

"Be glad to."

Ray couldn't help but smile at the challenge in his words. "Great. Now, get a move on, will ya? We need to get out of here. Your brother is most likely dirty, hungry for American food, and impatient to be rescued."

"He may feel differently when I get my hands on him." Eli snapped his suitcase closed and stood. "Let's go then. Time's wasting."

Chapter Six

Ray was again driving, this time a rental truck so there was no rust. Eli spent the two-hour trip attempting to pry additional information out of her. The more he learned, the more he wanted to know.

He'd been sly, cloaking his personal questions with inquiries about Mataya. Ray didn't appear to notice, but at the same time, most of her answers were so vague, she might as well have not bothered.

"Are you always this evasive?" He already knew she was a mercenary, so what else could she possibly need to hide?

Ray flashed him a quick glance. "Are you always so nosy?"

Eli denied that accusation with a shake of his head. "Interested, not nosy. You've got to admit, your chosen profession is out of the ordinary."

"Rescuing is a side job that I'm very good at. Not my 'chosen profession.' I haven't had an assignment in . . . quite a while." The words no sooner left her mouth than she scowled, as if she'd somehow said more than she intended to and blamed him for the slipup.

Eli wanted to keep her talking. "Not that many people in need, huh?"

She made a face. "You can be pretty naïve, Eli, you know that?"

"Meaning?"

"The world is full of fools and thrill-seekers. There's always someone who needs me. But I turn a lot of jobs down. You just happened to come along at a time when I felt I could use the extra cash."

"For what?"

She sent him a glance filled with exasperation. "There you go with those personal questions again. How I spend my money, or why, is no concern of yours."

He was ready to launch into another round of questioning when she raised her hand and pointed. "Look. We're here."

Eli scanned the area and saw nothing except endless flat grassland surrounding a long, curving lake. Only a few trees studded the otherwise smooth scenery. Not a single soul was in sight. He asked skeptically, "Where is here?"

"Buddy will be landing soon. He owns all this. Not that you'd ever know it to talk to him." And with a load of fondness: "Money hasn't changed Buddy. He's still as genuine and honest as ever."

Eli scowled. Did she mean to say *he* wasn't genuine or honest? Unlike calling him an idiot, this was an insult he couldn't let pass. Thinking of his own background, he said, "I gather the money came to him later in life?"

Ray nodded. "There's a definite difference between people born to money and those that get it through hard work."

He just knew she was drawing comparisons and that, in her eyes at least, he'd come up short. Before her assignment ended, Eli vowed she'd understand him better. He didn't like rehashing his past, but for Ray, he'd make an exception. Then she'd stop making snide judgements on his character based on his wealth. "Why does Buddy still go on assignments if he doesn't need the money?"

Ray pulled the truck off the road and into the grass, going a good fifty yards before she parked. She turned the engine off and propped her wrists on the steering wheel, narrowing her eyes against the bright sun. "Buddy does this only when I do." She hesitated, drew a breath. "He won't let anyone else fly me."

She grew quiet then, listening, and soon the sounds of a loud engine could be heard. Through the truck's windshield, Eli saw the approach of a Cessna Skylane. The wings dipped in an aerial salute of welcome. With an unlikely girlish squeal, Ray left the truck in a rush, running toward the lake.

A little stunned at her display—especially that feminine sound of excitement—Eli held back a moment to watch her long-legged sprint, the way she waved her arms. It was the first time he'd seen her in an actual hurry. He opened his door to follow after her.

The plane landed on fat pontoons, spraying water in a wide arc. It glided over the surface of the lake, circled, then came to a neat stop not far from where Ray waited.

A man close to Eli's age jumped down from the wing of the plane, slogging quickly though the dark, shallow water and hitting the land in a dead run. He had dark blond hair, laughing green eyes, and a powerful build.

With a shout of pleasure, he intercepted Ray's rushing form, swinging her in a circle then crushing her close.

Eli was not a demonstrative man. He wasn't overly possessive either. And damn it, he didn't put on Neanderthal shows for women.

But the need to snatch Ray away from Buddy burned in his gut. Until this moment, he hadn't really heard Ray laugh.

Her laughter now, carefree and full of joy, was with another man. A well-built, handsome man who she obviously adored. Well, shit.

Eli finally got close enough to be noticed by the entwined couple. He waited, tense, angry, and trying to hide it without much success.

Buddy looked up first and his eyes widened. Humor fading fast, Buddy set Ray away from him. Ray was in no hurry to release her friend, though. She still had her arm around him when she turned to introduce Eli.

"Eli Connors, meet Buddy Rhodes."

Eli gave a slight nod of acknowledgement.

Buddy fumed. "What the hell is this? You taking on partners?"

"No." Despite Buddy's bark, Ray still grinned. "Eli hired me."

"So why the hell is he *here?*"

Eli was annoyed enough to say, "Because *he* insisted."

With a snort, Buddy glared down at Ray. "And you allowed it?"

She shrugged, glanced at Eli, and said sheepishly, "It was a condition of the job and I needed the money."

Buddy's expression showed stunned disbelief for three seconds before he erupted in fury. *"Goddammit."* He stomped a splashing circle around Ray, muttering more lurid curses. Ray just waited, her mouth twitching in amusement until Buddy came to a halt in front of her. "Why the hell won't you just let me give you the money?"

At the less than gracious offer, Ray pokered up and punched him hard in the shoulder. "That's an old tune, Buddy. You've played it to death."

"Then let me loan you the money and you won't have to hear it again." He caught her upper arms in a bone-crushing squeeze. "There's no damn reason for you to continue doing this."

She gave him a shove to free herself, and his ass almost hit the water. "I agree. That's why I haven't been back in so long. But now . . ." She shook off her anger and made a wry face. "Matt has a lot of new expenses."

They carried on like siblings, relieving some, but not all, of Eli's jealousy. Feeling very much like a third wheel, he frowned. "Who's Matt?"

They ignored him. "Does Matt know what you're up to?"

"Are you kidding? His temper is worse than mine. He'll find out when I'm back and it's all over with. That's soon enough to deal with him."

"Who's Matt?"

"He ought to lock you in a room somewhere." Buddy cupped Ray's chin, forcing her face up. "That's what I'd do with your stubborn little ass. In fact, I still might."

Ray jerked her chin free. "Try it and I'll drown you."

"Who is Matt?"

Buddy gave him an evil stare. He propped his hands on his hips and remained stubbornly silent.

Ray turned to face Eli. "My brother. I told you about him, didn't I?"

"You mentioned him briefly."

"Well, it's time for college." And with a lot of pride, she added, "Matt's smart as a whip."

Buddy leaned toward Eli as if speaking a confidence, which was ridiculous because Ray could hear every word. "Ray here thinks her brother walks on water and has to have the very best of everything."

Ray punched his arm again, but this time playfully. "I do not. Matt would do great with or without me. He doesn't need an advantage, I just want him to have it."

So, she took care of her brother? Eli remembered that night in the kitchen when she'd talked about young men having more testosterone than brains. Apparently, she spoke from experience.

Buddy cupped her cheeks, a huge grin on his face. "Damn, sweetheart, it's good to see you again."

Ray's expression softened. "I've missed you, too."

And then Buddy lowered his head and kissed her soundly, right on the mouth.

The jealousy was back, black and mean. Eli had never suffered it before, but he knew instinctively what it was. That it was happening now, over a woman he'd only known a few short days, a woman who made it clear—ad nauseam—that she wanted nothing to do with him, didn't help to alleviate the problem.

Nor did the fact that Ray and Buddy left him to stew on his own. It was almost as if they'd forgotten about him.

After they boarded the plane, Ray went over her supplies. Eli should have been more interested, especially when she produced an array of awesome weapons including a razor-sharp bowie knife at least a foot long. But with Buddy hanging on her, all Eli made note of was his rising temper.

"Here." Ray thrust a webbed vest with a multitude of pockets at Eli. "You'll wear that over your T-shirt. Do you have any idea how to handle a gun?"

She made every question sound like an insult. Eli wanted to smack her. He wanted to turn her over his knee and—visual, erotic images crowded his brain and splintered his concentration. He was in so deep he didn't know if he'd ever find his way out.

Barely controlling his temper, he surveyed the weapons, then reached out and took a .357 Magnum seven-shot. Without a word, he stuffed it under his belt.

"I take that as a yes?"

"I'm better with a rifle, but yeah, I'll hit something if I shoot." Eli turned away from her grin—and caught Buddy's grin instead. They shared amusement at his expense and he didn't like it. "When in hell are we going to take off, anyway? Can't you just look that stuff over on the way?"

Buddy chuckled at his disgruntled tone. "Sure she could." There was a heavy, anticipatory pause before he said, "If she didn't get airsick every time we go up."

"*Buddy.*"

Eli stared at Ray. Her face was hot with color and she had murder in her eyes. It was Buddy receiving that lethal glare, though, not Eli.

Of course, he'd already noticed her little problem on the earlier flight. The way she'd clutched the armrests so tightly, he'd half expected her to pull them off the chair. When he'd taken her hand instead, her grip had been bruising.

He hadn't mentioned the weakness then, and he didn't say anything now. But her gaze swung around to lock with his, and she growled, "I'm fine five minutes after we land, so don't let it worry you. It won't interfere with my performance."

Turning her over his knee seemed more and more enticing. "I wasn't worried, Ray."

Perversely, she snapped, "Well, you should have been. You're the one paying me."

Buddy gave Ray an affectionate squeeze. "Stop chewing on the poor fellow and quit thinking of murdering me. He would have noticed once we were in the air, anyway. This isn't like a commercial flight. There's not a lot of space here to hide."

Ray shoved herself to her feet. The cabin was only four feet high, so she braced her legs apart, bent at the waist, and propped her hands on her thighs. "I'll have you know I napped on the flight."

"The hell you say!"

Buddy's obvious surprise assured Eli that it didn't happen often. He remembered how Ray had cuddled close to him in her sleep. Maybe Ray didn't want to admit it, but she felt the chemistry between them, too. Maybe she even felt safe with him.

That had to count for something.

With Buddy and Eli both scrutinizing her, Ray huffed. "Why don't you two go start the engines and I'll change."

Eli frowned again. "Change what?"

Buddy took his arm. "Her clothes. Ray can't stand restrictions. She'd rather suffer the bug bites than have her arms covered."

After they'd hunkered their way into the cabin,

Buddy offered Eli the copilot's seat. He took his own seat behind the controls. Blue, yellow, and red lights glowed around a green screen. "You ever fly?"

"A little. We have a Skylane for the ranch. Not as new or fancy as this one, but then we just use it to check fences and watering holes."

"Got a lot of land, huh?"

"Depends on what your idea of a lot is."

"If it takes a plane to keep track of it, I'd say it qualifies."

"Then I guess we've got a lot." Eli didn't want to talk about acreage or planes. His timing perfect, he glanced over his shoulder and saw Ray pull her shirt up and over her head. She had her back facing him, but that didn't do all that much to hinder his racing heartbeat. Her bra fell next and Eli was given the view of her smooth, sleekly muscled shoulders and graceful spine. His eyes narrowed in appreciation.

He'd known plenty of women in his days. Women from the streets, a little raw, starved for attention and excitement. Women from society, finely decked out, demanding and cunning. He'd known women in between, sweet and kind, easily hurt.

He'd never known anyone like Ray. The things she did and said, her brutal honesty, irreverence, and total lack of modesty appealed to him as much as her courage.

When Ray turned slightly to pick up a black sleeveless shirt, he saw the curve of her breast. Hell yeah, he liked her body a lot, too. Every move she made seemed fluid and sexy.

The roar of the engine coming to life brought Eli out of his daze. He twisted around in his seat, caught the knowing smile on Buddy's face, and scowled. "What?"

"She catch you peeking, she'll black both your eyes." Buddy winked. "I know because she caught me once."

Eli ignored that taunt to glance at her again. In distracted tones, he said, "I'm ready when you are, Buddy."

"A man who lives on the edge." Buddy thwacked his shoulder, almost knocking Eli out of his seat. "I like that."

The plane was small and open with storage space, only the two seats in front. Ray sat on the floor to put her boots back on. She stayed as far from the men as she could get.

Eli took in the new clothes with a discriminating eye. She was now dressed in a skimpy black tank top that left her throat and arms completely bare. She had a dark green vest similar to the one she'd given to Eli pulled on over it. At least that hid her breasts, which ought to help him keep his mind on the task at hand.

Very loose, well-worn fatigue pants were cinched around her waist with the bottoms tucked into a pair of scuffed brown lace-up boots. Her face appeared pale as she shoved ammunition into the vest pockets with practiced ease. Eli felt his heart twist, looking at her.

In that moment, he hated himself. He should have found someone else, should have canceled the damn idea as soon as she'd shown up. Strangely enough, it wasn't just because Ray was female. Another woman might not have affected him so strongly. But he'd connected with her, whether she wanted to admit it or not, whether he was comfortable with it or not.

If things somehow went wrong and she got hurt . . .

Buddy must have read his thoughts, for he roughly shoved Eli's shoulder. In a low voice that didn't carry over the roar of the plane, Buddy told him, "Relax. She knows what she's doing. This assignment is a breeze. Think of it as a vacation, okay?"

"Then why all the damn ammo?" Eli grunted. "She looks like a female Rambo, for Christ's sake."

Buddy snickered. "Hell, she's much cuter than Rambo any day. And she has a better rack."

"Buddy," Eli snarled in warning.

"Down, boy." Buddy laughed. "The weapons are just a precaution. There are scary critters, both human and animal variety, in Central America. Drug runners, crooked officials, thieves. Odds are you won't have to deal with any of them, but only a fool goes in unprepared."

"Then there *is* danger."

Buddy rolled his eyes. "Nothing she can't handle. Do you think I'd let her go in if I didn't know she'd come back out with her sweet little backside in one piece? Here." He reached across Eli to withdraw a small photo wedged behind a control. "There's my girl."

Eli accepted the photo. It showed Ray in full combat mode, complete with a bandana around her head, a black eye, and an enormous grin. She stood between two trussed-up, truly reprehensible looking characters. "What is this?"

"Ray's job that day was to distract the men while others got inside the compound and retrieved two little-known but valuable Russian diplomats. They weren't very gentlemanly about finding a woman alone and unprotected."

Eli squeezed his eyes shut, which only made Buddy laugh.

"She went along with it, even let them tie her to a chair with her hands behind her. But when one of the idiots tried feeling her up, she canceled all bets. There'd been just enough time to get the diplomats safely on their way and Ray knew it, so she quit faking Little Miss Innocent and let 'em have it."

"You said she was tied up."

"Her hands, yeah. But the fools hadn't figured on her feet. Ray's damn good with her feet. Better than anyone I've seen. She still had her steel-toed boots on, too, and she let the first guy have it right in the balls. Probably emasculated him for good. Ray said any guy who tried to force a woman deserved no better."

"I agree."

Buddy shrugged. "Me, too. The other guy hit her—see her eye?"

Eli saw, and wanted to kill someone.

"He got Ray's boot in his chin. She got on her feet while they were both down, broke the chair apart by crashing it into a tree, and once she was free . . . well, Ray can be like the Tasmanian devil. She's all fast motion, damn near a blur. And nimble—that girl can twist in ways that defies explanation." He winked.

Eli had a hard time restraining himself. Only the fact that Buddy appeared to have some influence over Ray kept the anger and unreasonable jealousy in check. "Why do you let her go? You seem to care about her."

"Hell, I love her. I thought you already figured that out."

Eli took the words like a blow on the chin. Every muscle in his body clenched in preparation for a fight. He'd claimed her; she was *his*—she just didn't know it yet. "You've got a hell of a way of showing it. I don't care how good you both think she is, she's still just a woman."

"Oh ho! Don't let Ray hear you say that. Her temper is a very nasty thing." Then he chuckled. "Besides, you misunderstand, Romeo. I love her, but like a sister. She was never my woman. There was a time when I would have changed that but . . . now I have my own wife who I happen to love a lot, and she loves Ray, too. So you can quit bristling."

Amazingly, Eli did feel some of the tension seep away. "You're happily married?"

"Hard to believe anyone would put up with me, huh?"

Eli smiled. "Maybe. But I was talking about how you interact with Ray. It sure as hell looked like more than friendship."

"Yeah, a lot more. Hell, more than family even." He pursed his mouth in contemplation of their relationship, but ended with a shrug. "I guess we have a pretty complicated past."

How complicated? Eli wondered.

"As far as the other, you need to give Ray more credit. She isn't like ordinary women. Not by a long shot."

Did Buddy say as much to Ray? If so, maybe that'd help to explain why Ray refused to see herself as a woman with a woman's needs. But despite her skills, she was just that—a woman. An extraordinary woman, but female all the way down to her toes.

Sensing that Buddy might reveal more than Ray ever had, Eli reluctantly settled himself. "I noticed that she has special talents."

"Naw. You've only seen surface stuff."

"She got into a barroom fight."

Buddy nodded. "That's my girl." He gave Eli a quick, knowing look. "Kicked some ass, didn't she?"

"She is fast."

"Like greased lightning," Buddy drawled with pride. "Was she smiling while she fought? Ray always smiles, which can be pretty damn daunting."

Remembering their skirmish in the bed, Eli heard himself say, "She didn't smile when—" Belatedly, he caught himself.

Buddy, of course, didn't let it go. "Oh ho. You two get into it? Oh, to have been a fly on the wall . . . But hey, if she wasn't grinning like a loon, then she wasn't really mad, and wasn't really out to hurt you. Trust me, you'll know if Ray is ever pissed and out for blood."

Since he had only pleasure on his mind, Eli shrugged. "Tell me how she's different."

"Her training, for one thing."

"I understand she was in the service, but she's never really said which branch."

Buddy snorted. "I'll just bet she hasn't. She doesn't like going into it much. Now me, I don't mind at all. Maybe that's because I'm more settled now. My life is totally different from then. I have a different job, a wife, and a home that I love. But Ray . . ." He glanced back to make sure Ray wasn't listening before continuing in a lower voice. "She went to work for that damned agency, so she still hasn't separated herself from that time."

"You were army?"

"We weren't really any particular branch, at least not the way you'd figure it. They used us for specialized missions. Very covert stuff. Hell, most of the brass didn't know we existed, and other soldiers would have only dreamed us in a nightmare. We were . . . like cleanup crews. When things didn't go the way the diplomats wanted them to, we bypassed all chains of command, went in, and set things right."

"If no one knew about you, then what happened if you got into trouble, or couldn't make it out?"

"You said it yourself. No one would ever know."

"Jesus." Eli felt sick—and shaken. What if Ray hadn't made it? What if something awful had happened to her?

"Ray was perfect for the missions. She's so focused, so self-contained, she fit right in." Buddy's hands tightened. "That wasn't the tough part."

Eli wanted to tell Buddy to turn the plane around, but he knew Ray wouldn't allow it. This was the closest he'd come to understanding her, so he might as well take advantage of it. "What was the tough part?"

Buddy gave a grimace. "We were trained as teams."

Eli knew he was missing something. "Isn't that how most military units work?"

"I guess. But usually they keep things platonic. They don't push intimacy."

He didn't know what to say to that, so Eli just waited.

"They called our unit the 'Adam and Eve.' They paired up men and women they believed were compatible, based on mumbo jumbo pulled from these long series of in-depth tests. There were six in our unit. We were trained to work hand in hand, to rely on one another. For everything. At the time, before I met my wife, I thought it was almost like being married—except that they dropped us off in volcanic situations and told us to not only survive, but to carry out our orders."

"You and Ray were . . . ?"

Laughing, Buddy shook his head. "Nope. Ray had already been paired with Kevin for about six months before I was recruited for the program. They were the original Adam and Eve team, the very first. But they worked out so well, other teams were formed until we had three separate units."

It sounded like something out of a far-fetched spy novel, giving Eli a sinking feeling about it all. He dreaded the answer to his next question, but he asked it all the same. "What happened to Kevin?"

Buddy no longer looked amused. "He was captured in Central America. It was so damn different then. The country was explosive. Leftist guerillas and the army were battling in the street, with innocents getting shot down in the cross fire. Tourists were raped in broad daylight. Right before Kevin was captured, a German businessman was brutally murdered. Six of us went in to retrieve a kidnapped ambassador, but only five of us came out."

"The government did nothing?"

"To them, we didn't exist. We knew if we were caught, we were on our own. Most of us accepted it. If Ray had been caught, she would have accepted it, too. But this was her partner."

"And she wouldn't let him go?"

Buddy's throat worked as he swallowed, his gaze faraway, remote. "Ray insisted on going back for him, but our superiors vetoed it. They were having negotiations, or so they claimed, and didn't want to rock the boat."

"Jesus."

Buddy wiped his brow, his eyes now narrowed. He took the photograph of Ray away from Eli and carefully, gently, replaced it. "She went ballistic. I'd never seen her like that before. Ray was always calm and methodical, but suddenly, no one could console her or calm her down. She resigned her position, said to hell with the military, and made plans to go get him."

Eli couldn't ask. His chest ached just thinking of how difficult it must have been for her, a lone woman in emotional turmoil. He was oblivious to everything else at that moment. He didn't see the clouds floating by, didn't hear the gentle roar of the engine, didn't notice the way Buddy watched him.

Needing the visual contact with her, he turned in his seat to soak up the sight of Ray. Sitting on the floor, she had her knees drawn up, her head resting on her folded arms. Her face was turned away from him. To the casual observer, she appeared to be relaxing, but Eli already knew her better than that. From the first, he'd seen so much when he looked at Ray.

Where her hands clasped, her knuckles were white. Muscles in her shoulders were pronounced, showing her tension. More than anything, Eli wanted to go to her, to hold her. He wanted to somehow offer comfort for what had happened so long ago.

But he didn't. He understood how Ray would react to a gesture of sympathy. She'd probably squeeze his larynx again. That thought made him smile gently. If Buddy hadn't been there, a witness to her weakness, he would have gone to her anyway and said to hell with it. But her pride was important to her, and that made it important to him.

"How can she bear to go back?"

Buddy rolled his shoulders. "She remembers how helpless she felt when she tried to get funding or aid for her own rescue attempt. She came to me as a last resort, but only to fly her over. She wouldn't let me go in with her. Hell, like I said, I was in love with her then. I'd have done anything she asked."

"Including waiting behind?"

"She'd have found another way—without me—if I hadn't agreed." He glanced at Eli. "So I snuck in behind her, just to keep an eye out. I'd already decided to kill them all if they hurt her."

Hating to ask it, but unable not to, Eli said, "And did they?"

Buddy snorted. "It wasn't pretty, what she found that day in the guerilla camp. Those bastards didn't stand a chance. Ray damn near took the whole place apart. Before she left, there wasn't a cell standing, a jeep unturned." He laughed. "Rambo looked like a pussy in comparison to Ray that day. She didn't need me, that's for damn sure. She razed the place— and still that didn't seem like enough for her. The rescue was successful, but she blamed herself for not getting there quicker."

A lump the size of a watermelon lodged in Eli's throat. "What happened to her partner?"

Quietly, Buddy said, "For about six months, Kevin was hospitalized. Ray paid all his bills, visited him daily, took care of him. But once he'd recovered, he couldn't bear any connection to what he'd once been, to what had happened to him."

"And Ray was a part of that."

"Yeah. He saw her only one more time, to thank her and say good-bye."

Eli closed his eyes and swallowed hard. "She must have been crushed. After all she'd done for him . . ."

"You don't know Ray if you believe that. She was hurt, that's true. She loved Kevin and had done her best for him. But to this day, she thinks she failed, that she somehow didn't do enough for him. That's what bothered her then, what bothers her still, even now." He drew a slow breath. "Especially when she goes back."

And Eli was the one taking her there, making her dredge it all up. He again looked to Ray. She had curled into a ball against the side of the plane, her entire demeanor one of misery. "When did all this happen?"

Scratching his brow, Buddy answered thoughtfully, "Must be seven, maybe eight years now. Not long before she got her brother. She was just a kid then herself, not much more than her mid-twenties. Matt saved her life, to my way of thinking. He gave her someone new to focus on, someone new to love. She's poured her heart and soul into caring for him, and she's done a great job." Buddy shook off his tension. "She's thirty-one now, but the years have only honed her talents. She's tougher than a junk-yard dog."

"She's not so tough," Eli said in a whisper. He couldn't take his eyes off her, seeing her discomfort so plainly depicted in the way she held herself.

"She's always gotten airsick. The guys used to tease her something awful about it."

"She let them?"

"She was one of the guys, Eli. She took it in stride, and dished it right back at every opportunity."

One of the guys. That said it more than anything else could.

The plane vibrated suddenly with turbulence and Ray jerked, a small moan escaping her. The tiny sound proved to be more than Eli could bear.

"Ignore us," he said to Buddy while moving

from his seat to go to Ray. He knelt beside her, smoothed back her hair. "Is there anything I can do to help, sweetheart?"

She groaned. "They shoot horses, don't they?"

Eli smiled, but his amusement was bittersweet. Damn, she amazed him. Even while so miserable, she dredged up a smart retort. "Let me hold you. Maybe you'll feel better."

"I doubt that."

"You can slug me later, but right now I'm going to insist."

With Ray grimacing and grousing and putting up feeble resistance, Eli wedged in behind her so his back was to the wall of the plane, his legs surrounding her. Then he easily lifted her onto his lap and settled her head against his shoulder. *He* certainly felt better holding her. He rubbed her back and kissed her forehead.

He heard Buddy start to whistle in a ridiculous show of inattention.

This new insight into Ray had only defined his feelings for her. He felt the silky sleekness of her hair, her soft skin, and knew it to be a stark contrast to her iron will. The things she'd done proved an honor and bravery that few men could ever claim. It went bone deep, was a core of the woman—and made her so very, very special.

It didn't matter that he'd only known her a few days; he loved her and he wasn't going to let her go.

Ray stirred, lifting her face enough to see him. "I do feel a little better now, Eli."

"I'm glad." Eli pressed her head back to his shoulder.

Now that she felt better, she felt defensive, too.

Eli wasn't surprised that she concealed it with sarcasm. "You know, maybe it's not such a bad idea that I brought you along after all. We've already found something you're good for."

Eli nipped her small earlobe. Her hair smelled like his shampoo—and that turned him on. He liked his scent on her. He'd like it even better when the scent of sex clung to her warmed skin.

"I'm good for a lot of things, Ray." He touched the rim of her ear lightly with the tip of his tongue, giving her a new focus, other than the flight. "I fully intend for you to understand them all. Soon."

He felt her slight tremble before she changed the subject. "What were you and Buddy gabbing about for so long?"

Eli glanced at Buddy. He wore a headset and was still whistling, but Eli wasn't fooled. Buddy was Ray's friend and she trusted him; that meant he wasn't a fool. He was aware of everything going on around him.

"We were just getting to know each other," Eli lied, then tilted her chin up so he could see her face. "I want you to promise me something."

Her beautiful dark eyes narrowed in suspicion. "What?"

The urge to kiss that mulish pout off her mouth was almost overwhelming. "Promise me you won't take any chances."

"What are you talking about?"

He pulled her closer, stifling her efforts to wiggle away. "I don't want you hurt. If things don't look right, or if you feel uncertain at all, don't risk it."

Ray appeared bewildered by his instructions. "I thought you wanted your brother out."

"I do. But not at any cost. Not if you get hurt. If it doesn't happen tomorrow, I'll find another way. But I want your word you won't take any chances. Promise me."

Ray stared at him for a moment, then stubbornly looked away. "I didn't come this far to fail. I will get your brother."

He'd been under so much pressure, felt so many new emotions, that it didn't take much to make him crack. Eli shook her, surprising himself as much as Ray. "You listen to me, you little witch. I'm paying for this rescue. You work for me. And I say no risks."

Her eyes widened and her mouth fell open on a disbelieving laugh. "You're insane if you think you can give me orders. Besides, I've told you everything is already planned, there's no real danger, and *I can take care of myself.*"

Eli's hands trembled as he framed her face, tugging her so close their breaths mingled. He was torn between wanting to kiss her and needing to make her understand. "I'll have Buddy turn this plane around right now if you don't give me your word. I mean it, Ray."

This close, Eli could see the way her pupils dilated, how the darkness of her eyes flared with irritation. He allowed her to pull back. Frowning, she looked toward the front of the plane at Buddy.

Eli had known Buddy was listening, but he hadn't known he could hear every word until Buddy said, "He is the boss, hon."

Eli had the feeling Buddy felt the same way, that he wanted to protect her, too. Thank God the man was married, so he didn't get *too* protective.

With Buddy backing him, Ray had no choice

but to give in. "I'm always careful, so it's a stupid promise. Still," she added when Eli started grinding his teeth together, "you have my word I'll be *extra* careful. Now, are you happy?"

He was about as far from happy as a man could get. Eli shoved her head back to his shoulder. "I won't be happy until we've finished this goddamned rescue and I have you and my brother back in the States." He thought about that and then added, "Where I can keep an eye on the two of you."

Ray stiffened, but he didn't give her a chance to protest. "No more denials out of you, Ray. You can't just forget you ever met me once this is over, so don't even try. I won't let you forget. And that, Ray, is my promise to you."

Buddy, the ass, starting singing a soft song—but no one could mistake the laughter in his tone.

Chapter Seven

As Buddy circled the river, looking for the best place to land, Ray pulled away from Eli. Letting him hold her during the trip had been wonderful, better than Pepto-Bismol for her upset stomach. But his promise, more like a threat, had stayed with her, churning her up whenever she tried to figure his meaning.

Regardless of what he wanted to believe, she knew she wouldn't see him after the mission. It didn't seem worth arguing about when the end was inevitable anyway.

But now they had arrived, so she was no longer willing to take comfort from him, no longer willing to divide her thoughts. She needed all her concentration and attention on burying the memories of that one awful mission—a mission she'd failed, no matter what anyone else said—so she could get the job done.

The landing was rough. The plane hit the choppy river with jarring impact, bouncing a few times before gliding smoothly. Ray heard Eli curse and glanced up to see him brace himself.

Scooping up a pair of compact but powerful

binoculars, Ray tossed them to him. "Here, put these around your neck." Then she picked up a backpack and turned to Buddy. "Everything's inside?"

"Hey, you know I take care of you, babe. I didn't forget anything." Buddy nudged the plane's pontoons up close to the shore. He left the cockpit to open the cabin door, then peered out into the deserted landscape.

Hot, steamy air poured into the plane, rich with the scent of the lush jungle, brackish water, and dense humidity. Animal sounds rose from the bush, a cacophony of cries and alerts. Ray stared out the door and let it all seep into her, familiarizing herself with the sights and sounds and smells of Central America once again.

Eli picked up the other sack. "This is going, too?"

Ray waited until her heartbeat regulated, then nodded. "Are you ready, Eli?"

"As ready as I'll ever be."

Ray searched his eyes. "It won't be easy, you know. The heat and the humidity is stifling. It's not too late for you to change your mind. You can go back with Buddy—"

"Do you try to piss me off, or does it just come naturally for you?"

Chuckling, Buddy said, "Oh, for Ray, it's a natural talent." He handed each of them a fat canteen, suggesting to Eli, "Sip your water often, but don't forget you'll probably be in overnight. Mataya is still too antiquated to trust their plumbing. If you do run out, there are purification tablets, but they taste like shit."

Eli acknowledged Buddy's warning as he watched

Ray load herself down. She stuck a dull black, full-sized Beretta similar to the one Eli had already claimed into a vest pocket. The knife, now contained in a leather sheath, got tucked into her boot with her pants leg pulled down to conceal it. Next, an Uzi SMG got slung over her shoulder and every pocket of her vest was stuffed with ammunition. She held several clips and two boxes of hollow-point bullets. She tossed another to Eli.

"Exactly how many people are you planning to shoot?"

At his dry question, she glanced up. "We're not shooting anyone if I can help it. And if we look prepared, it's less likely anyone will challenge us."

She made quite a picture standing there, loaded down with weapons, her expression hard and implacable. Eli was prompted to ask, "Do you really expect to be able to walk any distance with that much weight added to your body?"

Buddy laughed. "Ray wears a tool belt heavier than that anytime she's not here in Central American playing Tarzan, Lord of the Jungle."

Eli gave him a blank look.

"She's a carpenter," Buddy explained. "Does everything from small repairs to home construction. You should see her place. It's a beauty now that she's completely renovated it from the floors up—"

"Buddy."

He finally clammed up, but too late. Eli stared at Ray, but the image wouldn't quite gel.

"It's respectable work," Ray snapped in reply. "I get to pick the jobs I want, have flexible hours, and can take off when I need to." She added under her breath, "And I like using my hands."

Eli decided to withhold judgement on that until he convinced her to use her hands on him. "I didn't—"

"Forget it. We don't have time for it right now."

Eli wanted to say more, but Ray's narrow-eyed expression stopped him. "Fine. Give me some of that stuff to carry."

"I'm okay." She turned to Buddy. "What time do you have?"

They made certain their watches were accurate, and when Eli suddenly removed his, handing it to Buddy for safekeeping, Ray was speechless. Eli winked at her.

"I thought you never took the damned thing off."

Eli shrugged. "I can be reasonable."

Ray made an obnoxiously rude sound. "Sure you can. Try to remember that while we're here, okay?"

Buddy sat back and watched the squabble unfold. It amused him because he'd never seen Ray bicker with anyone. She gave orders and they were obeyed, period.

Yet with Eli, she acted more like . . . a woman. His eyes widened with that realization. Eli had said it, and now he saw it was true. Ray was being more womanly with him. Oh, not your average woman. That'd kill Ray. But she had definitely lost some of her edge.

He gave Eli another, more thorough glance. He'd already picked up on Eli's interest, of course. The man wasn't any damn good at hiding his thoughts. But he hadn't figured on Ray feeling the same. Plenty of men had wanted her over the years, but she found fault with all of them, to the point that she sent a few crying home to their mamas. When she tried, Ray could be damned intimidating.

She was picking at Eli, too, but he wasn't going anywhere. He returned her taunts, teased her, and protectively hovered over her. Well, well, well.

In provoking tones, Eli said, "Give me some of your baggage to carry."

Ray drew up in offense. "This isn't worth arguing over, Eli."

"I agree." He crossed his arms over his chest, prepared to wait her out. "Hand something over."

Buddy bit back a grin—and waited to see what Ray would do.

Making her exasperation plain, she jerked the strap of her canteen over her head, along with the binoculars and two weighty packs of ammo. She threw them at Eli, but to Eli's credit, he caught it all handily.

That only seemed to annoy Ray more. "Don't complain to me later when you start to wear down."

Eli gave her a tight smile. "Yes, dear."

It wasn't in Buddy's nature to keep quiet. Beyond that, Ray needed someone to tease her, to shake up her grave, often lethal life on occasion. Up till now, he'd been the only one to fit the bill. Well, Matt did sometimes, but mostly he gave his sister the respect and unquestioning loyalty she deserved.

Now here was Eli, twitting her endlessly, ogling her like a sailor on shore leave, and handing out orders that actually got obeyed. Fascinating. "You know, Ray, I've never seen you give over to anyone before. I wish I had my camera handy."

Ray lurched around to face him. "Don't start with me, Buddy."

Her tone was so bad-tempered, Buddy pretended

to back up in fear, only to jerk forward again and grab Ray for a bear hug.

Just to see how she'd react, he said, "Don't distract yourself over any fools, honey."

Eli ignored him, but Ray immediately came to his defense. "He's not as bad as I first thought. He just might do okay."

Eli rolled his eyes. "Such high praise. Don't make me blush."

Buddy choked on his laugh. Eli was both entertaining and daring. "I hope you're right, honey, 'cause I have a feeling old Eli here is going to be busier watching out for you than tending his own backside."

Ray grunted as she tightened the straps of her gear. "That's ridiculous."

Buddy nodded. "Yeah, *I* know it. And *you* know it." He nodded at Eli. "But I don't think *he* knows it."

Eli reached out and took Ray's arm. "Let's go. The sooner we get this over with, the better."

And damn if Ray didn't let him lead her right off the plane.

Jeremy paced around the yard, trying to get a better view of the current activity. Two guards, one of them so ugly and hairy he reminded Jeremy of the tarantula, were arm wrestling. The others gathered around, cheering them on, shouting and laughing. He couldn't be sure, but he thought they were taking bets.

The hairy guy won. He raised arms as thick as tree stumps into the air to celebrate his victory. Jeremy could have sworn he even had hair on the insides of his elbows.

They called for another challenger, who also lost. Jeremy was bored out of his wits and this was the first real entertainment he'd had. It wasn't much, certainly not what he was used to, but it beat listening to the jungle.

After the forth guy lost, Jeremy got caught up in the excitement. When they asked for another challenger, he swaggered forward. Hell, he'd arm-wrestled Eli in fun plenty of times, and though he always lost, he knew he wasn't a slouch. "I'll try it."

Everyone grew quiet. One guy snickered, then another, and soon they were all guffawing and pointing. Rapid Spanish phrases of insult swirled around him, but he caught the equivalent of "puny," "pale," and "scared of bugs."

Damn it, he was tired of their disrespect. He planted his feet and shouted, "You're nothing but a bunch of dirty farmers."

The hairy one smiled, showing big white teeth surrounded by a dark beard. He crept forward, the look in his black eyes evil—but when he got close, he pinched his nose and made a face. "You are the dirty one," the ape said. "Maybe we should throw you in the stream, whether you want to go or not. *Sí?*"

In the stream? With the leeches? Just the thought of those slimy, clinging little maggots made his skin crawl. Jeremy turned and ran back to his hut—and the sounds of raucous laughter lasted for a good five minutes.

It was quiet and hot, the air so thick with moisture you could drown on a deep breath. It seemed every two steps brought her a new scratch or scrape. Ray ignored the small wounds. Eli did not.

After one particularly thorny bush drew a streak of blood on her forearm, Eli caught her shoulder and drew her to a halt. "I'll lead."

Squinting against the glare of the sun, Ray faced him. "And how will you do that when you don't know where the hell you're going?"

"You can direct me." He lifted her arm to examine it with a frown.

Ray pulled away. "No."

He pulled her right back. While he dabbed at her scratch, cleaning it with water from the canteen and a bandana, he said, "It makes sense for me to be in front, Ray. My arms are at least covered, and I'm taller."

His touch was so gentle, it muddled her more than the heat. He finished and she moved a few steps away. "What does being taller have to do with anything?"

"Don't argue with me." The heat made him cranky, she decided, given his tone. "Just stay behind my back."

He stepped around her, not giving Ray the chance to protest further. She sighed in annoyance, but what the hell? If he wanted to take all the abuse from sharp twigs and itchy plants, why should she quibble?

Minutes later, she had to admit they could travel faster with Eli clearing the path. He was so big, he just stomped down stuff that she would have had to move.

The sun was high overhead, scorching in intensity, when Ray called a halt beneath a large shady tree to the side of the trail. They'd been walking over an hour and a half. "I have to eat."

Eli gave a weak laugh and stretched his back. "I

should have known food would be the perfect motive for stopping."

"Don't make fun. I need to keep up my energy level. You do, too, as far as that goes. Look how much you're sweating."

"I don't need to look, thank you very much." He peeled off the canteen and binoculars, then shrugged out of his vest. "I don't suppose there's a stream around here anywhere?"

"There is, but I wouldn't suggest you wander around alone." Ray, too, removed some of her load, but left her vest on. "After we eat, I'll show you where it is so you can relieve yourself and freshen up."

He winced. "I hadn't even thought about that." Now that he *had* thought of it, he asked, "Where will we be spending the night?"

"Wondering about the facilities, are you? Well, I can promise you this: there won't be any showers or flushing johns. You'll get to see firsthand what type of accommodations your brother's had. If we're lucky, we'll use a temporary shack used to store blocks of chicle."

"Chicle?"

"They take it from the sap of sapodilla trees and form it into these odd, loaf-shaped blocks. It's used to manufacture chewing gum. Chicileros gather it during the wet season. If I'm remembering right, the shack should be between the village and the camp where they're keeping your brother. But I don't even know if it's still there. If not, we'll bed down in a cave."

"You mean like with bats and wild animals?"

She'd expected him to be appalled, but instead Eli looked anxious. Ray shook her head. She wondered if she'd ever understand him. "This whole region is underlaid with limestone rock. It rains every damn day, washing away the land and leaving behind a network of caves and dolines." At his blank look, she explained, "Deep depressions."

"Sounds treacherous."

"Yeah. The landscape is called *karst*. Because of that, there's not much surface water, but we should be able to find waterfalls for bathing and plenty of caves to duck into if necessary. The cave may have a few vampire bats, but if we keep a fire going, we'll be safe enough. Besides, bats rarely feed on humans."

"Rarely, huh?"

Ray grinned. "It's been known to happen. But there are a lot of wild animals around, some worse than bats."

"Such as?"

She gave an elaborate shrug. "Oh, iguanas and nasty little spider monkeys. There're caiman in the river and jaguars everywhere." She used the back of her hand to wipe her brow. "You do realize this is home to the largest jaguar population, right?"

Eli surveyed the area. "I haven't seen any wild animals. I think you're just pulling my leg."

Ray hunted through her pack until she found a nutrition bar. She peeled back the wrapper and took a large bite before going to Eli. Chewing the tasteless, dry snack, she took his arm and led him to stand beneath a tall, mostly barren tree. Its branches spread out wide overhead but had little foliage.

"See that third biggest branch? The one that's mostly bare?"

Eli squinted upward, his hand shielding his eyes against the white sun. "Yeah, so?"

"See what's curled around that branch?"

Suddenly Eli's eyes widened and he took a hasty step back. "Son of a bitch."

For a big man, he moved pretty damn quick, prompting Ray to laughter. "What's the matter, Eli? You afraid of snakes?"

"A boa constrictor is not your everyday snake, Ray." He brushed her bangs off her forehead and said with something akin to amusement, "Only you would choose to have lunch with a monster like that looming overhead."

She was covered in sweat, scratched and dirty, and still he touched her with a gentleness she'd never experienced before. Ray moved back to her pack and sat on a large twisted root. She needed the physical distance from Eli to keep herself in check. "Contrary to all the Tarzan movies, boas don't feast on people and it isn't poisonous. As long as you ignore it, it'll ignore you."

He stared up at the snake. "I wasn't planning to invite it to lunch." Glancing back at Ray, he smiled. "You're unbelievable."

He said it like a compliment, filling Ray with soft emotions out of place in the humid jungle. It was kind of nice that even when she was herself, Eli wasn't put off.

"Here." Ray tossed another nutrition bar at him.

Eli eyed it with distaste. "Thanks, but I'm not hungry. You can keep it." And he tossed it right back.

"Now, Eli," Ray scolded, "don't be a baby. It's not that bad. Besides, you eat caviar and escargot, right?"

"Not on your life." He, too, found a chunk of wood to sit on, stretching out his long legs and leaning back on a tree. "I'm more a beef or pork man. Steaks, chops, roasts . . ."

Here she'd pictured Eli dining on fine cuisine, not hearty meat and potatoes. He liked the kind of stuff she cooked—whoa. She was not the type to cook her way into a man's heart. "I insist you eat. If you get weak on me, you'll only be a bother."

Eli clamped his lips shut.

"Going to be difficult, I see." Challenged, Ray crawled the short distance toward Eli. Anticipation swelled inside her. "You're going to eat this, you know."

He smiled, but his lips remained firmly closed. He even shook his head. Ray saw the awareness in his golden predator's eyes. He knew she'd attack—and he wanted her to. But she wouldn't make it easy. She wouldn't give him any warning.

Sitting back on her haunches, Ray frowned at him, pretending discouragement. Eli started to relax—and that was all the advantage she needed. She launched herself onto him, knocking him flat onto the mossy ground. Eli tried to twist away, but she anticipated that move and countered it by throwing one leg over his hips and hooking his opposite arm. He turned his head, thinking she meant to shove the snack bar down his throat. Instead, Ray pinned him to the ground.

He quit fighting her.

Both of them were panting hard. Sitting on Eli's abdomen, she felt his every fast breath. She had her knees pressed into the hollows of his shoulders and caught two fingers from each of his hands in one of her own. Her hold was tight, but not damaging. The position had her leaning over his face with her breasts on a level with his mouth.

Eli's expression told her he had no complaints over her methods.

Damn. She knew how to hold a man immobile, but not with him plainly enjoying it.

Eli eyed her breasts as if they were dinner instead of the partially crumbled snack bar. His eyes had darkened, grown intent in that sexual, masculine way that indicated interest. By small degrees, he'd worn her down with his attention, his compliments, his acceptance. And now, the way he watched her made all those feelings ignite. She wanted to feel his mouth on her breast, tugging on her nipple. She wanted to feel the wet heat and velvet stroke of his tongue.

The images were so vivid, the sensation so real, she gasped.

"Ray." He growled her name with rough need and started to slide his hands free. Belatedly she remembered her purpose and attempted to stuff the food into his mouth.

Eli turned his face away, snickering, his lips again sealed. Ray considered the problem, then used her free hand to tickle him.

Taken by surprise, Eli burst out laughing and she smashed a considerable amount of the snack against his teeth. "There. Now eat it."

Sputtering, spitting granola and nuts to the side, Eli said, "Tickling? *Tickling*, Ray? What kind of commando tactic is that?"

"An effective one, apparently." Still shaken from her intimate thoughts, Ray started to sidle off him and Eli bent, snared both her hands, and turned her beneath him. Shock rippled through her. He'd caught her completely off guard. Again.

Eli settled himself by stretching her arms high over her head and locking her wrists in one of his hands. She was strong, but when it came to muscle, Eli had her beat. She still could have gotten loose, but not without seriously injuring him. And . . . did she even want loose?

His eyes hot with triumph, he looked at her mouth. "You've just made me sweatier," he accused.

Ray strained against him, but that only heightened her sense of helplessness. Strangely, it excited her. A sweet tingling filled her belly and her nipples drew tight, making her breasts ache.

Eli bent down and she felt his gentle breath fan her throat. He inhaled slowly. "You smell good, Ray, all warm and damp."

She barely caught her groan of desire. "I should be planning, not playing." She squeezed her eyes shut, then forced them open again. "I think you're a bad influence on me, Eli Connors."

He stared at her, keeping her gaze captive while carefully shifting his weight until he'd nudged her thighs apart. All her logical considerations evaporated. With the hard ground beneath her, his weight should have been uncomfortable, but instead it seemed her body welcomed him, her curves fitting his angles with ease.

He had an erection.

She could feel the hard length pressed to the wide open junction of her thighs. She knew she was growing damp, softening. She liked how it felt, how he felt. A small moan escaped. Their scents mingled, hot and muggy.

Eli's free hand came up to cup her cheek. "There's nothing wrong with laughing occasionally, honey."

He made her want to. He made the idea of playing on the mossy jungle floor, covered in sweat, with a boa overhead, seem like a great idea. Insane.

His hand trailed downward, over the side of her throat, cupping her shoulder, fingers spreading out and moving down again until his palm grazed the side of her breast.

She hated the damn vest that kept her from getting the full impact of his touch. Yet, she was responsible for him and his brother until they landed back in the States. She had to keep her priorities straight. Playing touchy-feely now was not on the agenda.

"Maybe laughing is okay." She swallowed and forced the words out. "But we're on a timetable. We need to make it to the camp before nightfall. And we still need to visit Sarita."

As if the softness drew him, he gently stroked her bottom lip with his fingertip. "Two minutes won't hurt, will it? I like hearing you laugh, Ray—almost as much as I like feeling you under me."

Oh God, if he kept saying things like that . . . "We're supposed to be rescuing your brother."

"And we will," he promised. His gaze followed the movement of his finger tracing over her mouth. He leaned closer and his voice grew husky. "I need to kiss you, Ray."

God help her, she wanted him to.

"Don't slug me, okay?"

He had great faith in her abilities if he thought she could break free and offer up a fight when her every muscle felt like mush. Almost from the moment she first spotted him in that dark, dreary bar, she had wanted this. For the first time in her adult life, the need of the woman took precedence over the responsibility of the mercenary.

They could spare a few minutes. After all, it wasn't every day that a man wanted her like this, and it was even less often that she wanted him back.

Chapter Eight

Ray went still beneath him, her sable eyes slowly closing in surrender. The significance of that didn't escape him. He knew she could be free in a heartbeat if that was what she wanted. Ray wasn't a woman who lightly gave in. She was a woman of honor, independence, and integrity. Unlike other women he'd known, she would never chase a man because of his family connections or his wealth. She would never require a man for financial support.

When Ray accepted a man, as she'd just accepted him, it'd have to be because she wanted him and for no other reason.

It was a heady thing, gaining Ray's attention. Though it had only been days, it seemed he'd waited a lifetime to touch her, to kiss her. She was hot, exciting, a mystery and a temptation. Vulnerable and stubborn and brazen beyond all social bounds.

She was so much more than any woman he was ever likely to meet.

Unable to wait another second, Eli slowly bent down and touched his mouth to hers. He felt her breath, her quiescence, and just that small contact, because this was Ray, felt hot and deep and sexually ripe.

Driven by a pervasive need to gentle her, he coaxed her lips open. Ray needed more gentleness in her life, and he was determined to be the one to give it to her.

His senses heightened to the luxuriant scents of the jungle, the subtle rustling of life that surrounded them. He felt Ray's every heartbeat, her every breath, as if they were his own. He was aware of it all, but his concentration centered on her mouth, her response, and his own needs.

"Ray." Lazily, he nibbled on her bottom lip, all the while covering her, absorbing her. Ray made a small sound of growing urgency that tested his resolve to go slow and easy. The fragile bones in her wrists flexed when she curled her hands into fists. Such a wonderful, telling reaction.

With the tip of his tongue, Eli traced just inside her lips, gliding along the edge of her teeth, touching her tongue, tasting her and teasing her before giving in with a groan.

God, she tasted good. His body clenched with his tight restraint, and despite his resolve, his hips pressed down and in, mocking the movements of his tongue, stroking her as if the barriers of clothes didn't exist. He was so hard, so full that he hurt with his need.

He wanted to fuck her, to be inside her right now, feeling her sleek thighs against his waist, her fingers tight on his shoulders. He wanted to claim her so that Ray would have no further doubts that she belonged with him.

As his cock thrust against her, she gasped and strained, trying to get closer, drawing his tongue deeper into her mouth, sucking. Eli gave up. The gentleness would come later, he'd see to that. But for now, he needed to appease them both.

The damn vest frustrated him because it kept him from her breasts and nipples. Blindly, his mouth still covering hers, he groped and found her silken skin between the waistband of her fatigues and the tank top and vest. For such a stubborn, capable woman, Ray had incredible softness—her mouth, her sighs, her dewy skin.

Eli knew he was grinding into her, but Ray didn't complain. Bending her knees alongside his hips and bracing her booted feet on the ground, she lifted into him, riding herself against the length of his cock with maddening determination. She pulled her mouth free, arching her neck and groaning deep and low. Eli forgot about holding her wrists— he captured her face instead, keeping her still for another kiss. He couldn't get enough of her mouth, didn't know if a lifetime would be enough.

The second her hands were free, Ray clutched his shoulders, then slid her strong fingers up his neck to clench in his hair. The small pain brought Eli to his senses. Ray was nearly desperate with need, panting and groaning, mindless to everything around them. Because of that, Eli knew he had to stop.

The timing was all wrong, the place preposterous. When he made love to Ray, it wouldn't be on the rough, dirty ground with the threat of wild animals, drug runners, and deadly insects to contend with. Yet, all those things existed. If they made love now, she'd feel guilty afterward, thinking she'd failed in her duty to stay alert, to watch out for him and protect him.

She would never let him take full responsibility

for what would happen. She'd blame herself—and Eli couldn't bear to see that happen. She blamed herself for enough already.

Truth was, he'd intended only a quick taste anyway, a small kiss to tide him over till they found a better time and place. He should have realized how impossible that'd be with Ray. Just seeing her affected him too strongly for him to believe he could touch her without wanting more. A whole lot more.

He'd screwed this up and now it was only going to get worse before it got better.

Carefully, Eli again caught her wrists and drew her hands down to either side of her head. Her slenderness was deceptive, given the strength with which she fought him now. Not because she wanted away from him, but because she wanted to draw him closer. And knowing that made his decision harder still.

"Ray," he whispered, hoping to bring her around slowly. Her eyes were all but closed, her lips swollen and wet from his kiss, cheeks flushed. She looked so *. . . ready*. Damn it, why did he start what he couldn't, in good conscience, finish?

As Eli watched her, mesmerized with her shifting expressions of awareness, her lids lifted and those indescribable eyes focused on him.

Knowing she wanted him, that he could have her, left his heart near to bursting. "Hi," he whispered, then couldn't stop himself from another small peck before teasing, "That was some kiss, lady. Way hotter than the jungle."

Her frown came slowly, but it was more confusion than anger. "We shouldn't have done that."

We. Though he was the one who'd pushed her, she didn't blame him as the instigator. He learned new things about his little warrior every hour. And if she kept looking at him like that, he'd lose what honor he still held and end up right back where he started.

Forcing himself to roll to the side, Eli stared up at the sky. In the past few minutes, it had darkened, turning a turbulent dim gray that reflected his new mood. "Come on, Ray. Do you honestly think I could have waited much longer?"

She sat up beside him and brushed small pieces of dirt and debris off her arms. Her movements were awkward, stiff, lacking her natural grace, and she wouldn't look at him. "It was wrong, Eli."

"Felt right to me."

She rubbed her face and a new strain sounded in her voice—a strain he'd caused. "Even if we weren't here, in this particular place, it still wouldn't make sense for us to get . . ." She floundered, letting her words trail off until she finally said, "Involved," without a lot of certainty.

He, too, sat up. Her profile was stubbornly proud and arrogant. "You can deny it all you want, Ray, but we're already involved."

"No way." She turned her back on him.

"Yes." Sharper than he intended, Eli's voice cracked into the quiet of the area, sending two colorful birds into screeching flight. Ray started to stand, but Eli curled his hand over her shoulder, halting her retreat. Her denials infuriated him, and though he'd just been cursing himself for his actions, he thought about pulling her beneath him again.

When she was hot, she didn't deny a damn thing.

Before he could decide what to do, the skies opened with a torrent of rainfall that soaked everything in sight.

Ray had looked ready to belt him, but now she ordered, "Grab our stuff," while scrambling over the ground to do the same. Within seconds, they were racing deeper into the trees where the rain had difficulty penetrating the thick, waxy foliage. Ray finally stopped beneath a large overhang of vines and jagged gray rock. Looking slightly dazed, she crouched on the ground, her forearms draped over her thighs. Her inky hair was plastered to her skull.

With a shake of her head, she sent water droplets flying. "Looks like you won't need the stream after all."

Eli tugged at the neckline of his drenched shirt. "I guess this is the closest I'll get to a cold shower." Maybe the dousing would bring both his ardor and his temper into check.

"It'll only last a few minutes." The insulating drum of rain surrounded them, with only an occasional animal call to break the stillness. Ray didn't avoid his gaze, but her expression was as remote and cold as her voice. "If you want to take advantage of it, you'd better hurry."

Such a credible act, but Eli didn't buy it. No matter what veneer she wore, Ray was every inch a woman. And as a woman, she wanted him. He saw it in her dark eyes, the faint trembling of her hands, and the rapid pulse in the base of her throat.

"I think I will." Holding her gaze, Eli dropped his gear on the drier ground beneath the overhang. Reaching over his shoulder to his back, he snagged a fistful of his tee and yanked it off.

Ray's shoulders and jaw tightened. As if accepting a dare, she watched him.

Typically, men had little enough modesty to begin with, and Eli was still wearing the jeans. Yet, something about Ray's attention felt beyond sexual, making him keenly aware of his still-aroused body and her not-so-discriminating interest. He might as well have been buck naked, the way she affected him.

Extending his arms beyond the protective foliage and cupping his hands so that they filled with rain, Eli doused his face, his sweaty arms, and upper chest. The chill water trickled down his abdomen and over his belly, into the waistband of his jeans. It refreshed him—but didn't cool his lust one iota.

Ray's bold stare moved over him, following the water's path down his body. Her eyes grew heavy-lidded as she stared at his erection, now straining the damp material of his jeans.

Using both hands, Eli pushed his wet hair off his face. He was so hot, steam should have risen off him. He took the three steps necessary to have her within reach. "Next time," he gritted out, "I won't stop. I don't give a damn if we're sinking in quicksand."

That brought her gaze back to his face. "Get your shirt. The rain is slowing down already."

He watched her turn away—then pause.

"And Eli?"

"Yeah?"

"I didn't ask you to stop this time."

Once the rain ended, Ray kept a grueling pace for two reasons. One, she needed to occupy her mind so she couldn't think about Eli and how right it felt to be with him. It had felt right to be with Kevin, too, more right than anything else in her life at the time. She'd known him a year, been intimate with him from jump, and their worlds had meshed. He knew what she did, relied on her for that reason and more—and still she'd disappointed him, to the point he'd had to be away from her. She squeezed her eyes shut.

She still missed Kevin sometimes because she'd thought once, long ago, that he was the only man to really understand her. In the end, she'd repelled him by being who and what she was—a woman that reminded him of times he wanted to forget.

They also needed to make up lost time, but despite the fast pace, she couldn't outrun her thoughts and worries. Damn Eli, for putting her through this. Why hadn't he just taken her there on the ground, giving in to the animal lust so that at least she'd know what to call it. This . . . this patience and consideration left her uncertain and confused, and she hated it.

Added to that was the seductive memory of being under him, feeling his tongue and hands, the power of him, and his own desire that rivaled hers.

She pushed harder, determined to block those sensations so she could concentrate.

Eli didn't complain, but he did keep a protective eye on her, insisting she take a sip of water every so often, careful to block the heavier brambles and branches. In one way his concern was a bother, but in another, it wasn't so bad. Not since her parents died had anyone dared to coddle her.

Buddy was sometimes protective, but in a different, grouchy and bossy way. He'd seen her in action and knew her ability to watch out for herself.

Matt loved and respected her, but she never let the scarier side of her life touch him. He got good grades, kept his room clean, and did whatever chores she asked of him. That was more than enough.

Eli's attempts to protect her were downright dumb. She could make mincemeat out of him if she chose to. But it was also sort of . . . sweet. Ray grunted to herself. If he got much sweeter, she'd gain five pounds.

The sun hung low in the sky when they finally neared the small town. Thatch-roofed homes formed a semicircle around the courtyard.

His nose in the air, Eli asked, "What's that wonderful smell?"

Ray pointed to two women working over outdoor fires. "It could be the Creole bread or cinnamon rolls. They bake them in those steel drums you see, using coals from driftwood. You can also smell the citrus trees. But a few yards down, closer to the wharf where the fishermen are dumping nets of snapper and jack, the smell is something else entirely."

Eli laughed. "Everyone is smiling."

"Yeah. See those kids eating wild sea grapes? And the men hustling tourists to make a buck? It's a nice place."

"It's busier than I expected."

"Which is why it's a good thing you aren't wearing your watch, or someone would have already taken it and you wouldn't even have noticed."

"And he would have grinned the whole time?"

"Of course."

Just as Ray said it, a dark man approached with a huge smile, saying, "Cahn I geht a dallah, boss?"

Unable to discern the dialect, Eli lifted an eyebrow.

Ray laughed. "He wants money," she said in an aside, then dug in her pocket, fished out change, and handed it to him. "Here you go."

As the man left, she explained to Eli, "He called you boss as a sign of respect."

"Which raises his odds of getting the money?"

"Exactly. They call almost everyone here boy otherwise, which is just their way, not a slur." Eli continued to smile down at her, so she shrugged and added, somewhat defensively, "It's easier to pay and get rid of them than to fight it. The people here specialize in a certain type of hustler's shtick that's hard to resist, especially when you see them washing cars in the streets, toting luggage, anything to make some honest money . . ."

Eli put his arm around her, mocking her with soothing words. "It's okay, Ray. Being generous won't tarnish your reputation as a badass, I promise." He gave her a teasing squeeze. "Just keep track of any money you give away so I can reimburse you."

She should have known, Ray thought. Eli was a genuinely nice guy. Other than his bossiness, she hadn't found too many flaws with him yet. His body sure as hell pleased her, as did his sense of humor.

His mouth left her mindless. The way that man kissed . . .

She knew that if Eli hadn't called a halt earlier, they'd be late now because she hadn't been able to think of anything except feeling him inside her. Half the day had passed since then and she still wanted him. Her body was warm and needy in a way she hadn't experienced in far too long.

She was afraid the feeling would linger—until she finally had him. Which left her with a decision to make.

They'd just neared the brothel when Sarita

stepped out onto the front stoop. The slat-board building used for her business boasted a sloped porch with uneven planks. It was small, in need of repair, and still one of the better structures within view.

Sarita wore a short homemade dress of bright colors wrapped snugly around her tiny waist and cut low in front to show off her abundant cleavage. Her feet were bare, her hair was long and loose, and she had eyes only for Eli.

Because his attention caught on the bewitching woman, Eli didn't realize Ray had stepped in front of him until he almost plowed her down. Ray regained her balance and drove her elbow into his stomach with enough force to knock the wind out of him. "Watch it," she snapped.

Eli murmured, "Sorry," but still he couldn't take his gaze off the woman. With everyone else layered in sweat, she looked cool and seductive. This, he thought, must be Sarita.

"Todo tranquilo?"

His high school Spanish was pretty rusty, but Ray helped out just by replying.

"Yeah, everything's calm." She propped her hands on her hips. "Should we talk inside?"

"Sí." Sarita stepped back, pushing aside long strands of beads that served as a makeshift door. Every few feet, ceiling fans swirled lazily, keeping the air stirred. She smiled at Eli. "Belikin?"

Eli wasn't quite certain what she offered, so Ray said, "Belizean beer."

"Thank you, no." It was hard enough keeping his hands off Ray without mixing in the effects of alcohol. "Does she speak English?"

Sarita answered for herself. "I speak English, Spanish, and a little Creole. In my line of work, one must be able to communicate."

Eli laughed, amused at her flirting. "I have a feeling you could communicate with any man you met."

She replied with a suggestive smile. "*Sí.*"

Eli accepted the hand she offered, but she didn't conclude the perfunctory shake. Instead, she cradled his hand in both of hers and held it to her mostly naked chest.

Pretending to ignore that, Eli said, "Thank you for your help, Sarita."

Her smile widened. "My help will not be cheap. As my Miguel has complained, your little brother is the pain in the ass."

He knew it only too well. But while his brother sometimes drove him nuts, Eli loved him. These people didn't, so how would they react to being annoyed? "What has he done?"

"He complains. Often. About everything. And he whines." She looked at Ray. "Does this one whine, too?"

Ray looked stiff and angry, but still she said, "No, he doesn't."

Sarita's black gaze slid over Eli, specifically his chest, and she purred, "*Yo los aprecio peludo. Ellos son hombres verdaderos.*"

Between the Spanish he remembered and Sarita's gaze, Eli caught the gist of her comment, which was something about hairy men being real men.

Ray puckered up even more. "He's not *that* hairy," she snapped, and then, all businesslike: "Sarita, his brother is okay?"

"*El esta enfermo templado, un chico.*"

Fed up, Eli barked, "Speak English."

Sarita shrugged. "The brother is fine. Spoiled, but fine." Her dark eyes looked at Eli with accusation. "He is rude."

Incredulous at her daring, Eli glared. "Miguel *kidnapped* him. Was he supposed to be courteous?"

"Eli . . ." Attempting to warn him away, Ray took his elbow, but Sarita still held his hand, which left him caught between the two women.

"He is fed as well as our soldiers, but doesn't like the food. He is offered clothing, but ridicules the *style*. If he were not valuable, Miguel would have already fed him to the jaguars and he would be back here with me now, where he belongs."

That subtle threat both alarmed and angered Eli. Before he could say or do much, Ray was in front of him, chin thrust out, blocking his view of Sarita by sheer force of will.

Both hands flat on his chest, she rudely backed Eli into the rickety wall. "Don't make me regret bringing you along, Connors." When he tried to look beyond her, she grabbed the back of his neck and brought his face down to hers. "You heard Sarita. If Jeremy's able to bitch about the accommodations, then he must not be hurt or even feel too threatened. Right?"

Sarita laughed. "Only the insects scare that one."

With a roll of her dark eyes, Ray glanced over her shoulder at Sarita. "Yeah, but with the bugs you have around here, who wouldn't be scared spitless?"

With the two women now joking, Eli relaxed a little. "You have a plan for us to get him back?"

"*Sí.* Bridget will take them breakfast tomorrow." She grinned. "*Los hará enfermo.*"

Ray automatically translated. "It'll make them sick." Then to Sarita, "How sick?"

"Sick enough, the men will not notice or care when you take the brother. Their thoughts will be on their bellies."

Eli winced. "That's brutal. The men won't retaliate against you?"

Her eyes narrowed. "I will have the money you give me, *sí?* And they will be rid of the pest. A fair trade. But we will also nurse them back to health." She teasingly trailed her fingertips over her collarbone. "They will find no complaints."

"No, I don't suppose they will," Eli said slowly.

Sarita turned to Ray, all humor gone. "My Miguel, you will not hurt him as you did last time. He was weeks from my bed."

"Last time?" Eli asked, but the women ignored him.

Ray shrugged. "You know how it is, Sarita. I'm not anticipating any trouble, but I'm not going to let him hurt Eli or Jeremy either." She held up a hand when Sarita would have spoken. "Look, I won't touch him if I can help it, okay? As to the other, well, if I do hit him, I'll keep it above the belt. That's all I can promise."

Sarita considered things a long moment, then rubbed her hands together. "That will do. Let us finish this deal."

After they exchanged money and specific time frames, Ray and Eli shared a meal with Sarita. The main dish consisted of white fish seasoned with coconut milk and Cajun spices, served with tortillas. They both agreed the fare was far more delicious and filling than a granola bar. It was also far better than what the guerillas and Jeremy would be eating. Ray hoped Eli knew how special the meal was—for him. Sarita was pulling out all the stops.

She even offered them a room for the night, but Ray didn't trust her. Throughout dinner, Sarita had eyed Eli with interest. The woman made a living off her sexuality and feminine wiles, and though jealousy was new to Ray, she wasn't about to start sharing what she hadn't yet had herself. She'd gotten to know Eli well enough to doubt he'd take Sarita up on an offer, but no way in hell would she put it to chance.

She insisted they leave the village, saying it wouldn't be safe for Sarita for them to stick around.

Sarita must have figured things out on her own, given the small gift she slipped to Ray, along with some pretty explicit advice on how to handle a man like Eli. She ignored the suggestive comments but, feeling unaccountably territorial, Ray didn't mind if Sarita knew how she felt about Eli.

She just wasn't ready for Eli to know it yet.

They came upon the hut where Ray intended to spend the night about forty minutes after leaving Sarita. It still stood, but just barely. Ray laughed at Eli's startled exclamation as bats flew past them and something scurried across the floor.

"Behold," she said, her arms swept wide in a gesture of grandeur, "your night's lodging."

Eli took in the grass roof, the rickety walls, and the very close quarters. He slanted Ray a look. They hadn't spoken much since leaving the village and Ray had done her best to avoid his intense scrutiny, though she'd felt it often on the trail.

She kept her smile firmly in place.

"How far are we from the guerilla camp?"

"Half a mile, give or take." Ray dropped her load, flexing her shoulders to relieve the strain. She noticed with some disgust that Eli didn't seem the least bit tired, though he was every bit as dirty and sweaty as she was.

"It's getting dark out there now," he observed while peering into the dense forest behind them. In front of the hut was a long forgotten field, now overgrown with weeds and vines. Behind them, edging the tree line, was a gurgling stream.

The shack was mostly hidden from view by tall trees, their roots gnarled over the ground, some as thin as fishing line, others as thick around as Eli's leg. They had broken through the plank foundation of the small structure and invaded the interior like hardened, entwined snakes.

There was almost no furniture. Only a small metal cot, bare except for a well-worn mattress badly in need of airing and two rickety hardback chairs set beside a three-legged table. The shed had one narrow door in front and one window, minus the shutters, in back. Ray watched as Eli dragged the mattress outside and propped it against a smooth tree trunk so the air could circulate around it.

When Ray picked up the binoculars and started out the door, Eli caught her arm. "Where're you going?"

She wasn't used to answering for her every move. Still, Eli looked concerned, and so, surprising herself, she explained. "I won't be long, I'm just going to check on your brother, catch a lay of the camp before we head in there tomorrow morning."

"I'll come with you."

"That's okay." Ray turned to the door. "Sit down and take a load off."

Eli stepped in front of her. "I'm coming with you, Ray."

That imperious, demanding tone got to her. Damn it, wasn't it enough that she wanted him? That she felt like she *had* to have him? He already interfered with her thoughts and body. She didn't need him rubbing it in. "There's nothing you can do except get in my way."

Eli's expression hardened. "We're wasting time, Ray."

She knew he wouldn't give up, so she had to. She didn't want to have a big fight when she had other plans for the night. As usual, he had her doing things way out of the norm for her—like conceding. "Suit yourself, but stay the hell out of my way, and you damn sure better follow my lead."

He saluted her, and together they left the shed.

The jungle here was thick with ferns and air plants, the ground loamy and loose. They moved slowly for about twenty minutes, aware of small animals scurrying around them and birds overhead flying from tree to tree. Finally, they came to a steep, rocky incline. Ray turned to Eli, her eyes narrowed. "I have to climb up so I can get a good view of things. The camp should be right over that next ridge. You stay down here to . . . to . . ."

He raised a brow, waiting, and she blurted, "To catch me in case I fall." Her eyes widened. Oh hell. She couldn't believe she said something so lame. That delicious kiss earlier had her so rattled, she'd alternately berated, belittled, and badgered him, and now she was spouting pure nonsense.

She had lousy seduction skills for sure.

As Eli continued to watch her, it became obvious he hadn't believed that giant clanker anyway. Their gazes clashed for a long moment, and finally

Eli nodded. "All right. But you won't lie to me ever again, Ray."

His arrogance knew no bounds. She shot for sarcasm rather than admit to the lie. "I won't, huh?"

Eli tucked her hair behind her ear, his touch so sweet that her knees suddenly felt like noodles and falling became a real possibility. "No, you won't. Give me your word."

Her mouth fell open. "I'm trying to conduct a rescue here, and you're worried about something that won't even matter in less than a few days."

His implacable stare never wavered. "It'll matter, so promise me."

Bemused by his certainty of that, Ray pulled away to pace a small circle around the uneven ground. She knew things ended with the mission, so why wouldn't Eli accept it? And what did it matter to her anyway? She could enjoy him tonight, and hopefully that'd get him out of her system. If he fooled himself into thinking it'd be more than that, big deal. Once he was home in his safe little world, he'd thank her for not intruding in his life.

She stopped in front of Eli, who hadn't moved. "Have it your own way. I won't lie to you. But it'll be a moot promise soon enough."

Eli smiled with his victory. "Come on. Get your tail up this rock so we can see what's going on." Kneeling on the ground, he cupped his hands for Ray.

She shook her head at his easy acceptance, stepped onto his laced fingers, and felt herself hoisted a good distance onto the rock facing. Like a monkey, she scrambled the rest of the way up until she could see over the top. Her feet were wedged into small crevices, much like toeholds, and with one hand she held on.

She raised the powerful binoculars to her eyes, then searched out the camp. For long moments she didn't move. Memories of another day, another rescue, swamped her. The things she'd seen then left her stomach roiling and her forehead filmed in a nervous sweat. Stupid. That was then, and now nothing seemed amiss.

She continued to watch, forcing herself to study the layout of the camp. This one was different, more decrepit, proof of the guerillas' lack of skills. There were only half a dozen casitas, which would make searching out Jeremy that much easier.

Luck was with her when she noticed one man moseying around alone. His hair was brown but his skin was fairer than the others.

Head down, arms crossed defensively, he prowled around the yard, disheveled and obviously bored, not talking with anyone. For the most part, he was ignored.

In the fading light, Ray couldn't detect any signs of abuse, other than a few bruises and scrapes that looked older, probably from the barroom fight. Climbing down, she suddenly felt Eli grasp her waist and lift her the remainder of the way.

He didn't turn her loose, even when both her feet were on the ground. "Well?"

"I found him. He looks fine. He even has free run of the camp, though I'm betting he'll still be thrilled to see you." Ray turned to start the trek back to the shack. "From what I could tell, they aren't heavily armed. And after Sarita doses them, it should be a walk in the park." She cast him a quick glance. "But just in case, be on your toes tomorrow."

"I'll manage."

"That's pretty damned vague, Eli. I need to know if I can count on you for backup or if you'd be better off as a watch. This isn't a game, you know. Even with Sarita's plan, things could still go wrong and someone could get hurt. I have to make sure it won't be you or your brother."

Eli caught her suddenly, jerking her around to face him. "You're the one who's always trying to minimize my strength and intelligence. Having money doesn't make a man stupid or weak." His words were sharp but low. Ray thought she'd insulted him until he added, "And what about you, damn it? I don't want you hurt either."

Ray was stunned by his vehemence and ridiculous worry. "I'll be fine. I can take care of myself."

"You can, but I can't?" He stepped around her, no longer willing to follow behind. They traveled in silence until they'd reached the cabin.

Ray stared at his broad back, wishing she could kick her own ass. She'd insulted him again when she hadn't meant to. This whole seduction routine was a pain. "Eli?"

He ignored her as he stalked into the shack.

Ray entered cautiously. She had no real idea what to say to him to make things right. "I didn't mean to sound so condescending."

"Yeah, you did. You do it to distance yourself from me. As long as you're convinced I'm some wimp who can't blow my own nose without help, you can justify all that disdain you heap on me."

Ray hated these kinds of confrontations. She'd rather have a knock-down-drag-out fistfight any day. "I don't think you're a wimp."

"Yeah, you do."

His insistence irritated her. "You don't know what I think, so stop saying that."

"I know."

Ray fumed. "You do not!"

Eli looked up then, a slight smile on his face. "Do, too."

Ray opened her mouth to once again object, then caught herself. They were arguing just like children. Here she was, trying to plan a night of debauchery with the only man she'd found desirable in years, and he wanted to tease her.

"Jerk." She threw her binoculars at him.

Eli caught them easily, tucking them back into the pack while chuckling. "Better a jerk than a wimp, I guess."

Great. Now he was laughing at her. She searched through her bags for a change of clothes. Cleanliness was a priority if she hoped to get lucky tonight. She could handle the jungle, even the musty mattress, but she couldn't have sex while soaked in her own sweat.

Unable to look at him with those thoughts on her mind, Ray balled up the clothes and said, "I'll be back in a minute." And before he could ask: "I'm gonna wash and change clothes, and no, I do not need your help."

Eli glanced up with new attentiveness. "You're going to the stream?"

"I won't be long." She went out the door without another word.

Chapter Nine

Knowing he shouldn't watch, but unable to help himself, Eli went to the window. After brushing away a few dead bugs and spiderwebs, he leaned his elbows on the rough wooden sill, his attention glued to Ray's every movement. Brilliant stars and a fat moon lit the sky over the small clearing the stream made. Everything seemed softer at night, the forest lending black shadows to the surroundings. The air was only slightly cooler, still unbearably humid, and smelled of the dense foliage all around. Animals called quietly to each other, as if saying good night.

Eli was so horny, he could barely think straight.

Then Ray lifted her shirt over her head. Spellbound, he couldn't look away, didn't even want to try. She sat on a rock and worked her boots off, then stood and unfastened her pants. They fell to her ankles and Eli was given a breathtaking view of her backside, clad only in a pair of panties. Her skin looked opalescent in the moonlight, her hair liquid.

She didn't climb into the star-dappled water as Eli expected her to do, but instead stepped out onto a large flat rock midway in the stream and sat down. Her long legs stretched out before her and she cupped the water, splashing her body until she was thoroughly wet. She lathered her palms with the soap and began washing with a leisurely, lazy thoroughness.

She was so naturally graceful, her every movement utterly feminine despite a lifestyle that stifled feminine inclinations. She cupped more water, rinsing, until all the soap was removed.

Eli felt the wild thudding of his heart when Ray lifted her hips and skimmed her panties down her legs. He could see the smooth line of her back and the heart-shaped contours of her ass. She faced away from him, but he knew she used the tiny scrap of material as a cloth, finishing her bath—washing between her legs.

His body reacted to what he couldn't see, envisioning her hands where he wanted his hands, his mouth, his cock to be. His breath grew shallow with his imagination.

Ray looked over her shoulder then, suddenly aware of Eli's attention. Given the darkness and the shadows of the hut, he wasn't sure she could see him. He waited, his chest tight, but then she looked away, her head dropping forward.

With a muffled curse, Eli moved away from the window, belatedly giving her the privacy she deserved. Strung tight with lust, he was unable to sit still. He paced the cabin until she came in. She stopped in the doorway, damp, flushed, staring at him.

The urge to grab her close clawed at him. Never in his life had he suffered such a powerful craving. Without a word, he went past her, ready for his own dousing.

It wasn't cleanliness he had in mind, but rather a cold dunk in the stream to help suppress his unbearable need. He pulled his clothes off as he walked, and by the time his feet were on the bank of the stream, he was naked.

He made a loud splash when he stomped in, needing to exert some form of physical energy. The bottom of the stream was covered with smooth pebbles, and he sat down, trying to get as much cold water on his overheated body as possible.

He was surprised when Ray, silent as a ghost, suddenly appeared. She stood on the bank with her hands on her hips, wearing only the pajamas she'd bought at his store.

Did she intend to join him? Was she finally ready to accept him?

She cleared her throat. "Eli?"

He couldn't speak, but he turned his face toward her. She'd picked up his clothes and had them bundled in her arms.

"Did you happen to notice how I bathed?"

His muscles almost went into spasms. For the rest of his life, the sight of her bathing would torment him. He remained perfectly still in the water, not daring to move. "I noticed."

"Did you see me get all the way into the stream?"

"No. You sat there on that goddamn rock where I could see every inch of you under the moonlight." Why did she want to torment him now?

"You wanna know why?"

The water only reached his waist. Eli leaned back, dipping his body farther into the chilly stream, giving Ray an aggrieved frown. "You're obviously dying to tell me."

"I thought you might appreciate it if I did."

"So do I have to pry it out of you, or what?"

He knew by her tone of voice she was smiling. "Are you familiar with the red piranha?"

His heart nearly stopped. "Red piranha?" he repeated on a strangled breath.

"They mostly eat fish, you know. But since this stream is cut off from the main river, the piranha could be especially hungry, and none too particular about their diets. I suggest you hustle your sexy bod out of there before something takes a nibble."

Eli was cursing long and loud as he splashed out of the stream, stirring the water enough to send anything inhabiting it into hiding, including red piranha. Ray's laughter died the second she saw him naked, but that didn't stop Eli from feeling like an idiot. With the heat of Ray's gaze on his backside, he stormed into the cabin. Ray had left a utility light on, sending a small glow around the interior.

Jesus, no wonder she thought he was a fool. Around her, he continually acted like one. Red piranha. He shook his head.

More subdued, Ray strolled in behind him. She didn't say a word as he pulled on boxers—and nothing more.

In silent agreement, they prepared for bed. Eli hung one of his shirts in front of the window, using rocks to keep it firmly in place, hoping to discourage the bats from returning. Killer fish and insects were enough. He didn't need bats feeding off him. Satisfied with his makeshift curtain, he went outside to pound the dust out of the mattress before hauling it back in. It smelled better, but was far from clean.

They used water from the canteen to brush their teeth and less than fifteen minutes later, they lay spooned on the extremely narrow mattress.

Though neither of them had said much, their bodies were pressed together, the air was quiet, and Eli was hard. He didn't want to be, but around Ray it seemed he had no control at all.

The seconds ticked by with the impact of a drumbeat. The surrounding jungle was so silent, Eli could hear himself breathing. His muscles were strained enough to crack.

He suffered a riot of mixed emotions. The urge to retrieve his brother had amplified now that they were so close. Family was more important to him than most, probably because he hadn't always had one, and could never take it for granted. He wanted Jeremy home, safe and sound.

But underlying that was the driving, pulsing urge to tie Ray to him before it was too late. He'd learned early on to take what he really wanted in life. Regardless of what Ray thought, no one had ever handed him a damn thing, not money, not family, and definitely not love.

He'd found her, he wanted her, but she was an enigma, doing everything she could to maintain a distance from him. One minute it would infuriate him, but the next he felt such compassion, understanding her need to remain emotionally isolated. He'd felt that way himself once, long ago. He nearly smothered with the heartache of knowing what she suffered.

She considered this it, that once the mission ended, so would their time together. He wasn't giving her up that easily, but for now, he wouldn't push the issue. For now, he wanted her to learn to trust him a little.

Ray hadn't spoken a single word once they'd gotten into bed. She was stiff, painfully silent, and somehow distant.

"It's damned hot tonight, isn't it?"

Eli raised up slightly to look at Ray. Her voice had trembled as she'd spoken, giving testimony to her own turbulent emotions.

She turned her head to face him. Her eyes looked big and soft in the darkness. "This humidity is stifling."

Eli's testicles drew tight and blood rushed into his cock, thickening his boner, making him hurt. Ray couldn't know how just the sound of her voice ignited him. He could barely make out her features in the darkness, but in every masculine fiber of his being he was aware of her nearness. He could feel her heat, smell the light, healthy fragrance of her body.

He labored for breath.

"The air is almost . . . sticky."

Sticky, humid, hot—to Eli's lust-fogged brain, they sounded like provoking sex words. His groan erupted from his throat with explosive force. *"Ray."*

She rolled to face him and Eli moved over her, then groaned again, the sound raw and deep, this time from the feel of Ray's breasts, belly, and thighs moving against him. There were few clothes in his way now, and Ray showed no reservations.

Her legs stirred, tangling with his own. Eli immediately took advantage. He used his knee to force her thighs farther apart and settled himself against her. God, it felt good.

With his body surrounded, invaded by the smell and feel of Ray, he couldn't think. A roaring filled his ears with an urgency that kept rational thought at bay.

Rocking against her, feeling close to the exploding point already, Eli fought for common sense. "Ray, sweetheart, I can't protect you."

"I'll protect you," she murmured, kissing his chin, his throat.

Touched by her misguided sincerity, Eli said, "No, sweetheart. That's not what I mean." He drew a breath. "I don't have anything with me. I hadn't thought . . ."

She pressed her fingertips to his mouth. "It's okay, Eli. Sarita gave me a condom."

"She did?"

He felt her barely there nod. "She knew I wanted you."

God bless Ray, she'd finally admitted it. "I'm glad."

"That she gave me a condom?"

"That you want me. And yeah, about the rubber, too." Then he thought to add, "Only one?"

Her warm breath touched his throat. "Sorry."

"That's all right." And in a teasing threat, "I'll make it last." Contrary to that, Eli wanted them both naked, *now*. He stripped Ray's shirt up and over her head, pausing to feel her breasts and stroke her nipples.

"Eli . . ."

He shoved her pajama bottoms down her long legs. His palms brushed the silky skin of her hips, ass, and thighs. "I want to feel all of you against me."

"Yes." Ray helped him strip, but her enthusiasm left his boxers ripped. He almost laughed over that, until her hand circled his cock in a firm, careful grip. Oh no. No, if she started that, he'd never last.

He kissed the curve of her breast while pulling

her hand away, and moving it up beside her head. It was the sweetest torture being wanted so much by Ray. Coming up on one elbow, he wished like hell he could see her better, but he'd manage in the dark. First, he wanted her as hot, as turned on, as he was. With that thought in mind, Eli went about arousing her.

Despite Ray's efforts to hurry him, he feasted off her mouth; his kiss was languid, wet, deep, and thorough. He forgot about her lightning reflexes, though. Before he realized what she was doing, she caught his hand and pressed his palm to her breast. "Enough playing around, Eli."

"All right," Eli soothed, bringing up his other hand so that he held both breasts. "Is this better?"

For an answer, she arched into his palms.

He cuddled her, carefully shaping, caressing. Ray's breathing labored, mingled with soft sighs and small gasps, so different from her usually decisive, commanding tone. Using just his fingertips, Eli fanned her sensitive nipples, lightly pinched, tugged. Ray's body bowed in pleasure and Eli couldn't wait a second more. He dipped his head to search out one straining nipple.

Damn, she tasted good. He rubbed with his tongue, teased, and softly, wetly sucked. Ray went wild; her hands clutched at him, moved down his back to his hips, over his ass. He felt her fingers digging in, trying to drag him closer.

Knowing what she wanted, what she needed, Eli trailed his hand over her waist to her belly—and lower, to the crisp curls shielding her sex. The moment he touched her, Ray went still, even her breathing suspended. With one finger he pressed in, pushing past the soft, plump folds, and found her swollen and hot, slick with moisture. Perfect.

He fingered her gently, shallow little explorations that only excited her more. "I've wanted you forever, Ray."

Ray shook her head, the only denial she seemed capable of at the moment.

"*Yes*, Ray." Using only that one finger, Eli played with her, petting her inner lips until they opened, gliding up and down maddeningly close to her clitoris without touching her, going just inside, shallow and slow, then retreating. She tried twisting, moving her hips, but Eli followed her movements, keeping just out of reach.

"*Eli—*"

"Shhh." He slid three fingers deep, stopping at the sound of her long, drawn out moan. He held her there, feeling her fast breath on his face, the tightness of her body. Slowly out—back in again.

Her hips rose to meet him and she shuddered in rising need. The feel of her, wet and snug and slick, filled him with satisfaction.

"I've been looking for you at least a lifetime, Ray." Eli hadn't realized she was what he wanted until he found her.

With his fingers still working her, Eli licked her ribs, forged a path down her taut midriff. He took a soft love bite of her waist, her belly. She was all womanly grace and supple strength, sleek and smooth and soft. Her body arched sinuously with each touch of his mouth on her heated skin. The sounds of their breathing swelled, heavy and thick with desire.

Ray shivered, saying his name in urgent demand. Encouraging her, Eli moved his fingers in and out, thrilled with the way she tightened around him, trying to hold him, to keep him deep. When he felt she was ready to come, when her legs stiffened and her breath caught, he used his thumb to tease her pulsing clitoris.

"Oh, God. Eli, please . . ."

He looked up at her with lust and love. He had one arm around her hips, his other hand between her legs, fingers buried deep. "That's it, Ray, that's it. Come for me now." She gave a high cry and Eli's blood pulsed with hers. *"Yes."*

Her heels dug into the mattress and she threw back her head, crying out, trembling. Eli held her, keeping the rhythm of his fingers steady to give her more pleasure. When she finally quieted, he squeezed her close. Words of love crowded his throat, but he swallowed them down, forcing himself to be content with the sounds of her labored breathing, the scent of her heated body and excitement. She went limp.

He was far from finished, but he allowed her a few moments to regain her breath, to calm her racing heart. While she did so, he stroked her skin, touching her everywhere, kissing her in select places.

He bit her belly again, loving the taste of her, wanting to eat every inch of her.

"Eli?" Her limp hand lifted to his head and her fingers threaded gently through his hair in what Eli chose to see as a loving caress. "That was . . ." She sighed without finishing.

"Just a start." He raised up, gave her a long look, then kissed her long and deep. "I could spend years loving you, Ray."

She started a bit at that, but Eli didn't give her a chance to protest. He kissed her mouth again, then her throat, her shoulder, and her left breast. Lazily, he suckled her nipples, aware of the moment Ray responded with renewed interest. Her body was no longer so languid and her hands began their own exploration. Eli allowed her a few minutes to touch him, relishing the feel of her hot little hands skimming up and down his body. She tried to wedge a hand under him, wanting his cock, but Eli scooted down her body instead. He had a feeling this might be the only place where he could keep control.

She started to protest, until he licked over her ribs, then her hipbones and down. He dipped his tongue into her navel, pushed her legs wide apart, and kissed the delicate spot where her thigh met her groin. Ray caught her breath in anticipation of what he would do.

Not about to disappoint her, Eli nuzzled his face between her open thighs. His nostrils flared at the hot, spicy scent of her lust. Her pubic hair was already damp, making him anxious to taste her. He used both thumbs to open her more, leaving her clitoris exposed, ripe and tender. She was still slightly swollen from her earlier release, and Eli couldn't wait. He closed his mouth over her, drawing gently, flicking with his rough tongue, and Ray screamed in excitement.

Putting his fingers back inside her, Eli teased with devastating intent, stroking, sucking, treating her to a delicious tongue fuck meant to drive her mad.

This time Ray was totally uncontrolled in her climax. Her body quaked in small spasms, her cries were low and raw and filled with the same need Eli suffered. He could feel the strong contractions of her inner muscles gripping his fingers and he could taste her arousal as she came in long, delicious waves. He didn't want it to ever end, but eventually her body sank into the mattress.

She was crying.

Not sobs, but silent tears that left her cheeks wet and salty. Eli wasn't alarmed. She'd been so tense over so many things, the sexual release had probably released other emotions as well. He was glad.

Moving up to lie over her, Eli held her to his heart. That Ray would break down and cry with him told him everything he needed to know. She cared, no matter what she told herself. But if he made a big deal of this, she'd hate him for it. And he'd rather die than hurt her.

Kissing away the closest tear, he whispered, "You are so beautiful, Ray."

She shook her head. "I'm not."

Argumentative to the bitter end. Eli managed a weak, strained chuckle. His words were hoarse when he told her playfully, "You're also the most stubborn woman I've ever met."

"No, I—"

"Where's the rubber?" he asked, just to keep her on track. If he didn't get inside her soon, he'd be coming without her and that wouldn't do.

She sniffed, twisted to reach under the cot. "If you ever tell anyone—"

"What? That you're a sexual dynamo? That you taste so fucking good I almost came just from eating you?" He growled, ready to taste her again. "That you—"

"That I cried."

His heart swelled at the pitiful, embarrassed way she whispered that. "I swear to God, Ray, I will never hurt you." He took the condom from her and levered up to take care of business.

"I don't know why I'm sniveling. I'm not sad."

"I know, honey."

"I'm not worried or afraid, either."

Eli said nothing to that.

"It's just that you're so . . ."

"I understand."

She laughed. "Maybe I should say vain?" Ray sniffed again, then touched his chest. "I love how you feel, Eli." Her hands moved over his nipples, down his sides to again clutch his butt.

"All sweaty?" With the condom on, Eli lowered himself back into her arms.

"All heaving and horny and hard."

Closing his eyes, Eli struggled for control. It wasn't easy, but he managed to keep his entrance slow. After two orgasms, Ray was so wet and soft that he sank into her easily.

Once he was buried deep, he paused to kiss her brow, her ear, the tip of her nose. He loved kissing Ray and could have spent hours doing just that.

"You're a part of me, Ray." He cupped her chin and pressed deeper, touching her womb to emphasize his claim. "I won't ever let you push me away again. And I won't ever let you go."

With a heartfelt, uncertain groan, Ray tried to turn her face away—but she couldn't do it. Eli knew it wasn't his hold on her chin, but rather his hold on her heart that she rebelled against. Physical bonds she could break, but when was the last time someone had loved her?

Ray closed her eyes and her voice sounded with humiliation and despair. "You don't know what you're saying, Eli."

No, she just didn't want to believe what he said. "Don't be afraid of me, honey."

She thumped him in the ribs, but it was a weak attack, awkward from her position, making him smile. He was a part of her, body and heart, and even Ray's stubbornness couldn't blind her to that fact.

Still, long ingrained pride made her grumble, "I'm not afraid of anyone," at the same time her legs slowly twined around his hips and she locked her ankles at the small of his back.

"You feel good wrapped around me, honey." He began moving in a metered pace. He forced himself to go slow, enjoying the sweet friction, the wet glide, the gentle conquest of Ray Vereker, his own little mercenary.

Unappreciative of his efforts, Ray cursed him.

"So impatient," Eli murmured. His cock throbbed and pulsed, hugged by her hot velvet sheath. With each steady thrust, he felt her pubic hair, her smooth belly on his, her pointed nipples against his chest. "I've waited too long to hurry, Ray. Just relax and enjoy."

Instead, she dug her heels into the small of his back and strained against him. Damp from the heat and humidity, they rocked together, finding a rhythm that came to them easily, as if they'd been making love for years.

Eli slid his hands beneath her, cradling her ass, kneading and holding her close. His control began slipping so he raised her high for more powerful thrusts, each growing harder and deeper. Her strong legs squeezed him tight in her pleasure. Her hands held him as if she'd never let him go.

The urgency was back, worse than ever. His body pounded with heat, his heart thundered, and his muscles went rigid with the effort of restraint. He didn't think he could wait much longer, everything about Ray driving him past his control.

Then Ray said; "I want you with me this time," on a high wail, and it was enough. Eli exploded. His own shout was harsh and filled with satisfaction. He pressed his face into Ray's neck, filling himself with the scent of her, holding her as close as he could manage without hurting her.

It wasn't close enough.

He didn't know if he could ever be close enough. He only knew she was his now, and he would never let her forget that.

Ray hated to admit it, but she *was* afraid.

Last night had been pure, unadulterated, all-consuming bliss, far more than she'd counted on when she decided to give in to the attraction. *Attraction?* Ha! What a wimpy word for how she felt, for how Eli could make her feel.

She'd never imagined sex could be that way, both powerful and tender, mind-blowing and healing. Eli had the means to make her whole, content and fulfilled, which meant he also had the means to hurt her.

He didn't really know her, or he wouldn't keep talking about relationships and the future. She didn't fit in, not in her own world, and definitely not in his.

The bigger problem though, was that she no longer knew herself, not when she was with him, not with how he made her feel.

Last night was a memory she'd cherish. But it should never have happened. She'd given in, and in the process she'd made herself too vulnerable for comfort.

Usually she had no problem keeping her mind on what she was doing, using an internal clock to keep to her schedule. But after last night, she'd conked out for the duration. Even her concerns for the job hadn't been enough to rouse her this morning. It'd taken the noisy howler monkeys to jerk her awake. Now she was running behind, and as she shoved on her pants and tucked in her shirt, she stared at Eli, still sleeping.

He was a beautiful man. And not just in appearance, though God knew he had her panting for his body. He was intelligent and proud and almost as dangerous as she was. She'd misjudged him badly in the beginning. But now she knew Eli Conners could hold his own in any battle, be it a boardroom debate or a physical struggle in the middle of Central America.

But even putting those truths aside, he was still from the social elite. Other than a few admitted prejudices, Ray didn't know the first thing about the life of the rich and powerful. She'd hired herself out to them, doing their dirty work, but she didn't know what motivated them. What did they think when they got up in the morning? What did they discuss over lunch? She didn't know, would never know, and that was the crux of the problem.

Fully dressed, Ray walked to the bed. They had about five minutes before they needed to move out. She'd deliberately waited to wake Eli so he couldn't start hashing out the proverbial morning-after awkwardness.

Ray reached out to shake him awake, but hesitated. He was naked as a jaybird, and she liked it. Boy, did she like it. One muscled arm rested behind his head, and she stared at his biceps, pronounced even in sleep. The tuft of dark, fine hair beneath his arm was a strangely appealing sight, masculine and naturally sexy. So was the way his heavy brows relaxed in sleep, the rumpled lay of his hair, the soft soughing of his breath.

Looking at him made her suffer with regret, but

also filled her with warmth. She stared at his sex, remembering how she'd touched him there, how she'd tasted him, how he'd slid deep and filled her up.

He wasn't hard now, but was nestled softly in dark, crisp hair. It amazed her that a man's body could change so rapidly and so completely. It amazed her that Eli's body changed for *her.*

She wanted to touch him again, and found herself seriously considering it. Eli stirred, becoming erect right before her eyes. Her gaze shot to his face and she found him watching her, those hazel eyes hot and filled with such intensity that the impact of his stare sank deep into her heart. From the first, he'd possessed the power to see too much.

Eli slowly reached for her, but she stepped away. "We're late. We overslept. You've got"—she glanced at her watch— "four minutes."

Eli came out of the bed as if he'd been awake for hours, as if he hadn't spent most of the night making love to her. But he had. The lack of condoms hadn't stopped him. No, he just hadn't come inside her again, but he'd given her so much pleasure . . .

He stepped into his pants as he said, "I'm sorry. You should have awakened me sooner."

Ray cleared her throat. "No big deal, as long as you're ready to leave when I am. We want to catch them soon after they've eaten, when the effect of the drug is strongest."

Eli tugged on his boots, rummaged through the bag, then went outside. Ray peeked out the window. He relieved himself, then went to the stream to splash his face and brush his teeth. She shook her head. It would have been better if he'd been grouchy this morning. Then she could have convinced herself that he wasn't as wonderful as he seemed.

God, she was a fraud, damn near a coward. She almost hated herself.

He was back in the shack, ready to leave, and he hadn't even used a whole three minutes.

Forcing herself to think of the job at hand, Ray readied her ammo in case things didn't go as planned. She did it by rote, the familiarity of it just what she needed to soothe her frazzled thoughts.

"You look like a female Rambo." Eli made a sound of disgust. "Christ, I hate this, Ray."

Pretending confusion, she cocked a brow. "This?"

"Knowing the risks you take."

She shrugged. "It's what you hired me for."

Her cavalier attitude set him off. "That has nothing to do with here and now."

Ray was ready for a fight, needed one, in fact. It'd clear the air and remind her, and him, of where they stood.

Which was not together.

"Be honest with yourself about who and what I am, Eli. That hasn't changed just because sex got thrown in as a bonus."

His jaw locked. "Don't push me, Ray. What happened last night doesn't have a fucking thing to do with our arrangement."

His foul language didn't impress her. "No? Our reasons for being here haven't changed. *I* haven't changed."

In a show of frustration, Eli ran a hand through his hair. He looked disreputable and dangerous with his scraggly beard and glowing eyes. Then he tilted his head back to stare at the rotting ceiling. Ray watched his chest heave.

When he again looked at her, that turbulent emotion had been banked while the intensity remained. Eli looked at her mouth. "I'm sorry about being so . . . insatiable last night."

Her eyes flared at that low, intimate tone. Unfair! He couldn't go from mad to tender in a heartbeat, not when she'd expected more arguments, more anger. Damn it, she wasn't ready for concern, especially over *that*.

Knowing her face had gone hot, Ray considered tossing him out the window. "No. Big. Deal," she assured him through her teeth, letting him know she wanted it dropped.

"I should have let you rest." He took a step closer so that she had to look up at him. "The second time I woke you . . . I don't know, Ray. You'd curled up against me in your sleep, and I woke up hard . . ."

Oh Lord. "Forget about it." *Please.*

"But that third time was entirely uncalled for. I've never been that excessive before." His gaze searched her face, sending new heat to pool in her lower body. "I hope I didn't offend you, making love that way."

Offend her? The pleasure had been so sharp, she'd screamed like a banshee. Images of Eli rousing her from sleep, his mouth at her nipple, his hand already pressing between her thighs, warm and rough and unrelenting, made her breathing labor and her skin burn.

With their one and only rubber already used, Eli had become inventive, holding back his own release to make certain she climaxed again and again. But that third time, he'd lost it, and she could still remember the thick, hot feel of his cum on her stomach. The look on his face as he'd exploded made her want to crawl right back in bed with him now. Ray closed her eyes in self-defense, but it didn't help.

She drew a shaky breath before daring to face him again. As usual, he saw too much, more than she'd ever let any other man see.

"We have to go. Now."

Eli hesitated a heartbeat, reluctant to give up, before finally nodding. "I'm ready."

Ray knew he'd only put his questions on hold. He wanted to know what last night meant to her, but she didn't really know, so how could she explain it to him? She was usually so confident, feeling uncertainty and weakness just sucked.

Unfortunately, the day got worse instead of better.

When they neared the camp, it was to see half a dozen men tossing their cookies with the verve of a pie-throwing contest. Some half stood, others were rolled into balls on the ground. They had their hands clapped to their mouths, around their middles, and in some cases holding their noses.

"Good God, it's like the plague." Ray resisted the urge to cover her nose. "Sarita overdid it."

"I'll say." Eli curled his lip at the sounds the men made. "Hell, just watching them is about to turn my stomach."

"Wimp," she taunted, then had to pinch her lips together to hold down the orange she'd had for breakfast.

At that moment, they spotted Jeremy. He tottered over to the edge of camp, so green he blended with the jungle vegetation. He fell to his knees, wavered a moment, then began to heave violently.

"Huh. Montezuma's been busy with his revenge."

"Goddamn it, he must've eaten with the guerillas," Eli growled.

"And they told us he bitched about the food. Imagine how he'll feel now." Ray would rather have faced three armed men than a yard full of vomit. She *hated* nausea. "This is just friggin' great. Now I'll have to contend with him being sick on top of executing a rescue."

"You're all heart, Ray, you know that?"

Jeremy fell to his side with a groan that rivaled the others' combined. Ray did feel sorry for him, but merely shrugged. She had other things to contend with. "See the guard standing beside the ammunition shed, keeping out of reach of the sick men? He looks a little shaky himself, but I'd say he hasn't eaten yet."

"I'd say he won't eat for hours now."

Miguel stood at the other end of the compound, his hands on his head, his eyes wild with shock while his men fell like flies. He shouted and cursed at them in Spanish, to no avail. Either he hadn't eaten as much as his men, or he had a stronger constitution.

"Two men still standing," Ray said, "and the ape is Miguel. There're two jeeps parked behind that ammunition shed. That's your job, Eli. Ready one jeep for us to take. You can temporarily disable the other to give us a head start, but don't kill it completely. They need it to survive."

"And what'll you do?"

"I'll take care of the men."

Eli didn't like that. "You promised Sarita you wouldn't hurt anyone."

She glared at him for standing in her way. "Lucky for you, huh?"

Eli made a face. Ray was beginning to think he didn't take her seriously anymore. 'Course, why would he when he knew damn good and well she didn't want to hurt him?

They were hidden behind a line of trees, a thick layer of moss and dead leaves silencing their movements—as if anyone could hear over that awful retching racket anyway. Ray could guess what Eli would think of her plan, but she'd used the ploy before and it worked.

It'd be easier to get him out of the way first, so she ordered, "Slip around to the back of the shed. When I signal you, come in and grab your brother. I could do it myself, but since you're bigger, you'd be faster, and if he tosses his cookies . . . well, he's *your* brother."

Ray waited for Eli to move, but instead he asked, "What are you going to do?"

"Save your brother. That's the plan, right?"

"That doesn't answer my question."

Both tired and disgustingly emotional this morning, the last thing Ray wanted or needed was an excess of protectiveness from Eli. Leaning close so that their noses touched, she hissed, "I'm trying to get us the hell out of here with as little trouble as possible. Now. While everyone is still preoccupied barfing. So cut the bull, Eli. Can you carry your brother or not?"

"I can carry him. No problem."

"Perfect. Give me a few minutes, then after you've taken care of the jeep, circle around and be ready."

Eli nodded, now silent. But he still didn't move.

To hell with it, Ray decided. She handed Eli the Uzi, the binoculars, her canteen, and finally her vest.

Eli's brows came down. "Ray . . ."

"I know what I'm doing, Eli. For once, just let me do my job." Without a single look in Eli's direction, she grasped the neckline of her shirt and ripped it, tugging until her meager cleavage was visible, and farther down still, so that the insides of her breasts were on display.

Eli dropped everything to grab her upper arms in an iron hold. "Just what the hell is this grand plan of yours?"

"There're two of them."

He stared pointedly at her exposed cleavage. "So you think a ménage à trois will turn the trick?"

"For the love of . . . it's a *distraction*, Eli."

"I'll say."

She rolled her eyes. "Tell me, do I look the least bit threatening to you?"

His gaze drifted over her, bright with menace and a good dose of jealousy. "You look ready to fuck."

"Perfect. Then they won't be expecting me to steal their prisoner, now will they? Not that I couldn't easily put both those guys out of commission, but then they might not get back up, and as you said, I promised Sarita. And before you volunteer, I *know* you'd hurt them. So this is the best way."

His answer was to grab the back of her neck and pull her toward him for a deep, openmouthed, tongue-twining kiss. Stunned, Ray hung in his grasp. What kind of retort was that?

A possessive one, she decided.

Eli lifted his head and visibly struggled to get his temper in check. "I don't want to find a single scratch on you, Ray. Promise me."

Him and his damn promises. "Your brother is in that camp."

"And you're right here. Now promise me."

Her heart started racing and her vision blurred. He put as much significance on her as on his brother? Ray knew in that awful moment that she'd really screwed up. She'd done the unthinkable—she'd fallen in love with Eli.

Stupid, stupid, stupid.

Nothing had changed. She was still an outcast, an oddity. She could just imagine him trying to introduce her to his family. *This is Ray, a female mercenary. She excels in lethal hand-to-hand combat.* He'd make fools of them both.

Eli needed her arrogance now, and she gave it to him, truthfully. "If these clowns can hurt me, then it's time I retired. And it irritates the hell out of me that you can't find a little confidence in my abilities. Why the hell did you hire me if you don't trust me to do a good job?"

Eli looked agonized. "I trust you."

"About time." She shoved past him. "Now get about your business, but don't forget to watch for my signal."

She left, picking her way carefully toward the compound as if she had just found a much-needed sanctuary and was thankful. One quick glimpse over her shoulder told her that Eli had already disappeared.

Ray forced herself to look weak, limping slightly, her dark eyes pleading for help. The guard's attention diverted from the sick men as she came into view. His mouth spread in a wide, curious smile and he came to meet Ray at the flimsy gate.

Speaking rapid Spanish, he questioned her. Answering in kind, Ray claimed she had started work with Sarita but was accosted by two drug runners who hadn't paid like they should have. She pleaded for his protection.

He let her enter without a qualm.

Ray did her best not to look at Jeremy, but he was so white in comparison to the other men, he shone like a beacon. A queasy beacon. It was almost enough to turn her stomach, too.

Miguel had his back to them, issuing orders for the rest of the breakfast to be dumped. The middle of his tan shirt, straining across his broad, thick shoulders, was dark with sweat, and his shiny black hair hung wet against his scalp. No doubt, he was grumpier than ever this morning, trying to bring order to his camp. A good thing, too, because Miguel would recognize her, and Ray needed to be rid of the guard before tackling him to ensure no one got seriously wounded.

At her frown, the guard laughed. He misinterpreted her look as fear of the sick men. "You have nothing to fear, *chica*. It is just bad food." His finger came to rest in her cleavage, and he held her eyes as he dipped below the material of her shirt, dangerously close to a nipple.

Much more of that and Ray would be in the yard chucking with the men. She pulled away, doing her best to look teasing when she really wanted to snap a joint or two on his burly body. She only hoped Eli hadn't witnessed that little taunt.

Making certain to speak in Spanish, Ray began backing the man toward the ammunition shed. She praised him with false compliments and he gladly retreated with her toward what he viewed as intimate privacy.

The rickety door was locked, so Ray smiled and

danced her fingertips down the man's shirt, stopping at his belt with a suggestive grin. Fingers fumbling, the guard worked the padlock and swung the door open, caught Ray's hand, and tugged her inside. Ray didn't fight him, and he laughed in delight, cupping his hands around her bottom, squeezing, seeking. He backed her against an inside wall and leaned forward to kiss her.

Not in this lifetime.

Ray gripped his right wrist in both her hands. Their eyes met, his startled, hers determined.

She smiled. "Sorry, amigo." Whipping him around so fast he didn't have time to react, Ray hooked her leg in his, tripping him and shoving him forward hard at the same time. He landed on his hands and knees on the shed floor. Shock kept him immobile long enough for Ray to leap out and slam the door shut. She snapped the padlock closed.

Less than two seconds later, the man roared and landed against the door so hard, he nearly toppled the shed. He definitely didn't like being duped, and yelled as much in rather colorful terms. His shouts could be heard everywhere.

Miguel would be on his way. With a sigh, Ray turned to greet him.

His abundant body hair matted in sweat, Miguel stomped toward the shed to investigate. He had to dart around fallen men and twice-served breakfast remains. When he saw Ray, he skidded to a halt and his black eyes widened. *"You."*

"Hey, Miguel. What's up?"

Before he could stop himself, he took a hasty step back and almost fell. His bushy eyebrows met over his nose. Realization came quickly. "You want the American boy, *si?*"

"The wheels don't get rusty on you, do they, *compadre*?"

His shoulders bunched forward in aggression. "You can not have him."

"Who says I can't?" And with a laughing sneer: *"You?"*

"I have guards . . ." His booming voice dwindled at the sound of continued moans and other, more obnoxious regurgitating noises. He looked around the yard that now resembled a battlefield of fallen warriors. Suspicion dawned and he gave her a sharp, accusatory look.

Ray grinned. "How'd you like your special breakfast?"

Red heat washed over his face. "They will die?"

"Don't be an ass." That irritated her. She knew Miguel didn't trust her, that he was afraid of her. But she didn't do mass killings and he should have known it. After all, hadn't she taken it easy on him last time? Hell, she could have killed him and instead she merely incapacitated him for a while. "They'll be fine in a few hours—after I'm long gone."

He grunted in doubt.

"Admit it, Miguel. This is better than me leaving broken bones behind, isn't it?"

He wanted to debate her confidence on the outcome of a skirmish, but knew better. He shook a fist. "The boy is more trouble than he is worth. Yet he must be worth *something.*"

"Sure he is. Hand him over and I'll see that you get well paid." Since Eli had already given a fair amount to Sarita, it was a safe promise.

Miguel rubbed his flat belly, either from sickness or humor. "You think I am so stupid to trust you?"

Ray stared him in the eyes and took a menacing step forward. "You calling me a liar, Miguel?"

His grin slipped. "No!"

"Then give up now, before you or any of your amigos get seriously hurt."

"*No.*"

Ray laughed. "Oh, Miguel, I did make the offer." She took another step forward—and Miguel attacked.

Ray hadn't been expecting that because Miguel knew what she could do. Despite that, he grabbed her in a tight bear hug that cut off her supply of oxygen and pinned her arms to her sides. Stars danced before her eyes and her lungs burned, prompting her to quick action.

As if she'd passed out, Ray collapsed against him. Miguel staggered, cursing while trying to keep them both on their feet. The position threw him off balance. Ray twisted to fall to her back, used her knees to catch him in the middle, and sent him up and over her head. The big goon landed flat on his back behind her, winded and gasping for air.

Ray surged back up, exhilarated, bouncing on the balls of her feet, ready to go at it. Oh, if only she hadn't promised Sarita, she could have gotten in some good practice today. She was far more skilled than Miguel, but he was easily twice her size, which would help even the score. Palms up, she bent her fingertips, urging him to her, grinning with glee. "C'mon, Miguel. You wanna play? I'll play."

"No." He shook his head and again looked around, probably hoping for assistance. At that moment, another guard approached. He looked sick, but determined. Ray hated having the advantage again. No challenge in that.

She kicked out, catching Miguel in the ribs, forcing him back a pace or two. Just as quickly, she twisted and caught the other man in the thigh. His leg collapsed, landing him on his knees in the dirt. Ray brought her knee up into his chin. His head snapped back and he fell unconscious to the ground. Ray spared him a glance and saw he was breathing just fine. If anything, he was better off. Maybe he'd sleep until the sickness wore off.

She faced Miguel just as he charged toward her again. Grinning with a surge of exhilaration, Ray said, "You're up."

He gave a battle cry of outrage. Ray ducked around him, chopped fast, and hit him twice in the back. Miguel staggered forward, almost losing his balance. He spun around to face her, aware that she only toyed with him and not liking it a bit.

"Puta," he snapped and lunged at her. Ray dodged his meaty fist while delivering a chopping blow to his ribs again, then his stomach, making him huff.

He slowly straightened up, saw her stepping toward him yet again, and covered his crotch with both hands.

Laughing, Ray clipped him in the side of the neck just behind his ear. He went down face first—thankfully well away from the nauseous remains of his men. The whole thing had lasted less than thirty seconds.

Ray knelt to check him, saw he was okay, and started to raise her hand to signal Eli.

He was already sprinting across the compound toward her.

And wow, he looked pissed. His eyes were lit with an angry fire discernible even from a distance.

Ray slowly came to her feet, then propped her hands on her hips, trying to quiet herself from the rush of adrenaline. "Everything go okay?"

Eli charged right up to her and shouted, the words practically spit at her, "What the hell kind of plan was that?"

Chapter Ten

Jeremy forced himself upright, bewildered by what had just happened. There was Eli, as big and strong and imposing as ever. But he hadn't tackled the ape. No, the woman had done that. She'd taken on two men—three, if you counted the one bellowing from the shed, though he'd barely noticed her then, assuming she was with the whores who came to visit on occasion.

But this one hadn't had sex on her mind. No, she'd played with them, grinning with evilness, and then, with a hit or a kick, she'd laid each of them out. It defied reason and didn't make a bit of sense. Only in movies had he ever seen anyone fight like that. And all the actors were male.

His stomach cramped and he curled in on himself, fighting the nausea, but not for long. The woman ignored Eli and his awesome anger, and eyed him with pity.

That burned Jeremy's pride.

"Save your gripes for later, Eli. Let's move."

"Jeremy." Eli put his arm around Jeremy's shoulders, offering support while moving him away from the compound. "You okay?"

God, to be found this way, dirty and sick and weak. And to have *her* witness it, especially after she'd done things he couldn't. Things he wouldn't have dared try. Even now, she strode beside them, her gaze watchful, her manner arrogant. "If you don't count the stomach cramps." Jeremy glared at her. "Was she right? The food was poisoned on purpose?"

"Not poisoned. You'll be okay in a few hours. But yeah, it was deliberate."

Jeremy stopped, fighting off a wave of churning sickness. "I should have known better than to eat that slop they serve."

"That *slop* is what they live on," the woman pointed out.

"You should try eating it," Jeremy shot back.

"I have. Plenty of times." A movement drew her attention to his feet, and she said, "Watch yourself."

Jeremy glanced down and saw he'd almost stepped on that damned furry, creeping tarantula.

He couldn't help it. He stumbled back so fast he fell on his ass. But it didn't seem far enough away, so he continued to scurry back. *"Son of a bitch."*

The woman actually laughed. "For a sick kid, your speed's pretty good." Then she stepped forward. "I'll get it."

"No!" Dear God, if she touched it, he'd die. Eyes wide, he said, "Let's just go around it."

Eli scowled, used the side of his boot to shove the spider out of their way, and then helped Jeremy back to his feet. "Did you hurt yourself?"

Now seemed like a good time to disappear into the jungle. Jeremy gave it serious thought before remembering the jaguars and boas and other deadly creatures that prowled around. "No, but that damn bug has followed me everywhere."

The woman chuckled again. "It doesn't have a personal vendetta against you. It's probably not even the same one. Tarantulas are common around here."

Jeremy hated her.

Not only did she take care of his captors with no effort, she would have touched that damned spider that was almost as hairy as the head guerilla, Miguel. He shuddered.

Eli hauled him forward. "We need to get moving."

The woman started to put her arm around him, too, but Jeremy rudely shrugged her off, giving her a look filled with contempt. "I don't need your help."

"Coulda fooled me."

"I'm fine," he gritted out.

Laughing, she said, "Well, that's the sickliest shade of fine I've ever seen. And whew, you do smell ripe. They wouldn't let you bathe?"

Her continued good humor in the face of his misery raked along his nerves. Where were they going, anyway? It seemed Eli led them into the jungle. "Only in the dirty river."

"The river's not so bad."

He shuddered and explained, "It's loaded with leeches."

Her mouth twitched, as if she wanted to laugh at him. "Gotcha." And then with a glance at Eli, she teased, "There're piranha in there, too."

Piranha? God, he'd rather be dirty.

All around them, men were starting to collect themselves. Their severe cramps were abating enough to make them aware of intruders, but not enough that they wanted to do anything about it.

Suddenly the woman said, "Unless you want me to do a little more hand-to-hand, you'd better carry him, Eli."

Strangely enough, Eli didn't take her to task for her commanding tone. No, he just obeyed. Ignoring Jeremy's protests, he hauled him into his arms, carrying him like a damned baby. It was a humiliation he'd never forget.

Jeremy thought he even heard one of the men say "Good riddance" in faint, tainted English.

The woman led the way toward one of the guerilla's jeeps. His eyes widened when Eli plopped him into the backseat. There in the front floor was an odd-looking gun, far more modern than those the guerillas carried. "What the hell is that?"

The woman glanced into the jeep and shrugged. "An Uzi SMG. Your brother stored it for me." She slid behind the wheel, then had to keep sliding when Eli pressed into the jeep, moving her over into the passenger side.

"Hey. You're forgetting who's in charge here, Eli."

"Sorry, babe, no time to argue now." He gunned the jeep just as the man locked inside the ammo shed broke through the rotting wooden door. He had his gun drawn and was racing toward them.

"Hold on." Eli slammed the jeep into gear and hit the gas pedal, spraying mud everywhere, throwing Jeremy onto the floor and causing his stomach to pitch.

The woman watched out the back, that awesome, shiny silver weapon in her hand. She looked entirely comfortable with it, too. Seconds before

Jeremy crawled back into his seat, she said, "You might want to duck," and then she took aim.

The gun made an awful noise, scaring the bejesus out of him and forcing him to cover his head while cowering flat in the seat. His brother, however, was calm personified.

"Shoot anyone?"

She snorted. " 'Course not. I hit the ground just to make him run for cover."

Jeremy stared between them. He knew his brother could be ruthless on occasion, but shooting at people? "Just who the hell are you, lady? One of their whores?"

Now *that* got a reaction out of Eli. "She's Ray Vereker and she just saved your sorry ass. You might try thanking her instead of insulting her."

Thank her? For poisoning him? Eli had to be kidding.

Ray smirked. "Forget it, Eli. He can think whatever he wants. I already got my pay. That's thanks enough."

Jeremy raised his head in incredulous disbelief. "You *paid* her to come here?"

Eli steered sharply to the left, causing Jeremy to topple in his seat again. "The only reason I managed to get to you was because of Ray's experience."

Jeremy struggled to crawl back into the seat. The woman helped by grabbing the back of his shirt and hauling him up. She damn near strangled him in the bargain. "I'll just bet she's real experienced."

Ray laughed, looked at his face, and laughed some more. "Way to lighten the mood, kid." She reached back and punched him in the shoulder.

He knew she meant it as a joke, but she hit hard for a girl. After that, she twisted back in her seat, facing forward. Jeremy took that to mean the immediate threat was over and he sat back up.

Eli drove the jeep like a pro, but at each fast turn, Jeremy tightened his mouth. At the moment, he just wanted someplace to curl up with his misery.

"I'm sorry, Jeremy." Eli's tone was calm and comforting. "I know it's rough."

"Where are we going?"

"To a private plane, then home." Eli cursed as he maneuvered around a fallen log. "The road isn't much better than the footpath."

"But it's faster," Ray said, leaving Jeremy to wonder how they had gotten to him. At the moment, he felt too lousy to ask more questions. The woman, Ray, chattered on, giving Eli directions while keeping a vigilant eye on the surroundings. The gun stayed in her hand, and after her performance at the compound, he'd bet she hit anything she shot at. Jeremy couldn't figure her out. Just who the hell was she?

By the time they reached the plane, he was slumped in his seat, his face clammy, ready to die and get it over with. Never in his life would he eat beans or rice again.

To make matters worse, that damn Ray was full of energy and orders, and Eli just let her do it. It pissed Jeremy off and made him doubly cranky.

Eli parked, and then suddenly she was beside him, leaning in close, her velvet eyes black with concern. "You okay, kid? You look like hell." She stuck the back of her hand to his forehead—as if she had any motherly instincts! "You're not feverish, thank God."

"I'm sick because you messed with the food."

"Yeah. I sympathize with you. Personally, I'd rather be flogged than puke." She straightened away. "I've been nauseous twice in my life, and that was enough for me."

Jeremy stared at her. "Go away."

She shook her head at him and wandered off.

Another man, big and blond with a surly expression, appeared from the side of the road. He took one look at Ray's disheveled appearance and exposed chest and raised his brows. "This ought to be interesting."

"It's not."

Eli's tone shut down any further questions on Ray's appearance, though Jeremy suddenly realized that she might not always look that way.

Did she always kick ass?

Eli helped him out of the jeep. "We'll have you more comfortable in a few minutes." Supporting him with one arm, Eli steered him toward a Skylane resting in the river.

Before they could board the plane, Jeremy fell to his knees to be sick again.

Over his head, Ray said, "It was probably the bumpy ride that set him off again. I can give him a shot of Phenergan to settle his stomach once we're on the plane."

Eli laid a heavy hand on Jeremy's shoulder. "I'd appreciate that."

"Well, I wouldn't," Jeremy choked out while struggling to his feet. "She's not a doctor and she's already poisoned me once—"

"No one asked you." Eli shoved a canteen at him, then took his elbow and hauled him aboard the plane.

The pilot stayed up front preparing to take off,

and Eli stored the gear so it wouldn't roll around on the flight. Jeremy curled on a blanket on the floor, and seconds later Ray carried him a plastic basin.

Just watching her walk got on his nerves. She had a cocky gait, and even dressed in the ridiculous ruined clothing, she somehow looked commanding and completely in charge.

"Here you go, in case you puke again." She squatted next to him. "We won't be in the air long. Before you know it, you'll be in the States in a comfortable bed after a nice long bath. But for now, you need to scoot your pants down so I can give you a shot in your hip."

His bloodshot eyes widened. Drop his pants for her? "Hell, no."

"The Phenergan will kill the nausea and make you a little sleepy. You'll be able to rest."

No way would he rest with her around. "Get lost. I don't need your help."

Ray made a sound of impatience and those mysterious dark eyes narrowed. In a thousand different ways, she seemed far more imposing and dangerous than the guerillas had. "What's your problem, anyway?"

She managed to put so much silky menace in her tone, Jeremy hesitated before grumbling, "You."

"So you'd rather I left you in the camp?"

He forced himself up on an elbow, scowling ferociously. "Eli would have gotten me out, with or without you."

"But he didn't," she reminded him, all smug and mean. "He hired *me* to do it."

Jeremy stared at her torn shirt and curled his lip. She didn't have enough to flaunt, in his opinion. "Is that all he hired you to do?"

Eli suddenly appeared. "Jeremy, I swear, if you weren't so puny at the moment, I'd turn Ray loose on you." He put his arm around her and half smiled as he made that absurd threat.

Ray didn't think it was funny. "I wouldn't waste my time."

Jeremy watched her as she prepared the shot. With Eli looming over him, he had no choice but to take it. "I saw you throw those guys around like beanbags."

"Yeah, so?"

"I've never seen a lady fight like that."

Even to Jeremy's own ears, it sounded like an accusation. She jerked the top of his loose trousers down a good five inches. "Yeah, well, I'm not exactly a lady, so that explains it, doesn't it?" She stuck in the needle with a little more force than Jeremy thought necessary.

He sucked in a painful breath and cursed.

"Quit being a baby," she said. "You should feel more human in just a few minutes."

To hide his discomfort, Jeremy asked, "Where did you learn to fight like that, anyway?"

Ray smirked. "I was raised with two long-haired, vain cousins. They constantly primped in front of the mirror. I grew up having to fight my way into the bathroom every single day."

Jeremy stared at her incredulously, but Eli laughed. "Lighten up, Jeremy. And show some respect."

"Respect?" The woman looked to be a cross between a whore and a soldier. "You have to be kidding me."

"That's enough." No longer laughing, Eli pinned him with that penetrating gaze of his, then took Ray's hand, holding tight when she would have pulled away. He looked stern, but Jeremy could see the smile in his eyes. "I'll admit Ray may be just a bit unique. But you'll get used to her."

Both Ray and Jeremy blinked at his statement. "Get used to her?" Jeremy asked, appalled. Just what the hell did that mean?

At the same time, Ray shook her head. "That's not going to happen, Eli. We're parting company tomorrow."

Eli tugged her closer. "You're not going anywhere, Ray."

No one really noticed the lurch of the plane as Buddy took them airborne.

Ray growled, "The hell I'm not. I have to get back home."

"And where is home?"

"None of your damn business."

"I'm making it my business."

Jeremy had never heard anyone argue with his brother. Employees at the malls rushed to please him, ranch hands treated him with due respect. And women . . . well, they sure as hell didn't go nose to nose with him.

But then, Ray wasn't an ordinary woman, and she was definitely nose to nose, and furious, too.

"Why?" she demanded, succinct to the point of being rude.

Eli gave a negligent shrug. "I'm not letting you go."

She fell back a step, no longer so confident. "You're not?"

"No." Eli turned his hand to entwine her fingers tightly in his own. "You'll have to accept me, little soldier." Then he grinned. "Whether you like it or not."

Judging by the sound she made, she didn't like it one little bit.

Neither did Jeremy.

The plane ride hadn't lasted long enough to suit Ray, but at least Jeremy stayed groggy from the shot, which spared her from his insults and occupied Eli's attention. Buddy had tried to tease her into a better mood, but she wanted only to escape.

Was Eli out of his mind? Buddy didn't think so. The way he carried on, Eli was his new best friend, practically a hero, and already a member of the family.

Ray ignored most of the absurd conversation until after Buddy landed his plane near the rented truck. He helped Eli get Jeremy off the plane, then stood beside Ray while she watched the two brothers head slowly for the truck. Thanks to the drug, Jeremy was practically asleep on his feet, with Eli guiding him.

"Promise you'll invite me to the wedding."

Wide-eyed, Ray jerked her head toward Buddy to stare. Weddings were formal affairs with fancy white dresses and hordes of people and lots of pageantry. They were between two people in love, not in lust, and they meant . . . a lifetime. "There won't be a *wedding.*" She could barely get the word out without choking.

"That's not the impression I got from Eli."

"Eli's got jungle fever or something. Ignore him." She shaded her eyes, saw that Eli was about ready, and headed toward the truck. Buddy kept pace at her side. "He'll forget about wanting to see me two hours after he's home."

Buddy put his arm around her, drawing her to a halt. "I don't think so, hon, but I'm more curious about how you'll feel."

"Richer. We're getting well paid for this little caper. And you know, Buddy? I think he could have managed on his own."

"So he didn't need you after all?"

She shook her head, saddened with the awful truth. As Jeremy had said, Eli would have gotten him, with or without her. "Not for this—and probably not for anything else."

"No? Why don't I ask him . . . ?"

Before he'd taken two steps toward Eli, she jerked him back around—then threw herself against him in a tight bear hug. "I'd like to just leave with you."

Buddy's arms tightened until he lifted her right off her feet. "If you really feel that way . . ."

She shook her head and forced herself to step back. God, now she was even being clingy. Eli had changed her, and not for the better. She rubbed her face. "Ignore me. I'm just tired." And in love and heartsick and . . . "I'll have your cut wired into your account tomorrow."

Buddy nodded. "Promise me you'll think about things, Ray. Don't just write Eli off, okay?"

All she did was think about him. "Quit worrying, Mom." Buddy laughed at that and pulled her into another hug before turning her toward the truck and swatting her posterior.

"Be good. And give the man a chance!"

With a wave, Ray jogged toward Eli. She deliberately smothered those weak, tender emotions that made her question herself. She'd face this—*him*—just as she'd faced the rest of her life: with logic and determination.

"Ready to go?" Eli asked.

Ray nodded and got into the truck without a word. She started the engine and made a slow, bumpy path back to the road. In her rearview mirror, she caught Buddy's plane lifting into the sky. It was almost over. She'd done what she set out to do. She'd gotten Eli's brother, no one had gotten seriously hurt, and she'd get paid. Like she'd told Eli, it was a breeze.

Except for the fact that she'd fallen for him.

They rode to the hotel in complete suffocating silence. Ray now wished she hadn't planned to spend the night again, but her flight didn't take off till the next morning. Then she and Eli would head their separate ways. Could she get an earlier flight? It might be worth checking into once she reached the hotel.

She was just pulling into the lot, Jeremy slumped against her shoulder, when Eli said, "Ray?"

After that long silence, the sound of his voice almost made her jump. "Hmmm?"

"Don't you dare try to sneak out on me."

Had he read her mind? Just in case, she dredged up her most caustic look. "You still have to pay me, so I'm not going anywhere. But," she added with emphasis, "if I did, I wouldn't sneak."

"Glad to hear it." She drove up to the front door where they were met by the valet. "I'll take care of the money in the morning."

They each climbed out. Over the roof, Ray said, "I thought you could do it tonight."

Eli reached inside for his dozing brother. "Nope. I'm thinking of that money as insurance." He winked at her. "I need to talk to you, and this way I know I'll get my chance."

Or she could say to hell with the money, and leave while she still could. She already knew if a flight was available, she'd take it. She didn't want Eli's money—she disliked herself enough at the moment without taking pay.

Jeremy came awake with a start, staring around himself blankly before giving in to a wide yawn. Thanks to Buddy, he wore clean clothes and shoes, but he still looked like hell. And given the way his gaze sought her out, he still disliked her. But then what brother wouldn't react that way to the likes of her?

With a hefty tip and a brief explanation that his brother was ill, Eli got VIP treatment. He was shuffled to the front of the registration desk, their bags carried in, and before Ray knew it, she was again in a hotel room. This time she had her privacy and she wasted no time in calling the airlines.

There were no earlier flights. She hated to admit it, but she wasn't really disappointed. Regardless of what she knew to be right, her heart hurt when she thought of leaving Eli.

She lingered in the shower, changed into clean clothes, and then for almost an hour stood in front of a window that overlooked the parking lot, her emotions turbulent, waiting. Finally Eli knocked on her door. She knew it was him without looking. "Go away."

"Open the door, Ray."

She gave a short laugh. "No, I don't think so."

"Suit yourself, honey. But it's going to draw a hell of a lot attention when I knock the damn thing down."

She didn't think he could do that, but he would cause a ruckus trying. Feeling her heart pound heavily in a mix of excitement and foreboding, Ray gave in and turned the lock.

Eli stepped inside, closing and locking the door

behind him. Leaning back, his arms crossed at his chest, he said, "You look like a frightened rabbit."

That was all it took to clear Ray's mind. She drew her brows down and glared. "What do you want?"

"You."

She had to close her eyes against the husky timbre in his tone. She felt it all the way to her toes, invading her soul, her heart.

Eli moved while she stood there silently before him. Ray opened her eyes when she felt his hand touch her face. "You want me, too, Ray. Admit it."

She swallowed hard. "Don't you see, it doesn't matter what I want. I'm realistic, Eli. And you should be, too."

Eli didn't argue with her. Rubbing his thumb over her bottom lip, he whispered, "You are so beautiful."

Frantic, Ray shook her head. "I knew you would come. I kept waiting. All through my shower, I was listening for the door."

"I had to get Jeremy settled first or I'd have been here sooner. He's feeling much better now that he's showered and changed. He was actually starving."

Ray laced her fingers together. "A good sign, right?"

"Yes. He no sooner finished eating than he fell asleep again."

"That's the medicine and the adrenaline rush, and probably a lot of relief, too. He'll be groggy for a while I bet."

Eli caught her arms and drew her closer. "You did good today, Ray." He hesitated, then said, "I'm sorry I yelled at you. It scared the hell of me when Miguel grabbed you and that other guy joined in."

"They underestimated me."

Eli nodded. "I can sympathize. I made that same mistake at first, too. But"—Eli bent to kiss her gently—"I can't make that mistake again."

Warning bells went off in her head. "What do you mean?"

Eli straightened, a little regretful, a lot determined. "I'm spending the night here."

Ray's mouth fell open. How the hell could she leave if he stayed by her side? Duh. That was probably his intent. "Your brother . . ."

He shook his head. "Jeremy is going to be fine once he gets rested up and has a chance to eat his fill."

"He doesn't like me, Eli."

"It doesn't matter."

"Of course it does," she almost wailed. "He's your brother. How do you think the rest of your family will react if you drag home a hired soldier?"

Eli chuckled. "You make yourself sound like a hardened criminal. I'm proud of your abilities, Ray. That's all that's important."

Ray lifted her chin. "What about Jane?"

As if soothing a fractious child, his voice gentled. "I already told you I wasn't marrying her."

"No, you told me your grandfather was counting on you to unite the families. He'd be damned disappointed with the likes of me."

"Once he meets you, he'll be pleased. My grandmother, too."

His grandmother? Ray groaned and covered her face with both hands. This was a nightmare.

Eli pulled her hands down, then laid his finger across her lips. "Hush, now." Both hands cupped her face, leaving her to stare into his mesmerizing eyes. "God, I missed you, Ray. You've been so silent the past few hours, and I was too busy trying to get things settled to see to you. But I want you to know, I meant what I said. I'm determined to make you mine. Completely. And I don't give up easily once I set my mind on something, so you may as well save your arguments and agree."

"I won't be forced into anything."

"Of course not." He drew her closer and nibbled on her lips. "I just want a chance to convince you, that's all."

More like coerce her, she thought, as her thighs trembled and her belly curled. "Eli . . . you refuse to see what's right."

He smiled at her disheartened expression. "What I see, honey, is that you haven't once told me you don't want me."

Ray blanched over that. Blast it, she hadn't.

"You only claim it won't work. But I can make it work. You wanted me to trust you, right? Well, how about giving a little trust, too?"

This wasn't about trust, damn it. Why wouldn't he see that? Meaning to push him away, Ray put a hand to his chest, and saw that she was shaking. With need? It infuriated her.

But she couldn't bear to turn him away. Not tonight. She did need him. That should have made it easier for her to walk away. She'd been needy as a young child, and again when she was with Kevin. Both times had been miserable disappointments. Needing was bad—but with Eli, it seemed strangely exciting, like a dark lure.

She'd make him need her, too. For tonight, for right now. And then she'd leave.

She stopped trying to push him away and instead ran one hand over his shoulder. "You enjoyed using your teeth the other night, remember? I think you have a thing about biting."

At her obvious capitulation, Eli's eyes were suddenly blazing. "I wanted to eat you alive. I still do." His voice dropped even more. "You taste so damned good, sweetheart."

Stepping closer, Ray whispered, "I love the way you look at me, Eli. You have the most compelling stare. You're doing it now, aren't you? Trying to read me, trying to figure out how to get what you want."

One corner of his mouth tipped in a crooked smile. "You don't seem particularly concerned about it."

"I'm not." She leaned up and gently nipped the warm skin of his throat. He'd shaved and showered and he smelled deliciously of cologne and soap and warm masculinity. "Right now, we want the same thing."

He tilted her face up with the edge of his fist. His gaze was darkly sensual, hot. "I want to see you. All of you."

Ray toyed with the neckline of his T-shirt, sliding her fingertips beneath to touch warm skin. "And you, Eli? Will I see you, too?"

For an answer, Eli caught the hem of his shirt and pulled it over his head. Tossing it aside, he dragged Ray up close to his bare chest and bent to take her mouth.

Ray groaned at the tender assault. Her fingers immediately tangled in his body hair, then moved up and over his shoulders. Before Eli could become the aggressor, Ray licked her tongue over his lips, then thrust hotly into his mouth. Eli's arms tightened on her back.

Dragging her mouth away, Ray said, "I've been thinking about being with you all day."

Ray wasn't shy, had never been shy a day in her entire life. And right now, she felt especially bold. Eli watched her with a kind of predatory awareness, his erection obvious beneath the material of his jeans. Ray lightly dragged her nails down the length of him, then back up again. He shuddered and his hands fisted.

Going to her knees, she whispered, "I like to bite, too, Eli. But like you, I'm very careful, and very gentle." That was all the warning he got before she caught his muscled hips between her hands, leaned forward and opened her mouth on the front of his jeans.

Eli tightened, his breath coming out in a low rush. His palms settled on either side of her head, his fingers curling around her nape. Cautiously, Ray scraped him with her teeth and he groaned aloud. The sound was one of incredible pleasure and encouragement.

Ray smiled up at Eli. His cheeks were dark with aroused color, his eyes glazed and hot. With his bare chest swelling, he looked incredibly sexy and all too appealing.

Ray pulled the snap free on his jeans. For a brief moment, Eli closed his eyes then quickly opened them again. Ray slowly slid the zipper down, teasing him as he'd often teased her, then slipped her hand inside.

His size thrilled her, so powerful and hard, just like Eli himself. He was warm and velvet smooth, throbbing in her palm.

Rubbing her cheek against him, Ray whispered, "I've thought of touching you a hundred times since last night. I kept wishing it had never happened because it was so irresponsible of me. There was so much at risk. But I'm glad we had last night, Eli. And I'm glad we have now."

"We have a lifetime together, Ray," he insisted. But she chose that moment to kiss him, her mouth warm and wet and open. Eli tilted his head back and concentrated on breathing deeply. Her tongue stroked down his length, then back up again. When it curled over the tip of him, tasting, teasing, he growled viciously and locked his knees to stay upright. Ray loved his reaction.

She came to her feet. "Take your pants off."

Eli blinked at the startling command, then narrowed his eyes in sudden comprehension. Shaking his head, he said, "I have a better idea. Let's put this on even footing."

"I don't know—"

Eli reached for the hem of her shirt, then pulled it up and over her head. For several moments, he just looked at her, his gaze as tangible as the heat of his body and his fast shallow breath. He tossed the shirt aside.

His large hands covered her breasts, kneading, making her nipples pucker tight. The moment he felt that, he dragged his thumbs slowly over her nipples. "You're always trying to maintain control, aren't you, sweetheart?" He stared into her eyes as he toyed with her, lightly twisting, plucking her nipples, making her gasp.

"Someone has to be in control," she breathed. "Better me than you."

"Oh, I don't know. I like controlling you just a bit. I get the feeling it doesn't happen too often."

It didn't happen at all, and just maybe that was part of Eli's appeal. Her thoughts scattered, there and gone as Eli continued to arouse her. He kissed her temple, her cheek. His tongue flicked around her ear, then dipped inside, sending delicious chills up her spine. She moaned softly.

Chuckling, the husky sound melting her bones, Eli caught the lobe of her ear between his teeth and plied it with his tongue. Ray fisted her hands in the crisp, curling hair on his chest.

"Hey. Take it easy."

He was still amused, and Ray decided she didn't like it one bit. "I don't like you doing this, Eli."

"Doing what?" He gave her a look of feigned confusion while gently, insistently tugging on her nipples. Her back arched toward him on a groan.

"You know exactly what I mean," she insisted, panting now with the incredible sensations.

"Yeah, I know what you mean. You don't like it that I'm taking charge, that I can control the way you feel. You think you want a man you can lead around by the nose. But you don't, Ray. Not really."

Ray knew that wasn't true, that she didn't want some spineless mama's boy, but she couldn't seem to find the words to tell him so.

Eli gave a small, satisfied smile. "You're a strong-willed woman, Ray. You would detest a man who was weaker than you." Eli leaned closer and his breath fanned the sensitive skin below her ear with each whispered word. "I think you like having me take charge, at least like this."

He didn't wait for her to answer.

"If I touched you between your thighs right now, you'd be wet for me, wouldn't you, Ray?"

"Yes." She saw no reason to deny it. There was an undeniable thrill in being overpowered, in giving herself into Eli's safekeeping. She was so independent in her thinking and skills, she'd never encountered anyone who threatened her control.

Eli grabbed her by the waist and hefted her over his shoulder. "Just what I wanted to hear."

She stiffened in surprise and indignation. "This is not how I planned the night, Eli."

"I know." He tossed her gently in the center of the bed where she bounced twice before he came down beside her. Eli laughed, enjoying himself as he stretched her arms high above her head and held her wrists in one of his hands. "You thought to give a little payback, right?"

"You would have enjoyed my efforts." Now she would enjoy his.

"We'll save that for another day."

Ray already knew there wouldn't be another day, and that saddened her so much, she had to look away.

"Tell me you want me," Eli whispered.

Ray shook her head. "I already told you."

"Tell me again."

He wanted to trap her somehow. Even though she realized that, Ray still felt the truth closing in on her, choking her. "Go to hell."

Eli grinned. "You're something else, you know that, sweetheart? No, don't start fighting me. If you're not careful, I'm going to think you really want me to let you go."

Ray went still. She drew a deep breath and whispered, "No, don't do that. Not yet. Not tonight."

"Oh, honey. When will you understand?" Eli kissed her again. "I'm never letting you go."

But he would, Ray knew that. Kevin had been her equal in every way, her partner, her life mate.

And he'd walked away because she'd failed him, because he couldn't bear who she was and what she did.

There was no point in debating the issue tonight; it'd only spoil their time together. She watched Eli as his eyes swept over her, lingering on her naked breasts. Then he pressed her hands to the mattress.

"Don't move," he warned. "Promise me."

The man sure demanded a lot of promises. Hesitantly, Ray nodded. Submission wasn't easy for her, but it was incredibly exciting. Her heart beat a mad, fast rhythm with anticipation. Eli released her, waited a moment to make certain she'd obey him, then slipped his fingers into the waistband of her shorts, sliding them over her hips, down the length of her legs, and off her feet. He propped himself up on one arm beside her.

Ray held her breath as he touched her, his gaze following the movement of his hand. He caressed her breasts, thrilling her with the contrast of gentleness and startling aggression.

His fingertips explored her navel, the softness of her inner thighs, the warm, moist heat he'd already predicted would be there. Eli made a sound of satisfaction and murmured, "So wet."

One finger slid deeply inside her. Ray's body clenched, squeezing him until he, too, groaned. When his gaze came back to her face, he was breathing hard. In whispered words, he told her, "I have never seen a woman so devastatingly sexy."

His finger was still inside her, pressing gently, sliding in and out, and his body heat touched all along her side. Sensations, both physical and emotional, bombarded her in tidal proportions. Ray lowered her lashes, embarrassed at such a ridiculous compliment, knowing there was nothing sexy about her. But Eli wouldn't let her hide her feelings from him.

"Look at me, Ray." When she did, he continued as if he knew exactly what she thought, how she felt. "Your body is strong and healthy and silky smooth, just like a woman's should be. I can't imagine any woman more beautiful than you." As he spoke, he removed his finger and began stroking her rhythmically. She tried to counter his movements, tried to alleviate the ache that grew rapidly. Then his thumb came into play, sliding over her clitoris, and Ray couldn't bear the sensual onslaught a moment longer.

She lowered her arms and wrapped them around his neck, pressing her face hard into his shoulder. She shuddered, and the words wouldn't come easily, but she finally managed to whisper, "I think you're beautiful, too." Then she squeezed him tight, her breasts crushed against his chest, and she begged, "Make love to me, Eli. Now. Please."

In the next instant, he raised his hips, shoved his jeans off, and he was over her, pressing into her, holding her to his heart.

And neither of them once considered control.

Eli knew the moment he opened his eyes that she was gone. He stared at the shadowed ceiling, a little tense, a lot frustrated, but not at all surprised.

Or, for that matter, particularly worried. He would find her. And when he did, he'd hustle her sweet ass to a preacher so fast she wouldn't have time to come up with new ways to drive him crazy.

She was so damned unsure of her worth, at least where love was concerned. It amazed him, considering her natural arrogance and pride. But her life hadn't been an easy one. He thought of her parents' deaths, her aunt's cruelty, her work and Kevin's rejection—she couldn't trust in love. Yet. But somehow he'd reach her. He had to.

He was in love with her, of course. Head-over-heels, dropped-on-his-ass, turned-inside-out in love. He hadn't told Ray for the simple reason that she was skittish enough. He could just imagine how she would react to such an excess of emotion.

He smiled, remembering the night before. He had to stay on his toes to second-guess her, to keep from letting her categorize him as a rich milksop with nothing more substantial on his mind than his own pleasures. She would gladly take charge, then accuse him of being inept. She would willingly lead, only to claim he was malleable. She would call the shots, then claim their time together was over. It was herself she tried to convince, and he had no intention of allowing her to do so.

When he thought of making love with her last night—and it had been a joint effort, with no one leading or following—he had to smile. She wasn't selfish. Ray gave as well as took. And she'd been every bit as excited by touching him as she had been by his touches.

His body reacted predictably to those thoughts, and Eli decided it was time to get his plans underway. It probably wouldn't take him more than a week to find her, two at the most. Then he'd make certain to bind her to him, irrevocably. He could hardly wait to begin.

Chapter Eleven

After everything he'd said, his insistence, she'd thought for sure Eli would come after her. But five weeks had gone by without a word. She knew the advantages of the rich, being that they hired her for extravagant amounts of money. If Eli had wanted to find her, he could afford the means.

So, he must not want to.

Not that she should care. After all, she'd run off in the hope of escaping him.

Still, she was . . . *hurt*. How dumb that sounded. A specialized soldier had her feelings hurt. Well, boo hoo. Someone break out the violins.

She had bigger problems than tender emotions, anyway.

She'd gotten knocked up.

Preggo.

In the family way—which was too bizarre for words because she didn't know squat about families and even less about babies. They were small. Messed their pants. Needed a lot of things *she* couldn't give.

She held her head, feeling like her world had just tipped off its axis.

It was disturbing emotionally and physically. She was sick when she shouldn't be, the pregnancy wearing on her like a full day of strenuous work. She slept so much it was pathetic, and she puked even more than that.

The morning sickness had flattened her. According to her doctor, it had hit early. Lucky her. She'd barely been home a week when she'd missed her first period. Soon after that, she'd started barfing for no good reason—and it didn't stop. She remembered the sympathy she'd felt for Jeremy and how she'd bragged that she never got nauseous. That statement had come back to bite her in the butt big-time. And for her, there were no drugs to help. It wouldn't be safe for the baby.

So, among other ailments, she puked. Morning, noon, and night.

She knew herself to be in prime physical shape, but now she felt limp and tired and out of sorts.

And it was all Eli's fault.

Only *he* didn't know it. And she didn't know how to tell him, or if she even should. But not telling him seemed unethical and downright cowardly. And if she had to be bitchy and sick and limp, she could at least not be a coward.

What would he do? She shuddered, unable to imagine his reaction.

Despite feeling like something the cat mauled and then dragged in, she still insisted on going to work. It helped to keep her mind off Eli, and these days, she needed all the help with that she could get. Unfortunately, her current carpentry project was in a diner. She didn't care that it was classier than most, it hit her with the same effect as a greasy spoon.

Though she was working in the back, installing

crown molding and wainscot for their new meeting room, she could smell every single steak, lump of fish, or buttered vegetable that got ordered. She hadn't eaten that morning and still her stomach jumped and pitched and twisted.

She pushed through the discomfort, but by late afternoon she was uncommonly exhausted, and thankfully finished. The sight of half-eaten meals smothered in sauces she couldn't even pronounce had made her shaky.

And she had months to look forward to this?

Groaning and grumbling to herself, she found the manager and had him approve her work. She listened to his praise with only half an ear and a churning belly. He signed off on the job and gave her the remainder of her pay.

After a hasty thank you, Ray headed out. Her head pounded and it was difficult to swallow. She couldn't remember ever feeling so wretched.

Wearing her heavy tool belt, carrying her toolbox with one hand and holding her middle with the other, Ray sluggishly made her way toward the back exit where she'd left her truck. Just as she reached the door, a hand caught her arm.

The hold was gentle, but firm. "Hello, Ray Jean."

Ray froze in midstep, her groan low and heartfelt. She'd recognize that voice anywhere. But it couldn't be. No way. *Not now.*

Cautiously peering over her shoulder, Ray encountered Eli's hard, unwavering golden gaze. Uh-oh. He looked enraged. And wonderful.

God, she'd missed him.

Everything inside her turned upside down and like a volcano, she felt herself erupting. She dropped her toolbox, narrowly missing his foot but too sick to apologize. Covering her mouth, she raced for the rest room. She prayed she'd make it there in time. Humiliation would settle in later; for now all she could think about was getting away and finding some privacy.

Unfortunately, Eli followed hot on her heels.

She shoved the bathroom door open but couldn't shove it closed, not with him in the door frame.

"Get out," she managed to say—then could say no more as she fell to her knees hard in front of the toilet.

Misery washed over her. She'd shoot him. She'd dislocate his shoulder. She'd . . . *oh gawd*, she hated being sick.

At first Eli stood there like a halfwit, then he made several overtures, none of them helpful, and finally cursed. Ray slumped against the toilet, never mind the unsanitary conditions. If she could have moved, she'd have killed Eli.

With a limp hand, she reached up and flushed.

Eli knelt beside her. He caught her shoulders and pulled her against him. "What do you want me to do, honey?"

He smelled good. And felt even better. "Leave."

"Not on your life. No, don't stiffen up. Sit still and I'll get you a cool towel. Maybe that'll help."

He couldn't be that stupid. A cool towel? Yeah, right, that'd fix things right up.

He was back in only moments, handing her several dripping paper towels.

She pushed them away. "I don't . . ."

"Hush, sweetheart. Breathe slowly."

She well remembered his odd combination of gentleness and command. Since she wasn't up to killing him, she did as he told her, and even used the towels to wipe her forehead and mouth. The second she felt more collected, she leaned away from him. Propping her back against the cool tiled wall, Ray glared at him. Her hammer gouged her in the side and the tool belt made an uncomfortable lump against her back. "You could have given me some privacy."

"So you could run off again? I don't think so."

"Did I look like I was up to anything other than tossing up my guts?"

He stared a moment, fought the inevitable smile. "No. You didn't." His words were so soft they sank right into her. "You still look pale as a ghost. What's wrong with you? Flu?"

She couldn't deal with this in a public toilet with her feeling like crapola and him looking as delicious as ever.

Eli's hand touched her chin in a now familiar gesture, and he asked suspiciously, "Ray?"

She struggled to her feet, went to the sink, and rinsed out her mouth.

The heat of his body touched her spine, letting her know he was right behind her. "Ignore me all you want, babe, but I'm not leaving here without you."

"Fine." She used another towel to dry her mouth. "I was ready to go anyway." She avoided looking at him as she headed out.

He carried her toolbox for her, and she was just wasted enough that she let him. They went out the back door. Dressed in a dark green tank top and carpenter jeans, the early summer air felt nice settling over her bare shoulders and warming her face. She took a moment to enjoy the fresh air before fishing her keys out of her front pocket.

Eli took them away from her. "We'll take my truck."

These days, her temper was on a very short fuse. She counted to ten, knew she'd puke again if she starting fighting him, and nodded. "Whatever you say, Eli." There was still a definite bite in her tone.

"Well, now. That's a new attitude. I think I like it."

Ray narrowed her eyes at him as they crossed the parking lot. "Don't press your luck."

"We both know you're not in fighting form, Ray, so give it a rest." Eli opened the passenger door of a shiny black full-sized pickup.

Ray cocked her brow at him. "Pretty fancy."

With a negligent shrug, he said, "It gets me where I'm going." Without her assistance, he unbuckled her tool belt and put it in the back along with her toolbox, then helped Ray inside and closed her door. With the cumbersome belt gone, Ray caught herself resting both hands over her still-flat belly. It was instinctive, a damned maternal gesture or something that she'd been doing ever since finding out about the pregnancy. She quickly jerked her hands away, putting them on the seat beside her hips.

She'd imagined their reunion a hundred times, especially after she first left him, when she'd stupidly allowed herself to think he'd immediately follow her. But as the weeks had passed and she began to think he wouldn't come after all, she tried not to think about him—without much success.

This wasn't how she'd imagined it would be. He was calm and detached, not at all glad to see her. In fact, she wasn't even certain why he'd bothered.

"Is there some reason for this visit, Eli? Or did you just happen to be in the neighborhood?"

He ignored her questions. "Where are we going?"

"I was going home. But without my transportation now . . ."

"I'll go back for your truck later. Where do you live?"

Ray grudgingly gave him directions. She hadn't had an appetite in too long to remember, but the thought of warm tea seemed just the thing to settle her stomach.

Eli didn't say a word when Ray directed him to pull into her driveway. It wasn't exactly a huge house, but it was spacious, a renovated farmhouse with a wide, curving porch and an upstairs balcony. Ray saw her brother's car in the drive and wanted to sink into the floorboards. Since Matt had found out about her pregnancy, he'd been pampering her. Even though they were always considerate of each other, it wasn't something she was used to.

Just as Eli turned off the engine, Matt stepped out of the house. Tall for his age, broad-shouldered but lean, her brother made an impressive sight. He walked down the porch steps and waited, his arms crossed over his chest, for Ray and Eli to get out.

Eli immediately took Ray's arm again. "Company of yours?"

"My brother. Better get prepared for the inquisition. He's a bit on the overprotective side."

"And he let you go into Mataya?"

"He's only eighteen, Eli. I'm thirty-one. Do you really think I'd let anyone, even my brother, tell me what to do?"

"One can always hope."

With that last comment, Eli started forward, towing Ray with him. She tried to give Matt a silent message to mind his own business, but he kept his attention fixed on Eli. He stood in front of the steps, blocking the entrance to the house. Ray saw that Eli was only a tiny bit taller than Matt.

She tried for a casual smile. "Matt, you're home early today."

His gaze flickered to her face, then away again. "I fixed lunch for you. Soup. And before you tell me you're not hungry, remember what the doctor said about keeping up your strength."

Frustration rose the minute Matt mentioned the doctor. Now the questions would start, and she had no doubt he'd done it on purpose. The brat.

Eli stared down at her, one brow raised in honest concern. "You've been to the doctor? Just how sick are you, Ray?"

Matt spoke up. "Oh, she's not exactly sick."

Eli ignored him. "Ray?"

"It's nothing. An upset stomach."

Matt snorted, then reached out to take her arm. "You look like hell, Ray. Come inside and I'll get you some tea. Lunch will be ready in a few minutes."

Neither overbearing male seemed inclined to release her. Eli had one arm and Matt the other. They stared at each other in belligerent silence. Ray, never accused of being a diplomat, tried to think of some way to avoid a clash of wills, when suddenly her stomach settled the problem for her.

"Oh no, not again."

Matt said, "Out of her way," and hurriedly shoved Eli aside.

Ray dashed into the house—and she knew, there'd be no avoiding the truth now.

Appalled, Eli watched as Ray fled away. Again. Seeing her so pale and weak had already scared him. But for her to be this sick . . . He started after her.

Matt stopped him from following. "She'll be all right. But I can guarantee she won't appreciate you chasing on her heels."

"But . . ."

"No one wants an audience for what she's going to do."

Eli grudgingly agreed. "I suppose you're right." Then he started up the steps, saying, "She should be in the damned bed, resting. She had no business going into work." Without waiting for an invitation, Eli entered her home.

Matt didn't object. "She's stubborn."

"No kidding."

Eli looked around with curiosity. The house was sparsely furnished, antiquated and charming. It showed off Ray's considerable talents as a carpenter, just as Buddy had predicted. The house was neat as a pin, finished with crown molding, wooden floors, elaborate trim, and a lot of love.

It showed Ray's softer side—a side she'd probably deny—and he liked that.

Matt pointed to the kitchen. "You can wait in here for Ray. She'll be out in a minute."

"I don't know about that. She's been avoiding me."

"You don't say? And I thought it was the other way around."

"No."

At his one-word denial, Matt relaxed. "She won't avoid you this time. She's too afraid I'll start blabbing if she leaves me alone in here with you."

"Blabbing about what?"

"Not yet." Matt turned away, and Eli followed

him into the large country kitchen where an oval pine table and four chairs sat. The smell of homemade soup filled the air. Eli straddled the chair, watching Matt as he lifted the lid off a large pot on the stove.

"You're Ray's brother?"

"That's right." Matt turned and stuck out his hand. "Matt Vereker. I think I've already figured out who you are."

Eli took Matt's hand. "Is that right?"

"Yeah." His grin was wide and engaging. "You're the brave soul who wants to get closer to Ray. Right?"

"Ray talked about me?"

"Oh yeah. She talked. Didn't really say much though, just gave a few, er, necessary explanations."

"Why do I get the feeling you're trying not to laugh?"

Matt's cough sounded like a snicker. "I'll bet she was plenty surprised to see you after all this time, huh?"

"She shouldn't have been." Eli was already enjoying Ray's brother. He was as forthcoming as Ray, but with a more jovial persona. "I told her I wouldn't let her go."

Ray walked back in and slumped into a chair opposite Eli. The tank top she wore was snug on her breasts, making them appear fuller than Eli remembered. The soft, well-worn carpenter jeans hung on her hips, though, as if she'd lost weight. No matter the changes, she looked so damn good to him. Keeping his hands off her and sitting politely at her table was a challenge.

Matt immediately handed her a cup of hot tea. "Feeling better?"

Ray nodded as she sipped at her tea. Her hair looked lank, her cheeks pale, and Eli wanted to haul her into his lap and kiss her silly.

"You boys been getting acquainted?"

"Sure thing." Matt put his hand on her shoulder, then tilted his head toward Eli. "I was just about to ask what the hell took him so long."

"Matt!"

Matt pressed her back into her chair. "Under the circumstances, it's a damn good question, don't you think?"

Ray tipped her head back to narrow her eyes at her brother. "Don't you start," she said through stiff lips, "or you can just leave the room. Which probably isn't a bad idea, anyway."

Matt gave her a "yeah right" look. "Ain't gonna happen, Ray." He lifted his gaze to Eli. "I'm not sure yet that I trust him. Any guy who would—"

Ray lurched to her feet. "That's enough, Matt."

Confused by the undercurrents and by what wasn't being said, Eli also stood. "If you children can put off this little family squabble for a few minutes, I'd like to talk to Ray. Alone."

Matt again folded his arms over his chest, though now there was no real menace in the act. In fact, he looked highly amused at his sister's agitation. "I need to serve her lunch. She won't eat unless I force her to."

Incredulous, Eli stared at Ray. "She won't eat?" No wonder she looked skinnier. "And here I thought she was a bottomless pit."

"That was before."

Eli looked between brother and sister. One was smiling, one was furious, and the static in the air nearly had his hair standing on end. "Before what?"

Ray threw up her hands. "Well, I can see I'm not needed in this conversation. When you and my nosy brother get everything straightened out, let me know. In the meantime, I think I'll just go take a nap."

Eli drew himself up. "Take a nap?"

Ray didn't bother answering him. She stomped from the room, looking too wrung out and defeated and put upon.

Eli watched her go with a horrible, sinking feeling in the pit of his stomach and a vice around his heart. Had she caught something awful in Mataya? She'd only downed half her tea. She looked weak, didn't argue, and . . . He swung his gaze around to Matt.

"She sleeps a lot these days," Matt explained. "And she's emotional to boot. If I didn't love her so much, I'd probably strangle her."

"Emotional?"

"Yeah." Matt Vereker, a younger, masculine version of Ray, gave an ear-to-ear grin. "Pregnant women are like that, you know."

"Preg—" The bottom dropped out of his stomach. Eli fumbled for the chair behind him, then fell into it hard. His head swam. She wasn't seriously ill. "She's . . . ?"

"If you can't even say it, how the hell do you think Ray feels?"

He shook his head, then said, "Emotional?"

The grin widened. "Very. And sore and tired, and as you already saw, full of morning sickness that doesn't confine itself to the morning." Matt grew serious. "I've never seen her like this. She can deal with anything. She doesn't bat an eyelash when that damn agency contacts her, handles any weapon with ease, and could teach the local law enforcement a thing or two about hand-to-hand combat. But this has laid her low. If you hurt her—"

"I'm going to marry her." Eli shook his head, trying to take it in. "I was going to marry her before I knew, it was just a matter of convincing her. But this ought to help things along."

Matt appeared pleased by Eli's statement, then said, "You don't really know Ray if you think that. And I wasn't kidding about the emotional part. If you thought she was temperamental before, try getting on her nerves now."

Eli waved all that away. With a small, very pleased smile, he whispered in awe, "Pregnant." And then, thinking of how violently ill she'd been, he winced. "Poor Ray."

"Poor *you*. You're the one who put her in this condition, and she remembers that every time she pukes—which is pretty damn often."

"I can handle her."

Matt shook his head, laughing. "She did say you were brave."

Feeling steadier by the moment, Eli came to his feet again, started out of the kitchen, and realized he didn't know which room was hers. Standing at the bottom of the stairs, he shouted, *"Ray,"* loud enough to rattle the windowpanes.

The air seemed to still around him before Ray shouted back, "Stop that damned bellowing," from a door at the top of the stairs.

Eli took the steps two at a time. He couldn't wait to hold her, to tell her how he really felt, to touch her and kiss her and—given she was sick, a lot of that might have to wait. But not all.

He flung her door open, but held onto the knob for support. Knowing Ray would have his baby made his knees weak and expanded every tender, loving thing he felt for her.

Ray stared at him, her expression antagonistic. He remembered what Matt said about this throwing her, and quickly collected himself. She needed his reassurance and support to help her accept the inevitable.

He stepped into the room and quietly closed the door behind him.

Ray sat up and hugged a pillow to her stomach. Still scowling, she said, "You look so damned determined." And then, softly: "I missed that look."

That she'd admit to missing anything about him gave Eli hope. "You're pregnant."

Her chin jutted forward. "Surprise, surprise."

Taking two steps to tower over her, Eli gently grasped her by the upper arms and lifted her from the bed. "When did you plan to tell me, Ray?"

"Tell you? How did you expect me to do that? I don't have your resources. I couldn't track you down, and you sure as hell didn't follow like you said you—"

Despite her scowl, she looked hurt, and Eli decided the questions could wait.

Kissing her could not.

He leaned forward—and Matt swung the door open.

"Here's your tea, Ray."

Eli knew he only wanted to check on his sister, and he admired that. But at the same time Matt spoke, a feral growl sounded, and before Eli could turn to face the snarling threat, he got hit in the backside with a ball of fur brandishing sharp teeth. The dog—Ray's *pet*, he assumed—was latched onto his backside.

Eli lost his balance as he twisted around, but since he still held onto Ray, they both stumbled. The room was filled with sudden curses, barks, and shouted warnings.

And as if the day hadn't held enough surprises, Ray fainted.

Despite the toothy dog clinging tenaciously to the seat of his pants, Eli managed to catch her just before she slid to the carpeting. Matt tried to work himself closer to see Ray's face, and struggled to hold onto the dog's small, stout body at the same time.

Eli's own worry was immense. "Move so I can get her on the bed. And get that damned mutt off my ass."

The dog snarled and jerked and shivered, making Matt's job more difficult.

Very gently, his eyes never leaving her pale face, Eli placed Ray on the soft coverlet. She didn't stir. One small-boned wrist dangled off the side of the mattress, making her look almost frail when Eli knew her to be anything but.

He heard Matt commanding the dog to let loose, but it refused to listen. The stubborn animal swung jerkily back and forth, his teeth deeply snared in the material of Eli's jeans, only narrowly missing actual flesh. It might have been humorous if Eli wasn't so worried about Ray.

Impatiently, he reached back and pried the dog's jaws loose. It yelped in surprise, giving Eli his release. Giving the dog the full force of his intimidating stare, Eli commanded in a stern tone, "*Stay.*"

The dog stilled, perked his ears, whimpered, and then sat. His tongue lolled out and his head tilted to the side. He peered toward Eli, awaiting further instruction.

Matt was amazed. "That dog doesn't obey anyone except Ray. How did you do that?"

Eli bent over Ray, his hand gently cupping her cheek. "I've spent some time with your sister. I had to learn quickly to assert myself."

Matt chuckled, then peered over Eli's shoulder. "I can't believe she keeled over like that. But then, pregnancy does funny things to women. At least, that's what Ray keeps telling me. She's been really weird."

"Has she ever fainted before?"

"Are you kidding? Ray faint?" He snorted. "I shouldn't be surprised, though. She has a terrible time keeping anything down and she doesn't sleep well. She's always tired but still insists on working. And like I said earlier, she's in permanent PMS mode." He leaned back and crossed his arms. "I wouldn't say this if she could hear me, but I think she's afraid."

Eli made no comment to that. To him, Ray lived her life in fear, and the worst fear of all was that someone might know.

He patted Ray's cheek. "Come on, sweetheart. Open your eyes for me."

Ray moaned softly, turning her head away from him. She looked so damned debilitated with her face washed clean of color and dark circles ringing her eyes. Her bloodless lips parted on a sigh and Eli wanted to defend her against the world. He couldn't stop touching her.

As his thumb drifted over her smooth, stubborn chin, her lashes flickered. She blinked vague eyes open. "What happened?"

Matt leaned over her. "You fainted dead away and would have hit the floor except that Eli caught you, even with your dog chewing on his butt."

Eli didn't look at Matt when he said, "You spilled the tea, Matt. Why don't you get her some more?"

Seeing Matt rush from the room without question, Ray frowned. "Don't order my brother around. I don't like it."

"Should I have said please?" Eli smiled gently, and his thumb still drifted over her lips. He'd missed touching her so much. He'd even missed her quarrelsome tone and commanding manner.

Ray raised a shaking hand to her forehead. "That's never happened before." And then, with suspicion: "You're sure I fainted?"

"I sure as hell didn't knock you out, if that's what you're thinking."

She closed her eyes, but said, "Right. As if you could."

Eli sat on the side of the bed. He took Ray's hand, stroked her slender fingers. The dog came bounding past him, and with one less than agile leap, landed square on Ray's chest, making her grunt.

She smiled the sweetest smile Eli had ever seen her bestow, and said to the dog, "Hello, Precious. Were you worried about me?"

Eli shook his head. "Worried?" Then the name she'd used registered and he laughed in disbelief. *"Precious?"*

Ray continued to smile. "That's right. He's a very sweet dog. And he's always trying to protect me."

So, she allowed her dog that privilege, but no one else? "He attacked my backside. What did he think I was going to do? Sit on you?"

Ray glared at Eli. "You didn't scare him, did you?"

"No, I didn't scare him. I'm the one with teeth marks in my ass. And there is absolutely nothing precious about that damned mutt."

"I told you a long time ago that Precious didn't like men."

"Yeah, well, I think Precious and I understand each other well enough now." His gaze went to the dog, and it immediately laid its ears back and whined, then gave a tentative, lopsided doggy grin, complete with lots of tongue and drool. Satisfied, Eli scratched Precious behind his furry ears. "As to my injury, I think I'll survive."

Ray pushed up to her elbows. "I'm sorry."

Eli had the feeling she didn't say that too often, and that she was talking about quite a bit more than just the dog. He traced the dark shadows beneath her left eye with his fingertip. "What's going on, Ray? Why didn't you tell me you were pregnant?"

Hugging the dog, Ray avoided looking at him. "I hadn't heard from you . . ."

"You ran off."

"I know. I had to. But . . . you were so obstinate about things, I sort of expected you to try to follow me. When you didn't, and then I found out I was pregnant, I just wasn't sure what to do." She looked up suddenly. "I would have told you, though. Eventually."

She'd said a lot, and he needed time to wade through all the misconceptions and insecurities without making matters worse. He considered his next words carefully. "You should call the doctor and tell him you fainted. Maybe you need vitamins or something."

Ray gave him a wry grimace. "I'm already taking tons of vitamins. Believe me, I don't need any more. And besides, he'll probably tell me the same things he always tells me."

"And what's that?"

"Every woman reacts differently to pregnancy and every stupid thing that happens is normal. Bear with it and eventually it will go away." She made a disgusted face. "After I give birth, is what he means."

Eli couldn't hide his small smile. "Has it been so horrible, honey?"

"You're damn right, it has. I stay sick all the time, and I'm tired and my boobs hurt and my ankles are swollen and—" She stopped suddenly, her lips compressed as if she'd only then realized how she complained.

He wanted to hold her, to tell her to cry if she needed to. He started to tell her he loved her and would take care of her. But he knew such a sentiment would be abhorrent for Ray, so he quickly changed the subject.

"My grandfather was ill with pneumonia when I got home. It was pretty serious for a while there. I couldn't leave him, but I had people searching for you. The damned agency wouldn't give me a single hint about your location so I had to search every small town in Illinois."

"The agency protects me by keeping things private."

"I understand that. But it wasn't easy. I should have known you'd live in the most inconspicuous place imaginable. I'm not even sure it's on the map."

"You were really looking for me?"

She sounded uncertain, keeping him off guard.

"Isn't that what I just said?" He squeezed her hand. "Lady, I about went nuts when I couldn't find you right away. I went from swearing I was going to make love to you all night, to wanting to lock you in a windowless room so you'd never get away from me again. I may as well tell you, it's still a toss-up."

Ray didn't take that threat seriously. "How's your grandfather now?"

"Anxious for me to bring you home so he can meet the woman who's had me so distracted. It's not something he's used to. There was so damned much to do, tending him, breaking off the business arrangement with Jane, making certain Jeremy was settled. And all I could think about was you."

Ray affected a look of casual interest, though Eli saw through the ruse easily enough. "How did Jane take the news?"

"She still thinks our families should unite." He smiled. "I thought about siccing her on Jeremy, since he's been behaving like such an ass. Would serve them both right."

Ray licked her lips. "You may have jumped the gun here." She didn't meet his gaze, choosing instead to stare at her hands while she petted the dog. "I'm still not interested in a relationship."

It was in Ray's nature to put up one last grandstand. Eli didn't begrudge her the effort, but he had her and he wasn't letting her go. He already knew it, and he imagined Ray did, too.

Matt came back in with a tray. "I brought the tea and the soup. Usually once she eats a bit, it settles her stomach. I think working in that stupid restaurant is what really nauseates her. But she won't listen to me."

"I finished that job today, so quit harping."

"I was thinking about your work," Eli told her,

while moving the dog from her lap. He ignored her incredulous expression when all Precious did was wag his stubby tail in seeming joy, then plop down across Eli's feet.

After Ray scooted up to sit against the headboard, he placed the tray across her legs. "Why don't you teach self-defense or something? You'd be really good at it."

Matt chuckled. "She tried that once."

"Being my brother won't save you, Matt."

Matt just winked at her. "She even worked for the cops. But they kept sending her women to train and the women kept running off in tears. Ray here isn't all that good at tempering her strength or showing any sympathy with broken nails or messed up hair."

Imagining the whole scenario, Eli grinned. "Prissy women, huh?"

"*Regular* women," Matt claimed, "and not up to Ray's intensity." He leaned toward Eli in a conspiratorial way. "She had them all whining and crying within minutes."

"I can see where that might make things difficult."

Ray's expression had gone from embarrassed to annoyed to chagrined. "Why are we congregated in my bedroom? I'm feeling fine now. Let's go downstairs to eat."

Eli and Matt said, "No," at the same time.

"Not until we're certain you won't faint again." Eli handed her a spoon and sat back to wait while she ate her soup.

"I won't faint."

Gently, Eli told her, "I'm not sure that's a promise you can keep, honey."

Ray gave an exasperated sigh at his insistence,

then relented. Eli thought she must surely be exhausted to keep giving up so easily.

He waited until she had a spoonful of soup in her mouth, then said, "I have a suggestion. One for you both to consider."

Matt looked interested, but said nothing. Ray tried to ignore him.

"Come to my ranch with me. Ray can get plenty of fresh air and some much needed rest, and you can both get to know my family. They're dying to meet you."

Ray promptly choked.

Chapter Twelve

Very casually, Eli leaned forward to pat Ray on the back. He pretended not to understand the source of her distress. "Don't gulp your soup, Ray." Then he settled back in his chair and continued. "My grandfather is back home now, and my grandmother and Jeremy, of course. You won't find a place more conducive to rest, and the weather is beautiful this time of year. You could—"

"No."

Eli gave her a level look. "Why not?"

"Because . . . because . . ." She looked at her brother in near desperation. "Matt and I both have jobs. We can't just take off whenever we please."

Quietly, Eli contemplated the problem before giving his attention to Matt. "You're going to college soon?"

"This fall."

He nodded. "The men who work for me make good wages. It isn't easy work, but if you're interested, I can always use another hand. You can put in as many or as few hours as you like. It would be up to you."

Matt flicked a glance at Ray. Again, Eli noted the strong family resemblance between them. They shared the same dark eyes and hair, the same high cheekbones and stubborn chin. But where Ray seemed intensely purposeful most of the time, Matt had a natural geniality about him. Eli imagined Ray had done much to see that Matt maintained that carefree attitude—at her own expense.

Ray put her spoon on her tray. "It doesn't matter if Matt agrees. I still have a job to think about."

Eli hated pushing her when she wasn't up to snuff, but this was too important. "You also have a baby to consider. Look at yourself, Ray. You're exhausted and as pale as your sheets. You need to take care of yourself right now."

"I've always done just that, Eli. On my own. And without your help."

"Agreed. But now you have my baby—*our baby*—to think of, too." He stood next to the bed and looked down at her. "So you'll have my help, whether you want it or not."

"Is that so?"

He leaned down, caging her in with his arms. "I'm not going away, Ray. I don't know what it's going to take to convince you, but whatever it is, I'll find it."

Ray tightened her mouth mutinously. Then she suddenly blurted, "Your brother doesn't like me."

Incredulous, Eli straightened. "For God's sake, he doesn't even know you. I can't believe you'd be offended by anything he said when you knew what he'd just been through. He sure as hell wasn't himself, and your introduction wasn't under the best of circumstances." Eli shook his head. "I want you to marry me, Ray."

Her eyes looked ready to fall out of her head. "Marry you?" The words were little more than a horrified whisper. "But . . . why?"

Eli's thoughts scrambled for credible arguments. "I can help with Matt's college bills."

The color returned to her face in a rush. "We pay our own bills."

"Don't sound so damned offended. As my wife, you and your family would become my concern, so they'd be my bills, too. Matt would have a good job in the summer, and attend college the rest of the time."

"I can take care of Matt on my own."

Matt made a rude sound. "You two make me sound like an infant who needs to be taken care of."

"Speaking of infants, you *are* having my baby."

Her eyes narrowed. "Yeah, at this point, marriage isn't going to change anything."

Exasperated, Eli snapped, "I care about you, damn it."

There were three beats of silence before Ray replied. "You never said so before."

"Hell, Ray, you kept telling me to get lost. I wasn't sure you'd want to hear it."

Matt cleared his throat. "I wouldn't mind going with Eli. You're not the only one who likes to use his hands, you know. I do, too. What he's offering sounds better than working at the mall, which is about the only summer job I could get. And you did say you finished your carpentry job today . . ." At the expression she aimed his way, he rushed to add, "But naturally, it's up to you."

Ray sighed.

"I have to go out for a while," Matt said with sudden decisiveness. "Don't, ah, expect me until late. Okay?" He picked up the dog and started out the door.

"We'll leave early in the morning," Eli called after him. "I'd give you more time, but I need to get back for my grandfather."

Matt nodded.

Scowling, Ray said, "Matt, wait. Nothing's been decided . . ."

He was already gone, the door closed softly behind him. Eli blew out a deep breath. One down, one to go.

The love Ray felt for her brother, the protectiveness, was plain to see, and Eli decided to use that to his advantage. "You should consider Matt before making a decision, Ray. Don't you think he'll feel better knowing you're well taken care of? I saw how he dotes on you. He's worried."

"I know." Ray tilted her head back in frustration, then viciously punched the mattress next to her hip. That didn't appease her and she hit it again, then twice more.

"Feel better?"

"No," she snarled.

Knowing victory was imminent, Eli hid his satisfaction and reseated himself beside her. He removed the tray before she spilled it and took her hands in his, rubbing her knuckles until she relaxed, loosening her fists, then he kissed each palm.

It was time to get serious, and to do some apologizing. "What happened in the hotel . . . it was my fault. I should have thought of protection, but it never occurred to me. And that's strange because I've always been careful."

She shrugged. "Me, too. And it wasn't all your fault. I remember being there, Eli, a willing participant."

Always honest. She pleased him so damn much. "Very willing. But that doesn't excuse me. At the time, all I could think of was showing you how much I cared." He touched her cheek. "I really do, you know."

Ray shied away from his declaration. "Here I thought maybe it was the comfort of a real bed."

"With you, I'm finding time and place doesn't matter. In the jungle, that ratty little hut out in the middle of nowhere, it all seemed . . . I don't know. Surreal." He would have said magical, beautiful, incredible—but he didn't want to push her more than he already had. "At the hotel, I already knew you were planning to skip out on me. I felt it."

Ray looked uncomfortable at that. "You're too damned astute." And she grumbled, "I'm sorry."

He acknowledged that with a nod. "I'd like to make love to you in my bed, without worrying about bats or guerillas. I'd like to love you knowing you'll still be there in the morning, that you don't want to leave."

Her bottom lip started to quiver, totally unmanning him. "Ray." He scooted closer to her on the bed, pulled her into his side. "Honey, I know it's a little late to be asking you this, but how do you feel about having the baby?"

Her throat worked as she swallowed. She shook her head.

He frowned over her distressed expression. "I don't know what that means, babe. Talk to me."

She looked up at him. "What do I know about having babies or being a parent? I scare grown men, Eli. Matt wasn't joking about those women running off in tears just because I tried to instruct them. Can you imagine what I'd do to a kid?"

Eli felt caught between a laugh and suffocating tenderness. He pulled Ray into a hug, rocking her. "Everything will be all right, Ray. Trust me."

"You don't understand." Her voice was shaky and self-derisive. "Look at me, Eli. I'm a thirty-one-year-old part-time mercenary and carpenter. What a joke."

"You're a beautiful, sensitive woman."

Her laugh was raw, heartbreaking. "I don't have anything to teach a kid except how to protect himself and how to survive, and given a choice, I don't want *any* kid to have to worry about stuff like that."

Eli squeezed her tighter. "Those are important things to learn. But you're wrong when you say that's all you know." He caught her chin and brought her face up to his. "You know honesty and honor, pride, integrity, and the value of hard work. You, Ray Vereker, are going to be an excellent mother."

Ray blinked at him before laughing. "Did you fall off another planet, Eli? Because you sure as hell don't have your feet planted firmly in this one. And you don't talk like a rich man, either. What's all this about hard work? I thought your type disdained that sort of thing."

"One of these days, you're going to really piss me off, Ray, do you know that?" Though he knew she resorted to insults to distance herself, it still bothered him. He stood to pace restlessly around the room, finally stopping before a high window. Keeping his back to Ray, he said, "There are a few things you don't know about me. Since you'll soon be my wife and the mother of my child, maybe it's time you did."

She scooted up higher in the bed. "I didn't agree to the wife part, but I'm all ears."

Eli turned to face her. "I'll make this as short and uncomplicated as I can."

"I'm not going anywhere."

"I never knew my father, Ray." She didn't look shocked or judgmental, just curious. "He married my mother against my grandfather's wishes, and they ran off together. My grandparents still loved him, but they'd argued and . . . he became estranged from the family." Eli shoved his hands into his pockets and starting pacing again. He hated rehashing old news, and if Ray hadn't persisted in trying to make him out as some wealthy snob, he might not have told her. At least, not yet. "My mother hadn't counted on that because, just as my grandfather predicted, she'd married him for his money, not out of love. It didn't take my father long to realize my grandfather was right. She was . . . immoral, to say the least."

"How so?"

Eli shook his head and stared beyond her. "They divorced and my father went home, *before* my mother told him about me."

She straightened in the bed. "Eli, I swear, I would have told you—"

He smiled to reassure her. "You're nothing like her, Ray, I know that. You would never use a baby. But I can remember my mother laughing about it, saying she'd duped him and that soon she'd cash in. She said I'd take my rightful place in the family and there wasn't anything they could do about it. She made no bones about the fact that I'd be a pawn. Hell, she loved it."

"That's awful." She placed her hands protectively over her belly, and it pleased him. "So did she finally introduce you to your family?"

"I don't think she quite had the nerve. Whenever

she drank she'd make plans, but when she sobered up, she wouldn't mention it."

"She was an alcoholic?"

Inside his pockets, where it wouldn't show, Eli's hands curled into fists. "She wasn't really a drunk so much as a partier. I can remember one man after another trooping through. We lived with some of them, sometimes we lived in trailers, and once at a women's shelter."

"But Jeremy . . . ?"

"Is my half brother. My father remarried and they had Jeremy and were very happy together, from what I've been told. They died in a car wreck before I could ever meet them."

"Then you must have introduced yourself to your grandparents on your own." She gave Eli a look of admiration. "That had to be tough."

He laughed with self-derision. "It wasn't like that, honey. When I contacted them, it was with the intent of using them, just as my mother had always planned. You see, she'd long since washed her hands of me. She disappeared completely when I was seventeen. I just . . . I came home one day and she was gone. Not that I should have been surprised. She told me she'd leave if I didn't stay out of trouble."

Softly, Ray asked, "And you didn't?"

"Hell, no. If anything, it seemed I got worse, until finally I was arrested for hurting a guy during a brawl. I spent two days in county jail because I didn't have anyone to call or any way to make bail." His eyes searched her face, looking for some sign of what she thought, how she took his news.

"Why'd you hurt him?"

"Who?"

"The guy in the brawl."

"Oh." Eli didn't know why it mattered to her, but he said, "He was drunk and a bully and he was picking on this skinny little guy—"

Ray grinned. "I see. So you called your grandfather?"

"Not exactly. I'd been in trouble before with juvenile authorities, mostly just pranks, but I knew this time it would probably be bad. I decided I had nothing to lose, so I tried looking up my father."

Ray leaned forward on the bed, curling her legs beneath her and listening intently to Eli. "What happened?"

"My grandfather showed up instead. And let me tell you something about Granddad, no one uses him." Eli relaxed with that memory, smiling with genuine affection. "He took one look at me, saw a family resemblance, and claimed me as a Connors."

Ray nodded. "Smart man."

"So damn smart, it's scary. His bones are weaker now, but his mind is still razor sharp." He settled his most somber gaze on Ray. "You think my grandfather must be a snob because he's wealthy. But he went through the Depression a poor man. Everything he has, he earned the old-fashioned way—by nearly working himself into the grave. He's a self-made man and even though his attitudes tend to be hard in some ways, he's always fair."

"Was he hard on you?"

Grinning, Eli said, "He was a mean son of a bitch at first, but then so was I, and we fought all the time. He didn't put up with anything. Before I knew it I was sitting at a table for three meals a day, because Granddad said my grandmother expected it and he wouldn't let me disappoint her. When I wasn't in school, he had me working by his side at the ranch until I was so exhausted, I didn't have the energy to get into trouble. He also bought me my first horse, and my first car."

"Something fancy?"

He laughed. "A beat-up trap that we had to work on together. But by the time we finished, it looked and ran great. It got me through college, and when I graduated with honors, just to prove to him that I could, he told me how proud he was of me. I'd never heard that kind of praise in my whole life. The next year, after I'd trained in the business, he gave me responsibility and trust." Eli's jaw flexed as he remembered the swell of emotions he'd suffered that day. "He gave me his business to run."

Ray nodded. "I think I like your grandfather already."

Her comment helped him to shake off the memories. "He said the same thing about you when I told him about the piranha."

"You didn't," she protested. But she was laughing.

"It's been tough on Jeremy. He lost his parents when he was little more than a baby and then I showed up and stole half his grandparents' attention. I hope you'll give him some time."

"To do what?"

"To get to know you like I do."

"You don't really know me." As if admitting a grave sin, she said, "I screw up sometimes. I make big mistakes and I fail at things."

He shrugged. "You're human. It happens." Ray frowned in thought. "What?" He bent to capture her gaze. "Come on, Ray. Tell me what you're thinking."

"Why me? That's what I can't understand, Eli.

Despite everything you just said, you know good and well it won't be easy between us, especially on me. I won't fit comfortably into your life, so why don't you look somewhere else for a wife?"

Eli sat beside her on the bed. "I'm thirty-three years old, I haven't been a monk, but I've never met a woman I enjoyed as much as you. You make me proud, Ray, with all you've accomplished and all you can do. Not many people, man or woman, can claim your talents. You also make me laugh and you sure as hell make me hot. I like talking to you, holding you, and the sex is phenomenal." He stopped to smile. "Far as I can tell, your biggest complaint about me is my money."

She was still frowning over his straightforward compliments, but said, "Not just money, Eli. You're rich."

"Yeah. But you know, a wise woman once told me there was a big difference between people born with money and those that acquired it on their own. My father and Jeremy are the only Connors men able to take wealth for granted. And as for me, well, I think I fall somewhere in the middle."

"You've been rich a long time."

"I wasn't born that way. And though a lot of it was given to me, I've made quite a bit since starting to work with my grandfather all those years ago. I didn't have to create the opportunity, but I've definitely taken advantage of it. And I work damned hard to make everything run smoothly, for myself, for my grandparents, and for Jeremy. If that makes me a bad person, Ray, then so be it. But it doesn't change how I feel about you. And if you're honest, you'll admit you care about me, too."

She lowered her head. "I used to think about marriage. Even about babies."

Eli's heart beat faster. "Yeah?"

"A long time ago, when I was a different person. Young and stupid."

"You were never dumb, Ray."

She drew a careful breath. "When I was a kid, when my folks were still alive, I had all the same silly dreams most girls have. Then things changed, and I found out I'm different."

"Wonderfully different."

She didn't look up. "I had a partner once. I was crazy about him. I'd have *died* for him. But . . ." She shook her head. "I let him down."

The words sliced into Eli. "No, Ray. You did the best you could, and if things didn't work out, then no one was to blame."

She didn't realize he knew the story. She thought he was just speaking in generalities. Her gaze met his, somber and distant and so damn sad. "Don't you see, Eli. I disappointed a man who was so much like me, a man who knew what to expect from me. I tried, but I couldn't . . ." She bit her lips hard before continuing. "With you it'd be even harder. The things you'd need from me, I can't give, and I'd end up disappointing you, too."

Rage burned in his gut. "Just what the hell do you think I'll want you to do?"

"Dinner parties? Society events? I don't even know, because I don't know your world. I used to think I did, but now I'm not so sure."

Eli came to his feet. "I never thought I'd say this, but you're being a coward."

Her mouth tightened.

"You refuse to even try because you're afraid of

failing. Come to the ranch with me, see what it's like, then decide. Who knows, maybe I'll surprise you. If you don't want to stay, we'll work something else out. But that's not too much to ask, not of you, not of a mercenary who faces down armed guerillas, and not from the woman who's carrying my baby."

Eli held his breath, waiting to see what she would say. Regardless, he wouldn't give up on her. He couldn't. He'd never wanted anything as badly as he wanted Ray Vereker and the baby she carried.

She sighed. "I'm feeling better. And I'm starved. You want to go downstairs with me and have some soup? This bowl's gotten cold already. Matt makes great soup."

Lunch wasn't really the first thing on his mind. "You'll come to the ranch with me?"

She was already leaving the bed, her face not quite so pale now. "I'll go—for a while. And then we'll see. I'm not making any promises about marriage, though."

Eli was content with the bargain. Small steps, he told himself. Ray's life had been very unique and trying. He couldn't expect to change everything, certainly not her insecurities, overnight. "We'll leave tomorrow. First thing."

"Maybe. I have to make some arrangements first."

Her back was to him as he followed her out the door, so she couldn't see his wide grin of triumph. He even picked up her dog on his way down the steps, rubbing the shaggy little rat behind his furry ears. Precious growled deliriously, appreciating his touch but apparently not willing to let Eli know it.

He thought the dog and Ray shared some definite similarities.

"Soup sounds great."

Ray glanced over her shoulder at him, her eyes questioning.

"But after lunch, I intend to strip you naked, shower with you, then put you back to bed."

Ray shivered. "You know, I think I feel another faint coming on."

Eli chuckled as he slipped his arm around her waist. "Don't worry. I promise I'll revive you so you don't miss a thing." Then he kissed her brow. "Trust me."

Ray groaned as Eli pressed small, gentle kisses onto her belly. "I can hardly believe you're pregnant." He covered her with his hand, his fingertips touching her hipbones. "You're still so slim."

Ray arched into his palm. "I'll be fat as a cow soon enough."

Eli lifted his head to smile at her. "The idea of you all round and womanly with my baby makes me hot."

"That's no test. *Everything* makes you hot." She started to laugh, then groaned instead as Eli very gently and very slowly slid his finger deep inside her. He was being especially careful with her and it drove Ray nuts. "I'm not in a good frame of mine, Eli. You shouldn't play with me."

"I don't want to hurt you, Ray."

She curled her hand around his head, her fingers tangling in his soft brown hair. "You would never hurt me."

His gaze shot to hers, smoldering hot. "You believe that now?"

She nodded. He would never deliberately hurt her, but that didn't mean he could control the future, or shield her from the rest of his family. Regardless of what he said, Ray still couldn't imagine any family, rich or poor, taking her in stride. Even the people who didn't know her well—her neighbors, teachers at her brother's school—gave her a wide berth and watched her with the same caution they'd give a wild animal.

She used to do her best to fit in; now she just got by and took what pleasure in her life that she could. Eli was pleasure personified—so should she take him at his word?

Eli forced her mind from that train of thought when he nuzzled against her breast. She gasped, and he asked quietly, with great interest, "Are you tender already?"

He hadn't stopped touching her to ask that question, hadn't slowed the gentle, rhythmic thrusting of his finger, so Ray was only able to nod. But Eli was satisfied with her answer. He suckled her with gentle care, drawing her nipple deep into the heat of his mouth and very lightly stroking her with his tongue.

It was an exquisite torture, and her tolerance was excessively low these days. Ray decided she'd had enough. With little effort, taking Eli by surprise, she switched their positions. She might be pregnant, but she was no slacker.

Eli found himself flat on his back. Ray straddled his upper thighs, captured his hot, hard erection in her hands, and grinned wickedly as she felt him flex in excitement. "Let's see how you like being tormented, Eli."

"I wasn't tormenting you," he started to object, but ended by groaning loudly. Ray stroked him, smoothed her fingers over the tip of him, and then leaned forward to kiss his hard, hair-roughened belly, much as he had done to her.

"There's something you need to understand right now, Eli Connors. You're not always going to be in charge in the sack." She made that statement between careful nibbles on his hip, her fingers wrapped firmly around his pulsing cock, stroking, enticing. He strained against her. "I've let you have your way most of the time, but right now I'm not feeling so generous."

Eli caught her shoulders and pulled her higher so that she was poised just above him, her thighs open and vulnerable over his pelvis, her breasts within reach of his mouth. He raised his hips and slowly began to enter her.

"Honey, you can be in charge whenever you want," he rasped, holding her tightly.

Ray almost laughed, since Eli was again taking over. But as he filled her, lifting his head at the same time to cautiously capture a tender nipple, she decided she didn't mind at all.

Ray braced her hands on his tense shoulders, tightened her thighs on his hips, then thrust herself down, taking his length completely. The pregnancy had made her more sensitive and she yelled with the pleasure of it.

Eli's fingers dug into her soft buttocks as he held her steady for his accelerated thrusts. And Ray, smiling in satisfaction, let him have his way.

"I hope Matt doesn't get lost." She would have preferred for them all to leave together, but that hadn't been possible, not with Eli rushing, and Matt insistent on telling his friends good-bye.

"I gave him detailed instructions, Ray. He seems like a real levelheaded kid, so have a little faith, will you? He and Precious will make it in one piece."

"How much farther do we have to go?" It already seemed like they'd been on the road forever.

Eli shrugged. "A couple of hours. Why? Do you need another break?"

"No, but I can't blame you for asking. Being pregnant has done strange things to me. I swear I have a bladder the size of a titmouse."

Eli laughed as he reached over and squeezed her knee. "I don't mind stopping, honey, as long as you don't overdo. You're finally starting to look like yourself again. I don't mind telling you now, I almost suffered shock when I saw you at that restaurant."

"Most people have to work, Eli."

"Don't get defensive. That isn't what I meant at all. It's just that I'm used to seeing you carry a weapon, not a tool belt that probably weighs more than you do."

She punched him in the arm, earning a grin.

"And then your brother goes and tells me I'm to be a father." He shook his head. "It's a damned good thing I have a strong constitution, or you two would have been picking me up off the floor. Mortal men can only take so much."

It seemed to Ray that Eli had accepted the pregnancy much easier than she had. Of course, he wasn't the one suffering the side effects. "You're okay with the whole thing?"

His voice softened. "Are you kidding? I'm thrilled. I've already been imagining what he'll look like."

"He?" And just to be contrary, she asked, "What if it's a girl?"

"Then I hope she looks exactly like her mother."

If she had her way, her baby wouldn't have a single similarity to her. She wanted this child to be happy—she just didn't know if it was possible, not with her as the mother. "Does your family know you're bringing me back?"

"They knew that was my intention. My grandfather wished me luck."

Be careful what you wish for. "And Jeremy?"

"Try to be understanding with him, Ray. He's always had to be my little brother. There's a fourteen-year difference in our ages. When I showed up, Jeremy was only four years old and very used to being the center of everyone's attention. Even though Jeremy's always treated me exactly like a brother, I think it bothers him that I'm only his half brother, and yet everything that should have been rightfully his by birth has been handed to me. Until Jeremy finishes college, he's dependent on me and the company."

Ray scowled. "Nothing was handed to you. You worked hard for what you have. The fact that your father didn't marry your mother shouldn't have anything to do with it."

Eli laughed. "You don't have to defend me, honey. No one treats me like an outsider, least of all Jeremy. But it can't be easy for him being so much younger. He's forever trying to prove himself."

"And never quite measuring up?"

Eli shrugged. "I have a lot of years and experience over him."

"Not to mention a different background?" Ray

shook her head. "You know, Eli, I don't think being born rich or having things given to you is necessarily a favor."

"But our baby will have advantages, Ray. Things you didn't have. It'll be up to us to teach him about hard work, about earning and then appreciating what you get."

It'll be up to us . . . Ray squeezed her eyes shut on that daunting thought. She'd be responsible for a person, not just for a short time, but from birth on. This wouldn't be like crawling through a bug-infested swamp, or climbing barbed wire. It wasn't something she could resolve with a few well-placed hits.

This was important—and she could really screw it up.

"You look more like yourself now."

Ray jumped, then wanted to curse herself. "What do you mean?"

"Your color is back. You don't look so exhausted."

"Oh." Eli was so good at reading her thoughts, she often felt exposed, and wary. "It's a beautiful day, and for once my stomach is at peace. Probably because of all this fresh air."

"And here I thought it was me."

"You?"

Eli nodded, dead serious. "You've been worried, thinking about the future and how to handle raising a baby on your own. Now you know you don't have to. I'll be with you every step of the way."

He had read her thoughts! "Now you're the cure for morning sickness? Well hell, Eli, we'll neither one need to work. We'll make a fortune just passing you around to all the preggo ladies."

He didn't mind her teasing. "I'm only saying that you're more comfortable with me near."

True. With Eli's return, a bubble of happiness had slowly expanded inside her. At first, she'd tried to call it nerves, annoyance, but she knew deep down what it really was. And that forced her to accept how miserable she'd been without him. *Unacceptable.*

"Your ego knows no bounds, Eli."

"At least admit you missed me."

The smile came without her permission. "I did."

"Just a little?"

Her voice softened, as did her heart. "Actually . . . a lot." Eli looked so pleased by her admission, she was glad she'd given it to him.

Nothing had really been settled yet, but Eli was here, claiming he'd stick around. She didn't have to worry about being a bad mother, because she knew instinctively that Eli would be one hell of a dad.

Exhaustion pulled at her, and Ray settled back to take a small nap. She didn't feel nearly as self-conscious with the weakness as she thought she would, probably because Eli was so matter-of-fact about it. He didn't see it as a weakness, just the natural course of her pregnancy. His easy acceptance of her body's changes helped her to accept them, too. And that did make her stomach feel more settled.

At the subtle shake of her shoulder, she jerked awake with a start. She was so sluggish, she knew she'd been totally out. "What?"

"Time to get up, sleepyhead."

Ray stretched. Had Eli driven all that way without her company? God, she hoped she hadn't snored. He came around to her side of the truck and opened the door.

She rubbed the sleep from her eyes, stepped

out, and blurted, "I thought we were going to your home."

"This is it."

No. She looked around at the expansive yard, the white fences, and the enormous two-story building. It had to be a hotel. "How many bedrooms?"

"Ray . . ."

"How many?"

"Eight, and before you ask, there are five private baths. Which only means you'll be comfortable."

No, it meant she'd get lost trying to find her way around. She stepped away from the truck, staring around herself in shock. Behind the house were several more buildings—two enormous wooden barns, one with ten stall doors and one with twelve doors. There was a smaller shed, a sixty-foot round pen with six-foot sides, and a walk-through gate. More training areas, another building with an enormous loft, and a black walnut grove helped fill the landscape.

The house had two stories, each with a beautiful railed balcony and an abundance of sparkling windows. Stately oaks flanked each side with lush, mature landscaping, shrubs and flowers everywhere. The white brick with black shutters and shingles looked very elegant. The double front door was an aged oak with elaborately leaded sidelights and transom. Breathtaking.

And intimidating.

And now . . . open.

"Ah, here're my grandparents."

Ray held her breath as two elderly people emerged, the man dressed in a flannel shirt despite the heat, with suspenders and using a cane, the woman wiping her hands on a snowy, starched apron. They paused there in the sunlight.

It was like a fricking Norman Rockwell painting, complete with the homey feeling.

Shading his eyes, Eli's grandfather visually raked Ray from head to toe, then scowled ferociously at Eli.

Her old nausea returned in one staggering wave. Ray clamped her hand over her mouth, but didn't know where to go.

"Hold on." Eli grabbed her arm and hustled her up the porch steps so fast that his grandparents had to scurry to get out of the way. Belatedly, he shouted, "Excuse us, please," and Ray barely heard a woman's softly spoken, "Oh my," before Eli dumped her into a small guest bathroom. She fell to her knees before the toilet, hung her head, and quickly prayed for some way to disappear.

"I'll be right outside the door," Eli told her, giving her the privacy she badly needed.

Some minutes later, when Ray finally quit heaving, she crawled up to the cream-colored porcelain sink, splashed her face, and rinsed her mouth, then looked around for a way to escape. She did not want to face those old people again.

Unfortunately, the only window was octagonal cut glass, meant to let light in, not to let mercenaries out.

Eli tapped at the door. "Ray? Are you all right?"

Just dandy. "Unfortunately, it looks like I'll live."

She could hear Eli's smile when he said through the door, "That bad, huh?" Then the door opened a crack and Eli dared to show himself. "Come on out and I'll get you some tea."

Ray groaned and sank back against the sink.

"No way. I can't imagine what your grandparents think."

Ray's eyes flared and her spine stiffened when a female voice, cool and commanding, said from behind Eli, "They think Eli hasn't told them quite everything."

"Uh-oh," Ray whispered. "The fat's in the fire now." She would rather have faced a legion of guards in Central America than go through an inquisition with Eli's grandparents.

Eli laughed, caught her arm, and towed her out. "I wasn't given a chance, Gram. I didn't know until I found her, and there wasn't time to call. I was in a hurry to get home."

"To check up on me, you mean," came a grouchy male voice.

"It's a nasty job," Eli teased, "but someone has to keep you in line."

Ray stared. Up close, she could see that Eli's grandfather had enough eyebrow hair for three men. Deep, permanent creases left him in a perpetual scowl, and his watery brown eyes were direct and mean. But he stood straight and proud, and as Ray took in the sight of him, he thumped his cane on the floor, making her jump.

Eli rubbed the back of her neck. "If you're feeling okay now, I'll finish my introductions."

Ray nodded. No way in hell could she smile, but she did square her shoulders and lift her chin.

"Granddad, Gram, this is Ray Vereker. Ray, my grandparents, Hank and Lily."

"How far along are you, girl?" Hank demanded in a tone that brooked no arguments.

That particular tone prodded Ray. She narrowed her eyes and said, "I'm not a girl."

Lily smiled. "Obviously not, since you're carrying a baby. Still, we would like to know when to expect the birth."

Ray didn't know what to think. Eli stood there grinning like a half-wit, his hand still firm on her shoulder, and his grandparents were watching her expectantly. Grumbling, she admitted, "I'm about five weeks along."

Hank groaned, making her expect the worse. Maybe now he'd throw her out, or question her character.

Instead, he said, "That's not very far along at all. I may not make it another eight months!"

Taken aback, Ray said, "Uh . . ."

Eli shook his head. "She can't make the baby come any earlier, so stop trying to make her feel guilty."

Lily shushed both men. "Can't you two see she's ill? She needs to sit down, for heaven's sake, and she needs something to eat."

Ray's stomach gave a violent lurch at the thought of food. "No, thank you. I'm not hungry."

"Nonsense. You should nibble on dry toast or crackers whenever you feel queasy. It really helps to settle your stomach." Lily spoke with absolute conviction and confidence. "And you should concentrate on getting a lot of small, fresh meals, rather than three large ones. I can help with that. In a month or so, the sickness will probably be gone completely."

Ray's heart picked up speed. "Really?" This was more information than she'd ever gotten from her condescending doctor. That fool had acted like her pregnancy was a crime against nature. She would have stopped going to him—but that would mean breaking in a new doctor, and she had no time for that.

If Lily spoke the truth, she could handle a month. It was the thought of being sick for the rest of her pregnancy that beat her down.

Lily took her arm. "The time will fly by," she predicted. "I'll show you to the kitchen, since Eli doesn't seem capable of doing anything but grinning. We'll have you chipper in no time."

Chipper? Not likely. That wasn't a word that had ever been applied to her.

Still, she went along willingly. Lily offered her some bread and sharp cheese, and a cup of hot, sweet tea. It didn't sound particularly appetizing at first, but once she started, Ray ate every bite. And a moment later, she did feel much better.

Lily chatted at her while she ate, and the woman was constant motion. She'd no sooner sit down than she'd be up again to refill a cup, to offer more food, or just to fuss around. She cleaned the countertop at least three times, even though it was already clean. And she'd look out the kitchen window at a bird or a squirrel and smile.

Ray liked her. Before getting pregnant, she had detested idle time, too, so she could relate. "Your house is incredible."

"Thank you." Lily beamed. "It's seen its share of repairs and additions, but we've been here forever. I can't imagine any place else being home."

Ray nodded. Instead of being the mansion she'd envisioned, it was the kind of home every young girl dreamed about. It was homey, warm, and well lived in. There was a mudroom off the kitchen, and on the floor sat several pairs of scuffed, dirty cowboy boots. Rain slickers and windbreakers covered hooks on a wall, and there were shelves lined with fresh canned goods.

Lily was telling Ray about the time the creek flooded when Lily noticed her yawning. It was only four o'clock, but to Ray, it felt much later.

"You go up and take a nap. Getting plenty of rest early on is important. I remember I slept away the first three months of each of my pregnancies."

Ray didn't want to go to bed. "How many children did you have?"

"Only two. Eli's father, who sadly enough died some time ago in an automobile accident on the freeway, and a daughter, Jessica, who lives in California now with her husband."

"Do you have other grandchildren, then?"

"Oh, no. Jessica can't have children, though they did try for several years. And since Eli hadn't seemed particularly interested in any one woman, we'd about given up hope of enjoying any babies. You can understand why we're so pleased the two of you will be getting married and giving us a great-grandchild."

Eli chose that propitious moment to saunter into the kitchen. His eyes held Ray's as he said slowly and grievously, "The marriage part is still up in the air, Gram."

Hank, who had followed on his heels, was instantly enraged. "What the hell do you mean, up in the air? You got her pregnant and you're still dodging marriage?"

"Actually," Eli said, his eyes glinting with humor, "I'm not the one doing the dodging. It's Ray who refuses to say yes."

All eyes turned to Ray, and for the first time in a very long time, she felt herself blush. When she got him alone, Eli was dead meat. But until then, she didn't think his grandfather would appreciate a display of her combat abilities. And though she hated to admit it, she didn't want these gentle, loving people to know the truth about her.

At her venomous look, Eli told them, "Ray didn't think you would like her because she doesn't have a ton of money."

Ray sputtered.

"She also happens to be very independent and self-sufficient." Eli reached over and smoothed a knuckle over Ray's cheek. "She thought she'd have a hard time fitting in."

Ray was overwhelmed by the response that comment generated. Hank and Lily both rushed to reassure her. They wanted her to stay—but then, they didn't know what they were asking.

She hated deceiving them, allowing them to believe that she and Eli would make a nice little family. She hated letting them think she was an average woman with maternal skills.

Hank gave her another glare, and Ray decided it was simply his normal expression. "Where else would you go with my great-grandchild, I'd like to know?"

"It's not that easy," Ray admitted.

"You're pregnant and Eli's the father. Sounds pretty easy to me."

Eli grinned at her. He must have known the reception she'd get—and how starved she was for acceptance. She'd given up dreams of her own family a long time ago.

At that moment, the kitchen door opened. Jeremy stood there, his hands planted on his hips, his face stony. His smile was not a pleasant thing. "Well, if it isn't Ray Vereker. Who needs rescuing this time?"

"Jeremy." Ray pushed back her chair and came to her feet.

He looked her over. "Hey, you're dressed this time. But still wearing boots, I see. Army boots?"

Eli started to step forward, but Ray put her hand on his sleeve. She and Jeremy had to come to terms sooner or later. By the looks of it, he wanted it sooner—like now. "They're not military issue, no."

"You packing any weapons?" He grinned. "Got an Uzi hidden up your pants leg? Maybe a machete?"

He was full of the beans today, Ray noted. And he did look better, healthier than last time. Strange, but she kind of preferred him snoring.

She took a step toward him, her own smile a threat, and flexed her hands. "I don't need a weapon, remember?"

Alarm skittered across his features until Ray laughed, then his expression darkened and he turned to his grandparents. "Is she here looking for more money?"

Eli put his arm around Ray and said, "More? She never got paid the first time."

Ray shook her head. She'd taken off that night without the money they'd originally agreed on. To her mind, nothing had gone as planned, and she'd broken so many of her own rules she didn't deserve pay. As far as she was concerned, nothing had changed on that score. "I don't want it."

"Buddy might."

She lifted her chin. "I paid him out of my own account."

"Ray." Eli's tone was chastising but not really annoyed. "That won't do and you know it."

"What's all this about pay?" Hank demanded.

"She's a hired killer," Jeremy accused.

Ray felt her stomach sink. She could have truthfully denied the killer part, but said calmly instead, "I prefer the term 'mercenary.' "

Hank and Lily went wide-eyed.

"Whatever you call it," Jeremy said, "it doesn't change who you are."

"No," Ray agreed, "it doesn't."

That admission didn't appease Jeremy. "You still live and fight like a man."

"Better than a man, actually." In for a penny . . . "Which is how I saved your sorry butt."

"Saved me?" Jeremy laughed. "Yeah, right. You knew the guys who took me, and it was your friend who poisoned me." He shook his head, his look calculating. "I've thought about it, and I'm not so sure you weren't in on the kidnapping all along."

Chapter Thirteen

Eli immediately stepped in front of Ray, blocking her with his body. He could feel her tension, and he already knew her mood was volatile, thanks to the added pressures of impending motherhood. No telling what she might do.

His grandfather seemed genuinely annoyed now with the way things were going. "I don't know what all this is about mercenaries and money, but do you really think you have to protect her from your own brother?"

"Protect Ray?" Eli laughed. "Actually, I was hoping to protect Jeremy. He doesn't seem to have too much sense these days."

To his relief, Ray sighed. "For God's sake, Eli. I won't hurt your baby brother. I already told you he wasn't worth the effort."

Eli wasn't quite convinced. He turned slightly to confront her.

And almost missed Matt's arrival.

Chaos exploded as Matt stepped in carrying a large load. He "accidentally" rammed into Jeremy, sending him into a sprawl across the hardwood floor, and seconds later Precious was on him, grabbing him by the hem of his shirt and jerking about ferociously in a maddened frenzy. Matt raised one brow and said politely, "Oh. Excuse me. I didn't see you standing there."

Eli supposed Matt had overheard Jeremy's opinion of Ray. He reached down and snatched up Precious, patting the dog absently until it wagged his tail and licked Eli's face.

"Gram, Granddad, this is Ray's brother, Matt."

Jeremy scrambled to his feet, a little astounded by that disclosure.

Ray asked her brother, "What took you so long? With as many stops as Eli insisted we make, I thought you'd get here before us."

"I had a few errands of my own to attend to," he explained.

The look on Matt's face amused Eli. "Women?"

"Yeah. They're so sad to see me go." He grinned shamefully, and Eli couldn't help but chuckle.

Jeremy asked suddenly, "What the hell's going on?"

Eli narrowed his gaze on his brother. "Matt and Ray are going to be staying here awhile."

"Why?"

"Because I'm going to marry her."

This time it was Ray who interrupted. "That's far from a done deal, Eli, and you know it."

Eli sighed in vexation. Turning to Ray, he said, "You will marry me, Ray."

She folded her arms over her chest. "I don't think I feel particularly convinced your family wants me here. That was the purpose of this little visit, wasn't it?"

Eli scowled, and without taking his eyes from Ray's face, he said, "Granddad, do you want her here?"

"Damn right. I won't have my great-grandchild anywhere else."

Ray looked startled at the certainty of his response. She'd probably thought Jeremy's disclosures would have changed things. She just didn't know his grandmother.

"Gram?"

"Well, of course she's welcome," Lily muttered. Then she added, "And her brother, too."

All eyes turned to Jeremy. His face was red with anger and he remained stubbornly silent.

Ray shoved past him. "Come on, Matt. I'll help you carry your stuff in."

"Does that mean you'll stay?" Lily asked.

Ray threw a warning glare at Eli. "For a little while, anyway."

Eli caught her, then deposited the dog in her arms. "Why don't you go upstairs and get settled in? I already carried your stuff to your room. Jeremy and I'll help Matt unload."

Ray was ready to refuse, but Lily beat her to the punch. "Yes. That's a wonderful idea. I'll show you to your room."

Ray leaned close to Eli, so that no one else would hear her. "You won't always get your way, you know."

He chucked her under her chin. "Honey, if I had my way, we'd be married already. I think you should appreciate my patience and stop pushing your luck."

He corralled Matt and Jeremy and went out the door, whistling. No, things were far from settled. But he had Ray on his ranch and under his roof, and so far she hadn't maimed anyone. Things were moving right along.

*   *   *

Ray stared at the empty closet and dresser with disgust. She hadn't said anything to Lily, other than to thank her, but damn it, she didn't want to sleep without Eli now that she had him back. She'd envisioned them sharing a room with all the perks. She should have realized that wouldn't fly, not with grandparents around. Lily would faint if she knew what Ray had planned to do that night once she got Eli alone.

They had a lot to discuss, but both she and Eli managed to stay busy until dinner. She hadn't been nauseous again, so she'd unpacked her few things, taken a long shower, then looked around.

The fresh air was wonderful and she enjoyed seeing the horses Eli owned. One young man who was working with the horses told her that they had over seventy acres of rolling countryside. The property was completely fenced and had two beautiful ponds with natural springs. The barns all had electricity and running water. Someday she'd like to explore it all, but for today, she just strolled around, staying in sight of the house.

Beyond the black walnut grove was a variety of fruit trees, including pears, peaches, and apples. Wildflowers grew in abundance and a continual breeze stirred the air. Everywhere around her, nature seduced. Ray had worked up quite an appetite by the time she sauntered back to the house.

Lily was in the kitchen when Ray went in to wash up. She was preparing dinner, but refused Ray's help, insisting she should rest. Ray didn't want to sit idle, but Eli, Matt, and Jeremy were still missing. She finally found Hank in the parlor, feet up on a coffee table, reading a newspaper.

Ray interrupted him without a qualm. "Do you race the horses?"

He laid the paper aside, and his scowl looked more like a smile of welcome. "Naw. That's a whole 'nuther business. I mostly have horses because I like them and I'm good with them. I used to train them back in my day, gentling them to the saddle and riders. I have someone else to do that now with my bones so old. But I still get to baby them." He winked. "Eli keeps them around to indulge an old man."

"You?"

"See any other old men around?"

Ray was starting to like Eli's grandfather. "No, I sure don't."

He nodded. "We have grays, palominos, sorrels, and roans. I sell only to someone I know will be good to them, someone proven. Mostly we offer stud service. It's lucrative, but our major income is from the shopping malls."

Lily poked her head in the door. "Dinner is on the table. I hope you're both hungry."

Ray rose, and without thinking about it, offered Hank a hand. He kept her arm as he made his way into the dining room, but not because he needed it. If anything, he led the way.

Ray still wore jeans and a tee from her walk around the ranch, and she tried to pull back, but he didn't seem to notice. "Um, Hank, shouldn't I change?"

"What for?" He tugged her into the room. "It's just family."

Eli was already there. He'd made a small bed for Precious in the corner, and her little dog trotted over there and plopped down. He had good table manners, thank God.

"Precious loves the horses," Eli told her as he held Ray's seat out, then kissed her on top of the head. He, too, wore jeans, and to Ray, he looked more delicious than the food, though Matt probably would have disagreed, given how he sniffed the air. Jeremy appeared thoughtful and Lily was busy fluttering around.

Dinner wasn't formal. She'd sort of expected elaborate place settings and fancy tableware. Instead, heaping bowls of food got passed around the table amid the conversation that never slowed.

"Do you ride?" Hank asked her.

"I haven't been on a horse in years, but I think I could stay in the saddle."

Eli smiled. "Is there anything you can't do?"

She started to say, *I can't be June Cleaver,* but she caught herself. She didn't want to sound like she resented the baby, not when she already felt protective. "Plenty, but don't expect me to list it all."

Matt laughed. "Ray's an overachiever. I've never seen her fail at anything. If she decides she wants to do it, she does."

"Sounds like my Hank," Lily interjected.

Ray was considering her odds of failing as a mother when Matt asked Eli, "When're you two getting married?"

She went to kick Matt under the table, but accidentally got Jeremy instead. He jumped and grabbed for his shin. "What was that for?"

"What?" Ray tried to look innocent, but with Matt grinning, it wasn't easy.

Lily shoved a plate of biscuits under Jeremy's nose. Matt snatched one, then said, "Well?"

"My charms are starting to wear on her." Eli blew Ray a kiss. "It should be any day now."

His outrageousness had Matt laughing. "Good luck with that, because I gave a forwarding address and number to anyone I thought might need it."

"That's fine."

Ray pointed her fork at Eli. "You might not think so when his girlfriends all start calling here."

"I didn't just give it to girls. I gave it to our cousins, and to our neighbors, in case anything happened to the house."

Ray wondered what her brother was up to. She could see a mischievous smile in his eyes; she recognized that look and braced herself.

Matt patted his stomach, then complimented Lily on the fine meal. She beamed. It seemed Matt had won over the grandparents with very little effort.

"Oh, yeah. I almost forgot." Matt glanced around the table before settling his gaze on Eli. "I gave this address to the agency, too. Now that Ray is working for them again—"

Eli's fork hit the table with a clatter. Ray locked gazes with her brother, but he didn't back down. Jeremy scooted his chair back, wisely getting out of the line of fire.

"Ray isn't working for them anymore."

"She isn't?" Matt feigned a look of confusion. "Hey, I was as surprised as anyone when she started there again, but I got the impression—"

"She's pregnant. She can't be going into Central America."

Jeremy shot upright in his seat. "She's *pregnant?*"

Ray stabbed him with a look. "It happens to the best of us."

His incredulity faded beneath consideration. "Pregnant."

"You don't have to keep saying it," Ray snapped, now irritated with both young men.

"What if someone else needs her?" Matt asked Eli. "You gotta admit she knows her business. And

from what she told me, you were no slacker yourself. Did you know that's the first time she's ever
let anyone go in with her? Buddy used to hassle
her something awful about staying behind, but
Ray always claimed she worked best alone."

"Matt . . ." Ray warned, all but choking on her
unease. These people had already made her feel
welcome. They wanted her to marry Eli and be a
part of their family. They probably pictured her
driving some sky blue minivan and working the
PTA. She didn't want to disillusion them so soon.

As if unaware of her tension, Matt went on. "Ray
is like a one-man—er, woman—combat unit. She can
handle any weapon created but usually doesn't
need one. Not unless she's way outnumbered. And
she almost never gets hurt. But you know, she did
have a few bruises this time. She was probably distracted because of Eli."

Hank's bushy eyebrows rose so high, they mingled with his grizzled hair. For once, he wasn't
scowling. "Then it's true? You weren't just a guide?
You're really a mercenary?"

"What she is," Eli said, enunciating slowly, "is my
future wife and the mother of my child. That's all
that matters."

Ray pulled herself together. Tired or not, pregnant or not, she was still the same woman, and if
that wasn't good enough for all of them, then to
hell with it.

She pushed back her chair and came slowly to
her feet. As if waiting to be attacked, Jeremy also
stood, and Matt and Eli soon followed. "I'm not
ashamed of what I am, Eli—but it sounds like you
are."

Eli narrowed his eyes and took a step closer to
Ray, towering over her, reminding her of his size in

comparison to her own. Reminding her of his temper. She wouldn't back down from him. But after a moment, his probing stare settled into a gentle smile.

Still holding her gaze, he said, "Granddad, Ray used to be in the service. She was part of a unique experimental team called the Adam and Eve program. Ray was the first Eve."

An invisible fist tightened around her throat. How had he found out? That information was confidential—*Buddy*. He must have told Eli, probably thinking to help her out by explaining her odd habits.

Eli droned on about Ray's part in the military, expounding on her efforts to rescue her partner from Central America. Memories squeezed in around her, making her vision blur, her legs tremble. She stood in stony silence, unable to speak, barely able to breathe.

Eli made her sound like a heroine, when she knew that couldn't be further from the truth. She couldn't look away from him, but she felt Hank and Lily beside her, hanging on his every word. Ray wanted to smirk, to give some sharp reply, but somehow she couldn't work up enough sarcasm for even a measly huff.

Hank cleared his throat, finally freeing her from Eli's stare. He gave her a brisk nod. "I'm a military man myself. I don't recall hearing of any programs like that."

"It was very hush-hush," Matt interjected. "And it didn't last that long because the teams became so loyal to each other and so independent of the government, it was felt they were a risk to keep in use. Ray's the perfect example of how things went wrong. If the government had their say, her partner would still be rotting in Central America and they'd still be negotiating."

Tears burned the backs of her eyes, forcing Ray to blink fast. Oh, she'd gotten Kevin out, but not in time.

Hank said brusquely, "You did the right thing. Can't abandon a partner, now can you?"

Ray didn't know what to say. She glanced at Matt and actually felt his love, his support. He whispered, "You're a hero, sis. No reason to keep it a secret anymore. Not to your new family."

A new family. Her throat tightened.

"Your family too, Matt." Lily moved to stand next to Ray. She put her arm around her. "I can't say as I understand all this. Women as mercenaries? It boggles the mind. But I agree with Hank. You did the right thing."

Ray forced herself to look at Lily. To her own ears, her voice sounded cold and remote. "Most people consider me no more than a hired gun, doing the job I get *paid* to do."

Hank didn't care. "And why shouldn't you get paid? No one works for free."

"But she did." Jeremy had grown solemn throughout the discussion. He studied her in much the same way Eli always did, scrutinizing her so closely she felt exposed. "Why didn't you take the money Eli offered you?"

"I didn't . . . didn't stick to my plan. I broke my own rules."

"But here I am." Jeremy held both his hands out to his sides. "At home, having dinner with my family. I'd say you got the job done."

Having Jeremy defend her felt too weird. "Why the turnaround?" she asked. "Afraid I might decide to get even for all those wisecracks you've made?"

Eli drew her into a hug, squeezing the bluster right out of her. "I told you my brother wasn't a complete idiot, he just has moments of idiocy."

Jeremy said, "Ha ha."

Pointing his cane at his youngest grandson, Hank said, "You want her to stay, too, right?"

"Yeah." Jeremy's smile was slow and genuine and he looked more like Eli than ever. "I think she'll keep Eli on his toes."

"There you go," Eli whispered. He tipped up her chin. "We all want you."

Ray clenched her teeth. Blasted hormonal upheavals, she just knew she was going to start sobbing any second now.

Eli must have known it, too. "Come on. Let's go for a ride. We'll take the horses and I'll show you the property."

Precious jumped up, ready to follow.

"Do be careful," Lily warned. "You have to remember she's expecting."

With her mood swings, no one was likely to forget. Ray looked at Matt. "You want to come with us?"

"Not this time. I still have to unpack and get settled. Besides, I think I smell dessert." While Lily rushed to get him a slice of pie, Matt turned to Hank—who'd been trying to sneak Precious a piece of food under the table. "Was that a collection of WWII memorabilia I saw in the front hall curio cabinet?"

Hank jumped with a guilty start, then gave up and lifted Precious to his lap. The little dog was in heaven.

With everyone else well occupied, Eli tugged

Ray out the door to the back porch. The second they were out of sight, he pressed her to the wall and kissed her soundly. Ray could feel him grinning against her lips.

"Stop that, Eli."

"Don't be a sore loser, Ray." He locked his arms behind her back, keeping her from pulling away. "Admit it. You expected my grandparents to denounce you on the spot. Instead, you got a huge dose of respect, which you deserve, by the way."

Ray lowered her head, staring at Eli's chest. "Everything with you and your family is unexpected. Especially Jeremy's new attitude."

"You'd pasted on that serene expression you wear when you want to hide your feelings." He smoothed her hair behind her ear, a gesture she'd missed while she'd been away from him. "I could tell you expected to get bombarded with criticism, and I know you'd have taken it on the chin, shoulders straight, head up just like a good soldier. Then when Granddad practically saluted you, you looked ready to expire." He kissed her again, a loud, smacking kiss on her pursed lips. "Your excuses are disappearing one by one, sweetheart. Why don't you give in gracefully now and agree to marry me?"

She really wanted to. Little by little Eli had made the whole marriage scenario seem pretty appealing. Still staring at his chest, she muttered, "There's more to consider than just your family's opinions."

Eli bent to see her face. "Such as?"

Raising her brows, Ray said, "My opinion?"

"You're crazy about me. That's all that matters."

She couldn't help but smile, then admitted, "I am." And before Eli could take too much joy in that, she added, "I'll even concede that I could get along just fine if we always stayed on the ranch and only had to deal with the few people here. But what happens when you're needed in Chicago or some other office? And how many offices do you head, anyway?"

Eli sighed, taking her hand. "You're determined to find something to nitpick about, aren't you?" He started down the porch steps, heading for the barn. "I have three offices that I visit throughout the year. I can cut back on a lot of my travel, but I'll still have to visit occasionally."

Ray followed along, noticing how fresh and pure the air smelled. She breathed deeply of the scents of summer flowers and newly mown hay. The sky seemed endless, and the most startling shade of blue she'd even seen. "It's beautiful here. I don't know why you'd ever leave."

Eli urged her into a large barn, the interior cool and dimly lit. "You weren't here, so there was no reason to stay."

"I don't want you to change your life for me, Eli." The words were barely out of Ray's mouth before he pinned her to the rough plank wall, his hands caging her there. His mouth touched her cheek, her chin, finally settling on her lips for a longer, gentler kiss, void of passion, but filled with tenderness.

"You still don't get it, do you, Ray? I *want* my life to change. I want to have you here to come home to. I want a baby that looks like you. Or me. Hell, I don't care if he looks like Jeremy as long as he's mine. I want to take care of you. And," he added when she started to object, "I want you to take care of me." He kissed her again, this time with consuming need, his body leaning into her. "Marriage is sharing, Ray. With no one in charge."

She didn't know how to *not* be in charge.

"Tell me you'll marry me. Please."

Groaning, Ray laid her head on his shoulder. "I don't know yet if I can be what you want."

"Damn it, Ray." Eli gently shook her. "It's not something you have to consciously do. It would be harder for you not to be what I want. The things I love about you aren't things that will change. They're who you are, not what you are."

Ray went perfectly still. She stared up at Eli, wide-eyed, hardly believing her ears.

He lifted one brow warily. "What is it, sweetheart?"

Feeling unaccountably shy and uncertain, Ray whispered, "You said there were things that you . . . loved?"

Eli looked stunned that he'd admitted it, then he caught her face roughly between his hands. "God, Ray. I didn't want to scare you, but . . . hell yes, I love everything about you. Too damn many things to repeat."

"Such as?"

His smile was tender; and the emotion, it was all there in his gaze again. He had the most expressive eyes she'd ever seen. She'd noticed them the very first time she'd met him, within seconds of walking into that smoky bar which seemed at least two lifetimes ago.

"I love your temper and your loyalty. Your pride and protectiveness. Your honesty. Your confidence and strength and sense of responsibility."

Ray laughed, feeling a little self-conscious.

"I love your sassy walk and your lack of modesty, the way you seem so oblivious to your attractiveness." His eyes darkened. "And your delectable, healthy body. I especially love it. And the way you make love to me and with me. And—"

Ray smashed her hand over his mouth. "You're being outrageous, Eli."

He bit her palm, a small, damp love bite that had her catching her breath and groaning.

"I'm being honest," he said when she pulled her hand away. "Why don't you be honest, too? With yourself and with me."

His deep husky voice sank into her. All her reasons for keeping herself apart, for protecting her heart against Eli, were slowly being chipped away. Besides, it was already too late for denials. She'd loved Eli almost from the beginning. "Eli . . ."

A loud commotion in the outer yard drew their attention. Eli's name was called and he looked up with a distracted frown just as the barn doors were thrown open.

Jeremy peered at each of them, took in the intimacy of their positions, and turned slightly away, offering them a modicum of privacy. "Sorry for interrupting. Ted's here with a new mare."

Eli cursed. "I forgot about the mare. Tell him I'll be right out."

"Sure." Jeremy coughed. "Jane just pulled up, too."

Groaning, Eli said, "Tell her I'll be with her as soon as I get a chance."

Ray waited until Jeremy left before narrowing her gaze on Eli. "I thought you talked to Jane."

"I did. She's probably here on business." Suddenly Eli grinned. "You have no reason to be jealous, Ray."

It felt like her spine would snap, she grew so stiff. "Jealous? As if I would be."

Eli smoothed his hand over her cheek, his expression mournful. "I'm sorry we have to cancel the ride."

Ray shrugged. "No big deal. I already did some exploring earlier."

"This time would have been more fun."

"Yeah? How so?"

"I was planning to take you to the other side of the hill, strip you buck naked, and make love to you in the shade of a huge oak tree." His eyes glowed. "I need you, Ray."

His words made her breathless, but still she managed a chuckle. "Poor baby. Wouldn't your grandparents understand if you slipped into my room?"

"No, they wouldn't."

"Then maybe we can take a long walk tonight." Ray ran her finger down his chest and admitted, "I need you, too."

Eli sucked in a deep breath. "Damn." He kissed her one more time, and without another word, walked away. Ray took a moment to dwell on Eli's declaration of love. He'd told her he cared, and she knew he wanted the baby, but love? She hadn't expected it, but then, much of what had happened since meeting Eli Connors was unexpected.

Eli loved her, and Matt claimed she could do anything that she set her mind to. So maybe she could make this all work. She still didn't want to drive a minivan, but maybe she could get used to an SUV. It wouldn't be a truck, but at least it'd hold the paraphernalia associated with babies, like strollers and diaper bags and such.

Considering that the kid would already have great-grandparents, a wonderful father, and a pony or two to boot, it might just work out okay.

Chapter Fourteen

R ay left the barn just in time to see Eli and another man leading the new mare away. Jane was with them, walking close to Eli, brushing up against him. Eli stayed busy talking to the man and seemed to be ignoring her.

Several other men were now loitering around the fence, probably done working for the day. They boldly stared when Ray walked into view.

Not understanding their rudeness, Ray started to frown. Then she saw Jeremy striding toward her. When he reached her, he stepped between her and the other men.

"Could I talk to you a minute?"

Ray took in his anxious expression. "About what?"

"Actually . . . I wanted to apologize."

Ray just waited, not bothering to make it easier on him.

He cleared his throat. "I've been a jerk. Being rescued by a woman . . ." He rubbed the back of his neck. His unease was almost palpable, but he continued. "It's not a good excuse, but I was scared half to death and you came in like an avenging angel and it made me feel like a coward. You aren't afraid of anyone or anything—"

Ray cut him off there. "I wasn't afraid of that situation because it's familiar to me. It wasn't familiar to you. But Jeremy, everyone is afraid of something."

"Not you."

"You don't think so?" She made a face and found herself confiding to the most unlikely ally. "I'm scared to death of having this baby."

His eyes widened. "But I'm sure it'll be fine! You're as healthy as a horse—" She slanted him an amused look and he winced. "Sorry. I didn't mean that as an insult. It's just that you're in such great shape, and Eli can afford the best medical care."

"I don't mean that part of it. I mean . . . trying to be a good mother."

He blinked at her twice, then his shoulders relaxed and he smiled. "Every kid in the world would consider you the coolest mom around. Like Wonder Woman or one of Charlie's Angels. And hey, being afraid of that is at least understandable. It's a big responsibility. But I was afraid of a bug."

Wonder Woman? Ray grinned. "Tarantulas are not mere bugs. It took me a while to get used to them, too."

Jeremy twisted his mouth. "They're . . . hairy."

Ray shuddered. "I know. Nasty, huh?"

Someone laughed behind them, interrupting their new camaraderie. Ray looked over her shoulder and saw that the men who'd been ogling her earlier had come closer. One in particular leaned arrogantly against the fence, eyeing her up and down.

Jeremy said, "Oh, hell."

"Ignore them," Ray said, loud enough for the men to hear.

"Better listen to the lady, Jeremy, or she just might whoop up on you."

Jeremy turned fully to face the man taunting him. In a low voice, he said to Ray, "Mike and the other two came along with the new mare. They'll be out of here soon enough."

Mike asked, "Isn't she the lady soldier you've been talking about? I see what you mean now, Jeremy. She looks real mean." A round of laughter followed that observation, and Ray felt herself stiffen in indignation.

Mike stepped closer. "Honey, you can toss me around any time you want."

Jeremy looked ready to expire. Ray put her hand on his shoulder. "They'll get tired of acting like fools pretty soon."

Jeremy shook his head. "Eli is going to kill me if he hears what they're saying."

He looked genuinely upset now, glancing around to see if Eli was coming back. Ray sighed, feeling totally put upon. "Why would Eli be mad at you?"

Jeremy rolled his eyes. "Because I'm the one who told them about you."

Suspicions rose. "You didn't tell some far-fetched lies about me, did you?"

Jeremy gave her an incredulous look. "Why would I need to? The truth is outrageous enough."

Ray laughed derisively. "So it is." Then she took Jeremy's arm in an iron grip, smiling maliciously. "Why don't we go inside now, Jeremy? If we're not here to harass, they'll probably find something else to amuse themselves with."

"What are you going to do?"

"Don't worry. I've never murdered anyone yet. Though I'll admit you give the idea new appeal."

"I know I've got a lot to apologize for."

"No big deal."

"Then you don't care that they know?"

"I'm not ashamed of what I do, Jeremy." She peered up at him. "But I have a feeling you didn't exactly paint me in a fair light."

He looked embarrassed. "No. Probably not," he admitted. "At the time, I was still stinging from being rescued by you."

"Now, don't go looking so long in the face. I'm not going to—"

Ray didn't get to finish. Mike latched onto her arm. "Jeremy says you're real talented. If you wanted to jump me, I promise to hold still."

He was laughing at his own jest. Jeremy started to step forward, but Ray stopped him.

As she always did, she considered the situation and how best to handle it. The big, muscled oaf in front of her wouldn't be any problem at all. And to avoid further harassment, she should probably teach him, and the onlookers, a lesson. Otherwise, she'd be putting up with the gibes for years.

Assuming she'd be here for years.

She took a step back.

"Now, honey, don't go hiding from me. I just wanted to tussle with you a little."

"Hide?" Ray grinned, already enjoying herself. "I'm just clearing a spot."

"For what?"

"For you to fall."

Mike blinked at her, then roared with laughter, looking to his friends and including them in his humor.

Ray shook her hands, getting loose. "You ready?"

"Baby, I was born ready."

"Good." So fast that Mike didn't have a chance to react, Ray hit his shoulder, his chest, and his stomach—then kicked his legs out from under him.

As she'd planned, he went down.

His friends really found that hilarious. Mike didn't. He jumped back up, and again Ray hit him three times, dodging his big hands when he reached for her. After several stinging blows, one an insulting slap to his forehead, she ended up behind him, and this time she planted a foot in the seat of his pants, sending him face first into the dirt.

"Holy shit, she's good," one of the men said.

"I can't wait to tell everyone else."

Mike cursed and jumped back up to his feet.

Still grinning, Ray asked, "Had enough?"

He curled his lip, swiping dust off his chest and seat. "You damned bitch."

At the insult, Jeremy barked, "That's enough. You better back off right now."

As if sensing an easier victory, Mike rounded on Jeremy. "Who says? You?"

Jeremy took an aggressive step forward. Ray sincerely hoped she wouldn't end up having to defend him. But he proved a little smarter than she'd first suspected.

He threatened the man with Eli.

"You're talking to my future sister-in-law. How do you think Eli will feel about you bothering her?"

Mike looked stunned. "Eli is marrying her?"

"He is."

"Well, you never told us that." He glanced around the yard in a rush. "How was I supposed to know?"

"You know now."

Mike turned to Ray. "No offense intended."

"None taken." Seeing the man's unease, Ray started to wonder what Eli's reaction would be toward her.

She'd only been at his house a day and she was already making mincemeat of his friends. The more she considered it, the more apprehensive she became. She'd been wrong to goad the man into a confrontation and she knew it. She was pregnant, and pregnant women surely had to show more restraint.

That thought brought another—of her fat and round and unable to fight. The image wasn't a pleasant one.

As Mike started to walk away, taking his friends with him, Jeremy let out a sigh of relief. "Look, Ray Jean—"

The day's anxiety had taken its toll.

Jeremy only had time to gasp before he found himself caught in Ray's grip. She grabbed his arm and brought her leg up behind his knee. He landed on the ground, flat on his back, dust billowing around him and Ray looming over him. She came down quickly, her knee landing on his chest.

"Never, absolutely never, call me Ray Jean. I've taken a lot off you, Jeremy. But enough is enough."

Jeremy nodded while doing his best not to chuckle.

Provoked, Ray pushed down with her weight on her knee, making Jeremy gasp. "You think this is funny?"

He shook his head, nearly choking on his humor. "No." The word was strangled and Ray let up a little. Then Jeremy smiled. "I was just wondering if

you'd ever done this to Eli. You have, haven't you?"
A murmur rose from the onlookers, but Ray and
Jeremy both ignored it. "That's probably why he
fell in love with you."

Ray sat back on her heels, totally bemused. "You
Connors men are a strange breed, do you know
that?"

Jeremy laughed while rubbing his chest. "Ah,
can I get up now?"

Disgusted, Ray said, "Yeah, all right."

He sat up beside her. "Before I can ask if all's
forgiven, I'm afraid I have something else to apologize for, too."

Ray dropped her head forward. "I don't want to
hear this."

"I was the one who invited Jane here. I, uh, sort
of suggested she try to seduce Eli. You know, make
him see what a mistake he was making."

Ray turned her face away.

"Of course, that was before I realized it wasn't a
mistake at all."

Suspiciously, Ray asked, "You don't want him
and Jane to get together after all?"

"Are you kidding? Who would teach me how to
fight like you do?"

Matt said from behind them, "I will."

There was a definite touch of menace in his
tone.

Leaning on one arm, Ray twisted in his direction. She discovered that not only had Matt joined
them, so had the man who'd brought the mare,
Eli, and Jane. Oh hell. She had a damned audience.

Slowly, Ray came to her feet.

Eli wasn't just looking at her. No, he was staring
at Mike, at the dirt on his clothes and the red

handprint on his head. "What the hell is going on?"

As if to exonerate himself, Mike held up his hands. "I was just teasing her."

Eli's eyes went cold. In a deadly whisper, he asked, "Did you touch her?"

"No!" Looking around for help and not finding any, Mike stammered, "She . . . well, she sort of—"

"Kicked your ass?" Matt supplied.

Eli looked so furious, Ray rushed to reassure him. "I didn't hurt him, Eli."

Eli barely spared her a glance. "I've warned you before, Mike. This is the last time."

He'd had trouble with Mike before? Well, that made her feel better.

The man who'd accompanied Eli to the barn appeared furious. "All of you, get in the truck." And then to Eli, "I'm sorry. He can be such an obnoxious ass, but he's good with horses."

"He won't be if I see him again."

The man nodded. "Understood. I'll keep him away." Then he, too, left.

With the day deteriorating, Ray felt guilty and defensive. "There's no reason for all the fuss. I didn't hurt him."

Eli raised a brow. "He might disagree."

Watching Mike limp away, Ray couldn't argue.

"Don't worry about it. He's a bully and a jerk and I don't like him." Eli turned to Jeremy, still sitting on the dusty ground. "And what happened to you?"

Jeremy cleared his throat. "Uh, Ray and I had a little disagreement."

Incredulous, Eli said, "*You* were fighting with her, too?"

Ray stepped in front of Jeremy. Damn it, she was

starting to feel protective of the twerp. "There was no fight to it." Then she shifted the blame. "You've done a lousy job of teaching your brother, Eli."

Matt said, "I'll be glad, even eager, to instruct him." There was blood in his eyes.

"He didn't touch me, Matt, so knock it off."

Jane gave a snicker of amusement. "You really have been out here brawling in the dirt with men?" She managed to squeeze closer to Eli, pressing her breasts into his arm. "Unbelievable. But then, you are some sort of . . . well, *mercenary,* aren't you?"

She made it sound like a dirty word and Ray decided she'd had enough. Very slowly, with measured movements, she started forward. Her eyes never left Jane's face.

Eli sighed in vexation, then, while trying to pry Jane loose, he softly warned, "Ray, you're grinning."

"So?"

"So that means you want to fight." He said it as if she should have already known that. "But I don't think—"

She cut him off. "Forget it, Eli. You wanted me. You dragged me here and wouldn't let up for a single minute, even though I told you it wouldn't work out. Well, now you've got me. For good. And that means you're hands-off to other women. And most especially to her."

Chuckling, Jeremy hauled himself upright to stand next to Matt. "Will you really teach me to fight like Ray does?"

Matt shrugged, but his eyes never left his sister. "Why not?"

Eli sighed. "There isn't going to be any fighting."

"You don't think so?" Ray took another step forward, which sent Jane into a panic.

Harassed, Eli said, "Jane, for God's sake . . . Ray, stop terrorizing her . . . Matt, will you stop laughing." He was doing his best to get away from Jane and still give his attention to Ray. "You know you're not going to hurt her, Ray."

"And why not?"

"Because you're honorable and you fight fair."

"Wrong. I fight to win."

"But you've already won me," he reminded her with a smile.

Ray wasn't appeased. "Maybe you should have informed your girlfriend of that." She nodded her head at Jane. "She could have been spared this little scene."

"I did tell her."

"Then she's only got herself to blame." Ray reached for Jane, the gesture as far from friendly as she could make it.

Jane screamed bloody murder.

Wincing, Eli said, "Damn it to hell . . ." He bent, scooped Ray into his arms, and deposited her over his shoulder.

Bemused by how fast he'd moved and how he'd once again taken her by surprise, Ray hung still in his hold.

"I think we'll finish this conversation in private." Eli patted her butt. His other hand held her legs firmly pressed to his body so she couldn't kick him.

Coming out of her stupor, Ray twisted to see him. "Put me down, Eli."

"Patience, sweetheart. We'll be alone in just a minute." He started up the porch steps, but stopped when a loud wail came from the yard, followed by another burst of laughter. He turned. Ray lifted her head.

Jane was twisting in circles with Precious hanging from her tailored skirt, his growls as loud and ferocious as a six-pound dog could manage. Hank, who had turned the dog loose, stood off to the side, his hand over his mouth to hide his smile. Jeremy and Matt both tried to help her, but she kept scurrying around, making it impossible for them to catch hold of the dog.

Eli heaved a sigh of exasperation.

From her odd upside-down position, Ray said, "Will this ruin your business dealings with her?"

"Jane doesn't let anything get in the way of business. She may not look it, but she's a shark."

"Eli?"

He hugged her legs and pressed his cheek to her hip. "Yeah?"

"I could get away from you if I wanted to. You know that, don't you?"

With a laugh, he said, "Yeah, I know." He went into the house and upstairs, taking the steps two at time. Ray was surprised he hadn't jarred her teeth from her head. But then, from the day she'd met him, Eli had always been so careful with her, treating her like a woman first, a soldier last.

He went straight into his own room, then shoved the door shut with his foot. He didn't toss Ray onto the bed, but rather laid her gently upon it, coming down next to her and half-covering her to keep her still. Not that she had any intentions of moving.

"So," he said, his fingertips touching her cheek, smoothing her hair. "Am I in trouble now?"

She should probably be mad, Ray thought. Under normal circumstances she would be. She'd only wanted to scare Jane, as Eli had guessed. And she'd succeeded, if the woman's ridiculous scream was any indication.

"That depends. Why'd you run off with me? Did you think I was going to commit murder after all?"

He touched the tip of her nose. "No. Jeremy looked fine, and if you didn't kill him, you wouldn't hurt anyone." Eli kissed her, soft and easy, on the mouth. "I brought you here so we could be alone, of course."

Oh.

"Did you mean what you said? I've got you for good?"

"Yes."

"Because you love me?"

She looked at his mouth. "Yeah, I do."

He pulled back in surprise. "You mean that?"

Ray fought a smile. "I said so, didn't I?"

His voice deepened in that oh too familiar way. "You're going to have to say it a lot over the next sixty years or so." He leaned down to kiss her. "So now we know you love me, and you don't want to get away from me, so . . . will you marry me?"

"On one condition."

He gathered her closer, making her feel nurtured and protected and loved. "Anything."

Ray grinned at his fervent reply. "Teach me some of your moves. I don't like it that I always end up on the bottom with you."

Eli stared into her eyes a moment, then caught her shoulders in his hands and rolled so that Ray was on top, lying all along his length. "I promise to show you all my best moves, Ray." His hands settled on her hips, pulling her against him.

"Mmm. This is definitely one of your better moves."

"Yes. Now pay attention while I instruct you."
He leaned up to take her mouth.

The bedroom door opened and Lily waltzed in.
She was humming.

Ray shot away from Eli, then scrambled to sit upright, almost knocking Eli off the other side of the
mattress. She quickly straightened her clothes.

"*Lily.*" Good God, she'd been caught. "I—" How
did you apologize for romping in a respected
woman's house?

Ray wasn't given time to worry about it. Lily,
arms loaded down with three fat photo albums, sat
down next to her on the bed. "I've brought you
something to look at."

Eli straightened himself, trying for some aplomb.
"Gram. What do you have there?"

"Baby albums." Her smile was wistful. "Oh, how
I wish I had some baby photos of you, Eli. But I do
have them of your father, and I thought Ray would
like to see."

Ray put a hand to her throat. She couldn't get a
single word out. Not that Lily noticed. She spread
the first album open to a photo of a fat baby lying
on a blue blanket with his bare butt showing.

"Eli has his daddy's smile," Lily claimed.

Reluctantly, Ray accepted the album. The baby
staring up at the camera did, in fact, resemble Eli.
"Amazing. It's so small."

"He, dear, not it. And believe me, he didn't feel
small being born. He weighed a good eight and a
half pounds."

While Eli settled beside his grandmother, Ray
began turning pages. Each and every picture
seemed more adorable than the last.

"That's his first tooth. Oh, and look at that. His
first black eye. He was almost three when he fell

off the front step." Lily smiled, but said, "Oh, how I cried."

Ray glanced at her. "Why'd you cry?"

"Why, because I felt wretched! I'd let my baby fall and get hurt." She patted Ray's hand. "Having a baby is the most wonderful and the most fearful thing in the world."

Fearful? Yeah, she knew all about that.

"I remember being so scared when I carried, I cried almost every night. Hank thought it was just the pregnancy, and it might have been in part due to that."

Ray swallowed hard. "What was the other part?"

Lily sighed. "You'll think I'm silly."

"No," Ray promised her, "I won't." She was dying to hear what fears this kind, gentle woman could have had.

Embarrassed, Lily admitted, "I was a little country bumpkin who could barely stand up for herself, and yet I knew I'd soon be responsible for protecting a child. Me! All I knew about babies was that they were expensive and needed a lot of care. It was a terrible and overwhelming thought. Not that I didn't want the baby! From the moment I knew I was expecting, I loved that child with all my heart."

Ray laid her hand over her belly. She was aware of Eli watching her, his expression tender. "I love my baby, too."

"Of course you do. And you and Eli are in a much better position than Hank and I were. We'd been through the Depression. Plenty of times we had to struggle just to get by. I kept wondering how I could make my baby's life better, what kind of mother I'd be." She pulled out a hanky to dab at the tears swimming in her eyes.

Eli put his arm around his grandmother, smiling indulgently.

Shaken, Ray said, "So how'd you learn what to do?"

"Learn?" Lily laughed and patted Ray's knee. "Trial and error, honey. Trial and error. It wasn't until I had my second child that I realized there are no experts. Every mother comes into this with she same blank slate because it's such a . . . a *miracle*. There aren't any books or experiences to prepare you for how you feel when that tiny baby is handed to you to love and protect for the rest of his life." She dabbed her eyes again, still smiling. "But oh, do you protect him. I'd have fought lions for either of my children." She cupped Eli's face. "I felt that way when I met Eli. He was such a challenge, so defensive and hurt, and I loved him the minute I saw him."

Seeing the two of them filled Ray with hope. "Was it easier the second time around?"

"No, because each child is so different, it's like starting from scratch. You make as many mistakes, just different ones. No mother is perfect. All any of us can do is our best, and it never feels like enough. To us anyway. To the children, it's plenty. They need to feel loved and nurtured. They need to know that home is safe and that you care enough to set rules that are in their best interest."

"Does the fear ever go away?"

Eli glanced sharply at Ray. She didn't look at him. Not that it mattered. Eli could always see right in to her soul.

"It comes and goes in spurts." Lily took her hand, emphasizing that with a squeeze. "Like when they cry and you can't figure out why. Oh, that's just awful and it tears at your heart. Or when they get sick or fall. My daughter was an overachiever, much like you, but with academics. That girl would have a fit if she didn't get straight As. But she almost never got hurt.

"Now Eli's father was just the opposite. He was happy if he got a C. He was smart, he just had a different focus. And injuries? He kept me buried in doctor bills. He was fearless, always willing to be the first to try something dangerous."

"Like what?" Eli asked.

"Oh, there was the time when he was ten and he and his friends tried diving into the pond out of a tree." Lily covered her heart. "What a terror. I grounded him for two weeks, then got down on my hands and knees and thanked the good Lord that he hadn't broken his neck instead of his arm."

Trying to picture Eli as that little boy, Ray asked, "Where is this tree?"

"Oh no, you don't." Eli tweaked her hair. "I won't have you diving out of trees, Ray."

She reached past Lily to punch him, but she was laughing—and feeling much more confident about impending motherhood. Love she could give in spades. With Lily's influence and Eli at her side, the rest would hopefully fall in line.

"I still miss him," Lily whispered, staring at the photo in the book. "But I have Eli, and soon a great-grandson." She touched Ray's cheek. "I'm so glad you're here."

Ray's nodded. "I'm glad, too."

"Hank worked extra hard back then, making sure we'd have everything we need. He never wanted us to do without. That's a worry neither of you will have."

"He's a good man," Ray said, and meant it.

"Yes, he is." Lily stood. "Take your time with the

albums. There are years and years' worth of pictures in there. And Ray?"

Ray tucked the books close to her heart. "Yes?"

"If you want to talk more later, I'd be glad to oblige. There's little an old woman enjoys more than reminiscing, especially about her children."

"Thank you, I'd like that."

Eli sat stiff and proper until his grandmother's footsteps had faded down the hall. Then he fell back on the bed with a laugh. "I feel sixteen again, caught sneaking a girl into my room. Not that my mother would have cared, if she'd even noticed. But the girl's folks might have."

Ray looked at him over her shoulder. "What would you do if our son tried that?"

"At my age? I'd give him privacy." He grinned.

Ray turned back to the pictures. There were so many to enjoy. In some of them, Hank and Lily were included, young and vibrant and smiling. A loving, happy family.

"Eli?"

"Hmm?"

"I didn't want to go back, anyway."

Silence fell like a dead weight before Eli sat up beside her. He took the photo albums and laid them aside, then pulled Ray into his lap. "Where, sweetheart?"

"To Central America." She snuggled close, liking the way he held her. "I'm not hardened enough anymore for the job. I got distracted too many times during this last trip. That can be dangerous."

Nuzzling the top of her head, Eli said, "I distracted you."

"Right from the start."

Ray felt his smile against her temple. "So you're telling me that, at least this once, I'll get my way?"

Ray lifted herself to look at him. "I can't see me as some happy housewife, content to stay home every day."

"I hope not. After I told Granddad how handy you are with a hammer, he's been planning a lot of repairs."

"You're making that up."

"Am not. You can ask him yourself. But it's up to you what you do, Ray."

"What about my house?"

"I don't know. I thought about that, too." He put his forehead to hers. "We can keep it if you want, maybe live there part-time. I'm sorry, but I need to be near here as much as possible. Granddad has more health problems now and Gram—"

"Shh. I can be happy here."

"You're sure?" Eli cupped her face. "I love you, Ray. I want you happy."

It was ridiculous how easy tears came. She dashed them away, laughing. "I didn't want to fall in love with you. But I couldn't seem to stop myself."

"You never stood a chance."

"Yeah, right." Ray pushed him flat on his back and propped her elbows on his chest. "Because you're bigger and stronger?"

"No." He touched her mouth. "Just more determined. Your mission may have been to save people. But I had a mission, too. I had to accomplish what Central America couldn't."

"And what was that?"

"I had to capture a soldier. And she was the meanest son of a—"

Laughing, Ray clapped her hand over his mouth. She remembered Eli's request at the onset of their meeting. She'd bragged that she was the best the agency had to offer. And the meanest. It seemed like a lifetime ago, now.

Eli kissed her palm and tugged her hand away. "You succeeded in your mission. You saved my brother. But you got me in the bargain. I'd say we were both damned successful."

Ray thought to tell him that he'd saved her, too, saved her from her own wayward responsibilities to the world. He gave her the love she'd never thought to have, and the acceptance. But then Eli was kissing her, his tongue sliding deep, taking control as usual, and all she could do was hold on tight.

Her life was definitely going to undergo some changes. She looked forward to each and every one.

Keep reading for a
special preview of
Lori Foster's
Never Too Much,
available now
from Zebra Books.

That's when Ben saw her.

She came out of the shadows and started across the street toward him. Spellbound, Ben watched as fog seemed to part around her, giving her an ethereal appearance. Somehow her steps, slow and rhythmic, matched the beat of the music, and the beat of his heart.

The reflection of a streetlamp glinted off her reddish-brown hair. It was tied into a high ponytail that might have been neat at one point during the day but now straggled loose and sloppy around her face. A fringe of bangs, stringy with sweat, hung half in her eyes. She wore a dusty white sleeveless shirt under a pair of coverall shorts with unraveled hems and a pair of brown lace-up work boots over rolled gray socks.

Ben wouldn't call it feminine attire, but maybe fetish attire? Whatever. She sure got his attention.

He couldn't help but wonder what kind of panties a woman wore under a getup like that.

Despite being midnight and hotter than Hades, her stride was long and sure and fluid, matching that provocative music—"Bad to the Bone."

She had the walk of a satisfied woman, and it turned Ben on. He'd always found confidence to be very sexy.

Because he stood in the shadows, she didn't notice him until the last moment, when she was a mere three feet away. Their eyes met; their gazes caught and held. She faltered, then slowly, intently, surveyed him. Her lips parted in surprise.

Ben didn't move, didn't alter his relaxed pose against the building. But inside, interest roiled, kicked up his heartbeat and sent his senses—and his equipment—on full alert.

Knowing he looked too enthralled, Ben managed a more casual nod.

At his acknowledgment, the woman inched closer, but now her every step seemed weighted with caution and curiosity, as if she didn't want to look at him, but couldn't quite help herself. When she was directly in front of Ben, her wide lush mouth tilted and her eyes smiled. She shook her head, as if bemused.

Or disbelieving.

"You ought to be illegal." Her laughing comment, low and throaty, broke the spell. "It's a good thing I have a stout heart."

With that strange, yet provocative remark, she strode on past and into the building.

A little amazed at his aberrant reaction, Ben realized he hadn't said a single word, hadn't taken advantage of the situation or her comment, hadn't even introduced himself. He turned to view the back of her and his interest expanded. Her ass looked great in the coveralls, soft and cuddly and rounded just right. A nice handful. Her legs were strong, shapely with smooth muscles, lightly tanned.

The rousing music faded away, but the scent of

heated woman touched by the damp outdoors remained. Ben grinned in acute anticipation.

Oh yeah, this was what he'd been looking for. *She* was what he'd been looking for.

The chase was on.

Feeling like a bull in rut, he trailed into the bar after her. Impatiently, he waited while she looked around, located a booth at the back of the room, and headed in that direction.

With one nod, Ben let the waitress know he'd take care of this particular customer. He followed along and when she slid into the bench seat, Ben propped his hip on the table. He tried for a nonchalant smile of welcome, but he knew his eyes were glittering, that his smile was more wolfish than not. He couldn't help that; he hadn't felt this sexually alert in a long time. "Hi."

She glanced up, saw it was him, and pinched off her automatic smile in an effort to keep her expression impassive. "A Coke, please. Plenty of ice."

The interior lights this time of night were dim to accommodate all the drinkers. Ben couldn't see the color of her eyes, but the shape was exotic, tilting up on the outsides, heavily fringed with dark lashes. Ben studied her face and attempted to determine what it was about her that lured him.

Her mouth looked sinful, and very soft.

Her freckles looked playful, a bit impish.

Her body . . . Well, it was hard to tell in her sloppy clothes, but he sure as hell intended to find out.

Even with his obvious perusal, she looked away, reached for the menu, and effectively dismissed him.

Ben's interest escalated. Oh yeah, she was good at this, at playing the game. So, she wouldn't make it easy for him? Good. He nearly rubbed his hands together in anticipation of the coming night.

Feeling challenged and loving it, he straightened away from the table. "I'll be right back with your drink."

She didn't reply.

Taking her at her word, Ben filled a glass with crushed ice and then poured in the soda. She had her head propped up on a fist, her exotic eyes closed tiredly when Ben returned.

Her nails weren't painted. They weren't even clean. Wherever she'd worked today, it had been a dirty job, and the stains on her fingers proved it. But that didn't bother Ben. He was too pleased to make note of the lack of a ring. Not married, not engaged.

Perfect.

He set the drink down and waited.

Very slowly, her eyes opened. She had a sexy, full mouth, which stretched wide in a yawn before she mumbled through her hand, "Thank you."

Her voice was smoky and deep, her expression orgasmic. Or maybe exhausted. Hard to tell when he was so aroused.

Rather than take a drink, she lifted the icy glass to her forehead and sighed at the cool touch. "It's so hot outside tonight."

It was hotter than hell inside, too.

A drip of condensation rolled down the frosty glass, fell onto her upper chest, and trickled down between her breasts. Ben held his breath.

Damn, everything about her seemed devised to push his buttons. Only he couldn't ever recall a bedraggled, sweaty woman in work clothes turning him on before now.

In an effort to diminish the lust and further his

association, Ben cleared his throat. "You work next door?"

A proud, friendly smile lit up her eyes. "Yeah. I'm the new owner. We've spent the past couple of weeks getting the place into shape. But today we finally started business."

She owned the business. She'd be close by.

Damn. Any woman who would constantly be so close could be trouble. Starting something that would be difficult to end due to proximity would be plain foolish. He had to be cautious, to consider all the possible problems . . .

Using two fingers, she fished an ice cube out of the glass and sucked on it.

Ben drew in his breath. *To hell with caution.*

He held out a hand, anxious to touch her even in a platonic way. "Welcome to the neighborhood. I'm Ben Badwin, and I own this motel."

She looked at his extended hand. "Is that right? Wow, great place." She swiped her fingers across the top of her thigh, on the coveralls to dry them, then took his hand and pumped twice in a mannish way. "Sierra Murphy. It's nice to meet you, Ben."

Sierra—an unusual name for an unusual woman. Her hand was small, slim, warm. And callused. She looked far too young to own a business, and far too appealing to be working in the dirt. Reluctantly, Ben released her. "You're out late."